SPIDER'S
RING

Book 2 in the Detective Trann series

Christa Yelich-Koth

COPYRIGHT

This book is a work of fiction. All characters and events portrayed in this book are either products of the author's imagination or are used fictitiously.

SPIDER'S RING

Published by CYK Publishing
Oregon, USA

Cover art: CC Covers

Look for other books by Christa Yelich-Koth

www.ChristaYelichKoth.com

The Detective Trann series
SPIDER'S TRUTH
SPIDER'S RING
SPIDER'S QUEEN

The Land of Iyah trilogy
(YA fantasy)
THE JADE CASTLE
THE JADE ARCH
THE JADE THRONE

Eomix Galaxy Novels
(Sci-fi/fantasy)
ILLUSION (Book 1 of 2)
IDENTITY (Book 2 of 2)
COILED VENGEANCE

Graphic Novels
(Sci-fi)
HOLLOW

Comic Books
(Sci-fi)
HOLLOW'S PRSIM SERIES
(6 issues total)
Issue #1: *Aftermath*
Issue #2: *Reunion*
Issue #3: *Alliance*
Issue #4: *Trigger*
Issue #5: *Revelations*
Issue #6: *Fusion*

SPECIAL THANKS

To you, the reader: THANK YOU for wanting more from this series.

Sandra Yelich: Wow! The details in this book. THANK YOU for all your edits!!

Conrad Teves: For your amazing help with the cover art.

Thomas Koth: For beta reading so quickly with my ever-changing timeline.

Wes Albers: For answering my questions regarding police protocol.

1

September 10th
9 a.m.

Violet stared straight ahead in her prison cell, her face a mask. She'd been given her own space. Not because she'd earned it for good behavior. Not because she didn't play well with others. But because each cellmate of hers had requested a transfer within a month. Complaining of throbbing headaches, haziness, and nightmares, every cellmate begged and pleaded to be put somewhere else. Even though most were hardened criminals, some who'd even beaten and bullied the small-framed Violet, they all changed their tune, shying away and sometimes even apologizing.

The guards moved the first cellmate after four weeks,

thinking something must be making her ill when she complained about headaches. During Violet's second month, when the next woman complained of the same issues, they transferred both women to a new cell.

"Maybe it's something in the space?" the guard had guessed. "Mold in the walls?"

Within two weeks, cellmate #2 still complained, so they only moved her. When Violet's third cellmate came in, she started complaining after the first few days, and decided to take her frustration out on Violet. Bruised and bloodied after the initial beating, Violet did not strike back, choosing instead to ball herself up in the corner of her bed, ignoring the slurs and strikes from the ill-feeling convict, even after her hair had been ripped out and her elbow smashed into the wall.

Violet held her ground, knowing that if she defended herself, it would only make things worse. She may have had a lot of skills, but brute strength in a small space didn't make the list.

The guard ignored the beatings at first, as she too had little care for Violet's wellbeing, but eventually she knew someone would notice Violet's injuries and blame her for not keeping a better eye on her charges. She told this third cellmate that she could care less about how lousy she felt. Beating up Violet wouldn't get her transferred, it would only get her a longer sentence.

After the fourth week, the third cellmate quieted. A bit too quiet. She'd lie on her bed, facing the wall, muttering about drums. The constant drums.

A week later, screaming that she couldn't take it anymore, the cellmate ran face-first into the wall, knocking herself unconscious.

Since that moment three months ago, the warden stepped in and decided Violet shouldn't have any more playmates. No one could explain the issues with the cellmates, but regardless, the staff didn't want to deal with Violet anymore.

Violet had smirked to herself. Even inside a prison cell she could control the situation. She hadn't been as adept as Truth at using suggestive rhythmic and auditory cues, but her crude hypnotic abilities had worked well enough. The guards now allowed her to be alone. To think. Which was all she wanted.

At this moment, Violet's black hair, wavy and messy, hung in front of her face, but she stared through the curtain. Walls of concrete the color of grayish mud surrounded her. Sounds of women in other cells melded into a background din. The scents of moist cement and urine continually wafted into her space. Narrow, steel bars separated her from freedom. Eighteen identical bars, six on the door, twelve for the room. Each day the same view. Each day the same thoughts swirled, as stuck in her brain as she was stuck in this cell.

Six months she'd been trapped in this room. Six months since she'd almost had everything. And now?

Slowly, she dragged a ragged nail along her forehead, as if pretending to slice it open. She couldn't get inside though to change things. She was stuck, in this body, in this prison, in this life.

And all because of two people: Detective Sean Trann and Doctor Charlotte Salla. The cop who'd thwarted her plans and the coroner who'd lived.

Footsteps caused her gaze to flicker to the left, where the door to her unit stood. *Must be a guard.* She could tell by the metered clomping. But someone else followed, someone with daintier footsteps—the clicky-clack of heels on the concrete floor.

The guard came first, with wide hips, an even wider belly, and a dull, gray uniform. One hand lay on her nightstick—as if Violet would ever try to escape. What would be the point?

"You've got a visitor," the guard said, her southern drawl as heavy as her weighty breasts.

Violet blinked, but said nothing.

"Good luck, lady," the guard said to the woman behind her. "Call if you need me." She clomped away.

The remaining woman stood upright, tall and lean. Quite beautiful really, with arched eyebrows, creamy dark olive skin, and big, thick, chestnut curls to her waist.

"Good morning, Violet," she said. Her voice sounded crisp and cool, with notes of a Brooklyn accent attached. "My name is Marina Beguilous. I know you've had other lawyers over the past few months, but there has been a change. I've been assigned to your case as your representation. Your trial begins in three weeks."

Violet's mouth trembled with strain as her lips drew up into a shape they hadn't created in over six months.

A smile.

2

September 25th
9:45 a.m.

Homicide Detective Sean Trann drummed his fingers on his desk.

His partner was late.

Again.

This made it the third time this week and the calendar only showed Wednesday. Sean didn't always stick to the rules either, but this lateness was becoming more than just an annoyance. It had started to affect their work.

Not that Detective Max Payne didn't irritate him all on his own. He hit on any woman that walked by. He told the worst dirty puns, which no one ever laughed at. He never went out of his way to help anyone. And he punched Sean in the shoulder every time he came near.

Not that Sean couldn't handle a hit every now and then, but Payne happened to smack Sean in the same place on the same shoulder every time—a shoulder that had a bullet in it a few months before his partner joined the Boston's District One Homicide Department twelve weeks ago.

The two of them had only officially been partners for a couple months. Sean hadn't been approved to be on active duty until then, so they were still pretty new as partners went. When Payne had initially come in, transferring from Texas, he had temporarily joined up with Detective Wilt while Detective Tay had been on medical leave from her own injuries. Being shot both in the gut and having an ear blown off would keep anyone away for a while. Sean had "gotten away" with only being shot in the shoulder and grazed in the side, a fact Payne liked to remind him about.

After six months, the shoulder didn't bother Sean that much anymore—except it ached like hell on rainy days—but he knew when Payne saw him, he purposefully chose that exact spot to smack.

Sean had been staring out the window, remembering the reason why he'd gotten shot in the first place, when a solid object rammed into his right shoulder.

"Damnit!" Sean cursed, grabbing his throbbing arm with his left hand.

"Easy, there, softie," Detective Payne said. "Didn't mean to scare the skirt off ya."

Sean gritted his teeth and stretched his cheeks into a

grimace of a smile. "Morning, Payne. You're late."

"Couldn't be helped," Payne said smugly as he dropped into the chair on the other side of Sean's desk. He propped his boots on its edge, flaking mud into Sean's coffee mug, and lifted his muscled arms to run his hands over his shorn, dark hair. "Had this tasty little treat I took home with me last night and she insisted on riding the buck again this morning. I figured it was the least I could do before kicking her to the curb. I mean, she was fun for a roll or two, but I'm not going to seriously date some cocktail waitress hottie." Payne winked.

Sean took the jab in stride. When Payne first joined the department, he'd come in right after the case involving the serial killer, "Spider," had wrapped up. Except instead of one killer, Spider had turned out to be a strange Triad of three women, bent on exterminating physically unfit individuals from the planet.

Payne, of course, thought the entire thing sounded hysterical. Hot women running around killing not hot people? "Only women are crazy enough to do that," he'd said.

The whole spectacle had been plastered across the news for weeks, including behind-the-scenes moments with "real witnesses to these allegedly murderous women." Sean had been photographed walking into the police station, which was followed by twenty minutes of some journalist telling everyone everything about his life up until that point. This included the fact that he'd once been engaged to a cocktail waitress, Angellica, a year and a half ago, who had been found dead at the scene and accused of being one of the murderers.

Though his current dating plate remained empty, he'd

tried to keep anything concerning his personal life quiet since Payne heckled him about everything—from his black Jaguar, because it had been a gift from said ex-fiancée's father, to his tiny apartment, so no wonder he couldn't get anyone to go home with him.

Still, it could have been worse. At least Payne was a good cop.

"I don't care about your social life," Sean said. "You can't be late anymore."

"You squealing on me to the Sarge?" Payne said with a sneer. "What are you, twelve?"

"No, I'm twenty-nine, a homicide detective, and your partner. I'm just trying to do my job, which I *can't* if you aren't here because I can't start without you."

Payne pursed his lips. "So, Sergeant Millan doesn't know about my lateness?"

"Not yet. And he won't from me. But I'm not the only person who works here. Other people can see what time you stroll in."

Sean could see the internal debate going on inside Payne's mind. On the one hand, he didn't want to give Sean an inch. Why would he? In his mind, it must be an insult to be paired with a partner ten years younger than him and not be the senior detective. But on the other hand, Sean knew Payne couldn't afford to have any more strikes against him. He'd already been transferred twice and any more trouble would get him demoted to office duty. Which, for a detective not ready to retire, was worse than getting fired.

"Fine," Payne said grudgingly. "I'll be at work on time

from now on."

"Good." Sean tossed a file across the desk. "Here's where we are today."

Payne flipped open the file and read the contents, switching immediately into what Sean thought of as "Payne-Cop-Mode"—intense, focused, and all about the job.

"Homicide. Serena Watkins. Age twenty-two. From South Boston. Found in her garage. . .this morning?" Payne looked up from the page. "You already visited the crime scene?"

"I called, you didn't answer."

Payne grumbled a response before speaking up. "Must not have heard the phone."

Sean fought the urge to scoff. "Regardless, we think it's the boyfriend, a seventeen-year-old named Jerry. Just waiting on an address and then we'll head over to his place."

A female voice spoke from the doorway. "Morning, Detective Trann."

Sean glanced up to ID the voice, which belonged to the temporary receptionist, Judy. Wearing beige slacks, a loose black sweater, and her hair in a bun, she briskly walked in and dropped a piece of paper on Sean's desk. "Morning, Detective Payne," she said to Sean's partner, ignoring the leering stare he always gave her when she walked by.

"Good morning, Judy," Payne replied, licking his lips as she walked out. Sean shook his head. Anything with a female ass turned that man on.

Sean missed the usual receptionist, Mags. Not that there was anything wrong with Judy, it was just. . .she didn't seem to have much personality. She came in, did her job, and went home, but didn't really seem to care about being at work. He supposed many temps might be like that. It wouldn't pay to get too involved since you end up leaving soon anyway. But if Sean were being honest, Judy may have been the most boring person he had ever met. She rarely said more than ten words in a whole conversation, and if they didn't have to do with work, the words revolved around her three cocker spaniels, Zippy, Zappy, and Zoozoo, or something like that.

"I swear," Payne muttered, "she does not know what she does to a man."

Sean cleared his throat, anger sparking inside him. "Cut that shit out, too. She's a coworker."

Payne laughed. "Sure thing, Tinkerbell. I mean *Trann*."

Sean kept his temper in check as they left his office, but just barely. He didn't know how to deal with someone like Payne. If he reported him for unbecoming conduct, Payne would barely get a slap on the wrist, and it would make Sean's life worse. You had to count on your partner when on a job. If he got on Payne's bad side, it could mean his life.

Not that he thought that would ever happen. In the field, Payne was as professional as could be. In fact, he was a crack shot and always stayed cool, no matter the situation. It frustrated Sean to no end that reporting him would mean losing a good partner where it mattered—out in the real world.

Still, maybe he could somehow get him to curb his behavior.

The two of them weaved their way through the roadmap of cubicles and desks to Millan's office. Even with the window open to Boston's fall air, the room still smelled of stale cigarette smoke. The "No Smoking" sign had been conveniently covered with a poster.

Nobody in the office said anything about it, as the Sergeant only smoked with the window open, and only before the work day started. Plus, Sean couldn't blame the guy. Sergeant Frank Millan had quit smoking when he'd had a cancer scare, shortly after Sean joined the Boston P.D. a year and a half ago. It hadn't been the first time the doctors had warned him to quit—the 30-year-old habit was bound to have consequences for anyone—but that wasn't the reason Millan had stopped.

A week after his visit to the doctor, he found out he had a fourteen-year-old daughter from a woman he'd been involved with before his current wife. The situation had been complicated, and never explained fully to Sean, who didn't want to pry, but the woman never told him he was a father. Millan and his current wife were unable to have children. So the news of being a father hit him hard, and he'd quit smoking right then and there.

Despite their age gap, Sean felt fairly close with the late fifties, African-American man, but he never knew the reason why Millan had quit, until the sergeant restarted the habit a month ago; his newly-found daughter, who'd just turned 15, was learning to drive with her mother when a drunk driver ran a stop sign and killed them.

Needless to say, smoking was the first thing Millan turned to when he'd heard the news.

"Morning, Sergeant," Sean said as he entered.

"Morning, Trann, Payne," Millan replied, nodding in each man's direction. He rubbed his gristly facial hair absentmindedly. "What's the progress on the Watkins case?"

"We were just about to head over to the boyfriend's house for questioning," Payne replied, before Sean could speak.

Sean gritted his teeth. As usual, Payne stepped in as if he'd been part of the case all along.

"Sounds good. Keep me updated." Millan dismissed them with a flick of his hand. Before they left, the sergeant called out, "Hey Trann, hold on a sec."

Sean told Payne he'd meet him outside, then pivoted around and halted. "Yeah?"

"I almost forgot. This came for you." He held up a manila envelope.

Sean took it. "Who's it from?"

Millan rubbed his chin again. "General Attorney's office."

Sean's stomach dropped. He held the envelope with only his fingertips, as if it were soaked with poison slowly leaching into his skin. "It can't be time already."

"Trial got moved up a few months. The news is too big. Everyone wants to see her trial and the governor wants a win. Up for election soon, I bet."

With a curt nod, Sean left the room, feeling a bit numb. Instead of heading towards the front door of the precinct where Payne waited, he beelined to the front desk. The area looked barren and clean, with only one picture of Judy and her three dogs in one corner, a small cactus in the other, and a computer in the middle. "Hey, Judy, hold on to this for me, would you? I'll pick it up when I'm finished with my shift."

She took the folder, a quizzical look on her face.

Sean nodded in Payne's direction. "Prying eyes and all that."

"Of course." Judy tucked the envelope into her desk drawer. "By the way, an email came to the front desk addressed to you. You want it forwarded?"

"From who?"

"A graduate student from Boston U. Their class has to interview a cop about a case they worked on."

Sean nodded. He'd done this sort of thing before for students—they would shadow him or he'd run through procedures for a class of theirs. He'd even guest-lectured once at the University. But he *really* didn't want to talk about the Spider case. "Yeah go ahead and forward it. I'm sure it's about Spider. I'll tell the student I can't talk about the case, and since it's going to trial, I probably shouldn't anyway."

"It's not about the Spider case."

He paused. "No?"

Judy shook her head. "It was some case from when you worked in Philly. I guess she discussed it in the class."

"Trann, let's move!" Payne called out, sticking his head in through the front door.

Sean scratched his nose. "All right, fine. Send it over," he said to Judy. "I'll read it later."

She smiled. "Will do. And I'll keep the envelope safe until closing time," she said, pointing to the drawer.

He'd already almost forgotten about it. "Thanks," he murmured. Sean stretched his neck from side to side and caught up with Payne. Memories from six months ago threatened to flood his mind, but he forced himself to keep them at bay by focusing on the current case. He didn't want to deal with the trial. Not now, not ever.

Not that he didn't want to end the Spider case once and for all, it was just. . .it brought up so many emotional things.

Angellica.

Counselor Eth.

Charlotte.

With a shake he cleared his head and caught up with Payne outside. They hopped into Sean's Jaguar and drove over to the address Judy had supplied for them.

3

September 25th
4:20 p.m. Local Time

Charlotte's breath crystalized into a white puff of frosted air. The Russian temperature of 30 degrees F in the city of Saint Petersburg bit into the few exposed portions of her face. She stood, her stare peering past the cars rolling by and the people who scurried along the banks of the Neva River. Recently fallen snow created pockets of white diamond-encrusted gleams against the background of flowing water.

Instead of focusing on the hustle and bustle of civilians, Charlotte's gaze beheld two large sculptures, based on Roman-styled rostral columns. The large pillars towered over the edge of the river mouth, red as candy apples, with carved sea creatures and anchors along their sides.

A shiver passed through her that had nothing to do with the freezing temperatures. The columns were not her destination, nor were they pertinent to her current task, but they triggered something in her. Six months ago, she'd been pulled from an underground compound in Boston, nearly dead. The entrance to that compound also contained a large, pillared monument: the Soldiers and Sailors statue. The site of these current behemoths, though red and adorned with nautical figures instead of wreaths, felt too close to home.

Could one of those same pockets of murderers be lurking underneath these columns right now? Plotting who they planned to kill next? Believing they had the right to dictate who deserved to live and who wasn't worth the space they breathed?

Her small hands clenched into fists inside her gloves and tears blurred her vision. The wind cut through them, creating icy trails on her face as they rolled down her cheeks.

The past three months had been such a blur of travel, government officials, and cheap hotels that she'd barely had time to think about her situation, much less what she'd gone through six months ago. Her right fist edged its way up her body, pressing against her puffy jacket, below her right breast. She dug in her fingers, imagining she could still feel the pain from the knife which had protruded from that spot those few months ago.

A knife that should have killed her, but didn't.

Because she was supposedly the Messiah of the Triads.

A voice behind her startled her out of her thoughts.

"Charlotte? We're ready to go."

Charlotte hastily brushed away the frozen streaks on her face with her fingertips and turned around.

"Lead the way please, Mags." Charlotte stepped lightly through the snow behind the short, dark-haired woman in front of her, whose affection for quirky outfits showed in her red plaid snow boots. Mags clomped along, right at home in the winter conditions, having grown up in Canada.

Although appreciative of the company, Charlotte and Mags hadn't gelled very well on the trip. It could have been due to the constant time changes or the multiple flights, train rides, and drives in a rental car, but Charlotte wondered if their personalities were too different. Though both women were incredibly smart and had multiple college degrees between them, Mags had chosen to use her genius level of intelligence in math and computers to work as a receptionist for a police department. This "lack of caring" about her potential confused and frustrated Charlotte. Mags could be doing anything she wanted. Why did she waste her time at a front desk?

Charlotte caught up with Mags right before they reached the road where a small blue coupe waited, a fresh dusting of snow across its top and hood. A white car with blue stripes—standard issue police vehicle—sat behind their coupe. The driver looked up as they approached their car, a clipboard in her hand. She waved through the windshield and Mags gave a half-hearted salute.

"Any luck?" Charlotte asked Mags. She never used to believe in luck, but since their hard work hadn't been paying off, she hoped luck would cut them a break.

Mags shook her head, causing bits of snow to fall off the fringes of her faux-fur lined hood. "Another bust. Officer Petrova seemed a bit annoyed, to be honest."

"I do not blame her. That makes three locations here in St. Petersburg that we claimed had ties to Triads and the fifty-seventh in total for us," Charlotte said, a frown touching the edges of her mouth. "All of which led to nothing."

"You know my thoughts about that," Mags said quietly.

They reached the car, Mags taking the driver's side.

"I believe you may be right, that if there were any other active Triad sects, they were somehow alerted when Truth's Triad was exposed. Or, that the entire situation was a hoax. Still, it seemed imperative to keep up the attempts." She sighed. "I would hate to think stopping would cause us to miss out on capturing even one sect."

The two of them got into the vehicle, slamming their doors closed against the icy wind. Mags turned on the car and cranked the heat up to HIGH. Chilled air blew through the vents, slowly warming up as they left their parking spot. The police car behind them followed.

"What do you wanna do?" Mags asked.

Charlotte didn't have an answer. This was the furthest spot from their original beginnings in Boston, when they thought maybe they could catch a few straggling sects and arrest them, but it appeared that news of their intentions had spread. None of the possible sects seemed to have any trace of headquarters or a set-up for women to kill anyone. And all the places they'd searched bore no resemblance to the elaborate compound in Boston.

Mags hadn't acquired a complete list from the computer system she'd hacked into—some sort of failsafe had corrupted or deleted most of the data they'd found in the underground lair of Truth's Triad—but she had recovered 60 random addresses.

Sixty out of the 500,000 Triads Truth claimed existed.

This visit to St. Petersburg made 57 concluded attempts out of 60. All of them so far had been dead ends.

There'd been nothing. The addresses led to random places, no two alike. Some were warehouses, some companies, some apartment buildings, some non-existent buildings— merely an open field, ravine, or river. They had no idea what those addresses referenced. Charlotte had been sure they would lead to the other Triad groups, but after the first few failures, the addresses could have been anything: previous victim locations, alternate headquarters, even places where a sleeper agent lived or worked at some time.

Charlotte removed her black gloves and rubbed her temples. Nothing made sense. What Truth had told her about all the killings, all the other Triads, about being the Messiah— the concepts seemed so impossible. There was no proof. No other found sects. No one she was supposed to "lead."

Her eyes closed at the thought. Truth had been so sure Charlotte would be the savior of all the groups, to lead them all in killing those unworthy to live, reproduce, or influence humankind. Not that Charlotte would ever do such a thing, but why make up such an elaborate fabrication about a "messiah" to command half a million Triads of women killing others across the world?

Had Truth merely been insane? A liar to throw Charlotte off the track? But the track to where? None of it made sense.

And what about the ancient tome Charlotte had been shown which, according to Truth, was a written account of how these women were supposed to help keep human evolution in check? The Book currently sat in the evidence room of the Boston P.D. Since it was real, could everything else be real, too?

"We should be thorough," Charlotte said out loud, "and continue with the remaining three locations. I would not want to miss one chance to find a Triad just because the previous addresses have led nowhere."

Mags remained quiet for a few moments, longer than Charlotte expected before saying, "You got it. I've always wanted to go to Moscow. Just three more to check there and then we can go home."

Home.

Charlotte's thoughts immediately shifted to the one person in particular she both wanted to and dreaded seeing when they returned: Detective Sean Trann.

Mags continued. "We might even be there by Friday. I'd love to surprise Juliette on her first day back."

Charlotte knew Mags had kept in close touch with her coworkers of the Boston Police Department. Charlotte had tried, at first, to keep in contact with her own coworkers and some members of the Boston P.D., but as usual, the conversations dried up quickly. The only person she really looked forward to speaking with had been Sean. They chatted and messaged several times in the first few weeks of the trip, but between the time differences, the jet lag, and the frustration at failure after failure, Charlotte had basically stopped reaching out. Sean's attempts at contacting her had lessened as well, being busy with new cases and dealing with a new partner.

As their communication dwindled, she began to worry that there'd been no real connection with Sean or anyone else in the department, except about the Spider case, which seemed to be coming to a screeching halt. Doubts swirled in her mind each night as she fell asleep, listening to the soft snores of Mags in the other bed. Everyone had been brought together because of the case, but were they, or *could* they, really be friends outside of it?

And now she had to return home as a disappointment. She had no proof of any other Triad. She'd made such a big deal out of this trip and why?

Because somewhere inside she *liked* the idea of being a messiah who had power over these groups of women. She imagined she'd sweep in, tell them to stop their evil ways, and be a heroine. The thought had been nothing more than a fantasy, she knew that on a logical level, but the purpose she felt, the contentment at having such a large and important role lit her from the inside like an ember building to a roaring flame.

But there'd been nothing. She wasn't important. It had only been the ravings of a lunatic who decided to kill people because they weren't "perfect."

Huge snowflakes floated through the air as they drove,

reminding her of being inside a giant snow globe. Russia so far had been beautiful, but it gave the impression of vastness and loneliness. Going home should fill her with warmth and safety and security. All it did was make her feel anxious. Anxious about dealing with reality, about going back and not being special, and about seeing someone she thought she could have a connection with and realizing he was just another man she'd pushed away. . .

Luckily she didn't have to worry about that until they made their last three inspections.

Charlotte sobered up and shifted her focus once again onto business. They still had three more chances. Perhaps they'd be successful and she could still have the fantasy.

"After we arrive at the police station and finish our paperwork," she said, "go ahead and set up the next flight to Moscow."

4

September 25th
3 p.m.

Sean knocked on the front door of a small, shabbily-painted red house. A strange cuckoo clock mailbox hung on the outside wall, the clock apparently broken as the wooden bird hung limply from a curled wire. Crisp, fall air swirled around him and Payne, kicking up stray leaves and a plastic bag which danced in a circle on the porch.

Payne called out, "Jerry Newman, open up. This is the police!" They waited for a few moments until they heard the sound of the locks clicking open behind the door.

Payne gently moved his hand to the top of his holstered

gun, on guard.

The door opened and an elderly woman with flyaway gray hair and thick glasses answered. "Who's there?" she cawed.

"My name is Detective Trann," Sean began, "and this is my partner, Detective Payne. We are here to speak with a Jerry Newman. Is he here?"

The old woman frowned. "Jerry? He's my grandson. What kind of trouble he in now?" Her broken English had a bit of a slur and Sean didn't fail to notice the way one side of her face didn't quite move in sync with the other.

Recent stroke, he thought.

"Ma'am, we'd like to speak to him directly."

"Jerry!" she yelled, turning her head a fraction. Payne made a face at the high-volumed word.

"Yeah, Nana?" came a voice from the top of the stairs.

"Some po-lice here to see you."

The young man (Caucasian, sneakers, jeans, white T-shirt—Sean immediately logged these details in the moment) stopped halfway down the steps. He assessed the scene, and immediately ran back up the stairs.

"We got a rabbit!" Payne shouted. "Back!" he hollered to Sean, then took off through the room to the staircase.

"Damnit!" Sean cried out, running off the porch and around to the rear of the house. Sure enough, as soon as he turned the corner, he saw the young man land awkwardly on the ground, his ankle turning underneath him.

Yelling in pain, the suspect hobbled a short distance, but he was no match for Sean, who identified himself as police and called out for him to freeze, then caught him quickly, ordering him to the ground.

With a few quick motions, the kid was on his knees, and Sean's handcuffs were around his wrists. By the time he'd recited the young man his Miranda rights, Payne caught up with them.

"Nice job," he said, smacking Sean on his good shoulder.

Sean smiled. "Thanks." He helped the kid stand and the three of them returned to the front of the house. Payne called in the arrest and they waited for a patrol car to arrive and take the suspect to the station.

After admitting Jerry and signing the paperwork at the precinct, the rest of Sean's day was fairly uneventful. He replied to the grad student, who said she could only meet on weeknights, and offered to buy him dinner on Friday for his time. He'd done a couple interviews over coffee so a free meal sounded great. He'd replied "Works for me," and sent the email into the ether.

At a few minutes to five, he collected his things for the evening. He was just walking out of the precinct when he felt a tap on his shoulder.

"You almost forgot this," Judy said, handing him the manila envelope he'd given her earlier in the day.

He paled. "Ah. Yeah. Thanks."

An hour later, Sean sat on a stiff, brown loveseat, staring at a psychologist.

After the shooting incident six months ago, he'd been ordered to sit through therapy sessions once a week to work through the experience. The psychologist had approved him for duty three months ago, but she still had to monitor him for three more months after his return to work before officially clearing him. The elongated counseling time was a new practice for the Boston P.D., but the Chief of Police had instituted the new policy, claiming that trauma and unresolved violent issues in cases caused multiple problems with officers when not properly dealt with by a professional.

Up until this point, Sean had dutifully done his required task—talked about whatever the therapist asked about: his time as a police officer, his relationship with Angellica, his move to Boston, the Spider case, etc. As much as he didn't really care about seeing the doctor, somewhere deep inside, he did think talking about everything had helped. He hadn't realized how unhinged he'd felt during that whole month, how much the Spider Triad had screwed with his emotions and mind.

In the past several months, he'd felt calmer, more grounded at work and home, and knew he really wouldn't need these sessions anymore.

Except today, Sean felt uneasy.

He held the summons envelope in his lap, unable to look at it.

His initial thought of why he didn't want to open it had revolved around the fact that he didn't like trials. Something about them made him feel uncomfortable, sitting up in front of everyone on display. But he'd never hesitated to open a summons in the past. He'd never felt dread thicken in his gut before.

His psychologist, Dr. Carla Moria, simply waited.

The first visit with her caught him off guard. He'd been expecting some tightly-pulled-back hair lady with glasses and a permanent sneer on her face. Instead, he got Carla, a thirty-something-year old woman with curvy lips and an even curvier body. She looked more like a South American pop star then a cop therapist.

But the attraction quickly took a back seat. Carla didn't pull any punches and Sean could tell she wasn't someone to hit on or piss off. Besides, the giant glistening ring on her hand signified her marriage to someone who made at least three times more income than Sean did.

Carla pointed at the envelope. "You might as well spill. It's obvious that's bothering you." Her words rolled off her tongue with a Spanish lilt to them.

"It's my summons," he said, his stomach tight. "For the Spider trial."

Her eyes widened. "So soon? I thought you told me it probably wouldn't take place for another few months."

"Millan said it's been pushed up from the governor's office. I'm sure it has *nothing* to do with his reelection coming up." Sarcasm dripped off his last sentence.

"*Ay, Maria,*" she muttered in Spanish. "That whole experience felt so unreal, watching it on the television." She paused. "I never told you, but I knew one of the victims. Well, sort of. One of the women who died, I am good friends with her mother."

Sean nodded. Six months ago, details of the case had

leaked. For weeks after the deaths of Truth and Anya and the arrest of Violet, the news had been flooded with stories about the events. The victims from that month, plus those from the previous year, were redisplayed across screens all over the world. Particulars emerged, including the tell-tale spider webbed mark on a victim's shoulder after being shot with a paralytic dart, the existence of the underground compound underneath the Soldiers and Sailors statue in Boston, and that only persons with some sort of physical defect, either external or internal, were targeted.

People had panicked. Calls came in from all over with claims about loved ones having been killed by someone in a Triad, especially if they'd died randomly or strangely. "Accidental Death" as a reason wasn't good enough anymore. Other calls came in about people feeling like they were being stalked or followed because they had "imperfections." Picket lines paraded in front of police stations and graffiti colored the sides of the coroner's building. Even Sean's apartment had been staked out for a couple weeks by journalists wanting to know the "inside scoop" on the Spider case.

Sean knew the upcoming trial would just revive these hysterias. He'd have to go through it all again. Well, at least no one would get murdered this time.

Carla's words refocused Sean's attention. "We spent so much time talking about what happened to you during the cases, we never discussed how you might feel about the trial."

"Well, I'm glad it's happening, of course. I mean, it'll keep Violet behind bars."

"*If* she's convicted."

The words hung in the air, frozen like a monster in a nightmare Sean couldn't escape.

"I never thought of that." The idea seemed preposterous. Of *course* she'd be convicted. There was evidence. And witnesses. Hell, even Sean had watched her blow Counselor Eth's head off. She wouldn't get away this time.

The clock on the wall clicked softly behind him, ticking away moments of belief.

Doubt slithered its way into his mind.

"How could that be possible?" he asked, his voice quiet. "How could she *not* be convicted?"

Carla shuffled her papers and shrugged. "I don't know, Sean. All I know is she and those other women got away with murder for years. I worry Violet will have something up her sleeve. In the meantime, let's talk about this most recent case, the Watkins woman. . ."

5

September 26th
8 p.m. Local Time

Charlotte stood in line at the Sheremetyevo International Airport in Moscow, her thoughts a whirling mess. Smells of plastic seats and the tense faces of stressed-out travelers reminded her of every other airport they'd visited in the past three months. They all blurred together, like a never-ending carousel where she constantly got off and on but wondered if she ever really went anywhere.

Sixty. They'd finished the sixtieth place on Mags' list and nothing. All like the others—plain, boarded up, vacated, or didn't even exist. The list made no sense and had led nowhere.

Charlotte's eyes remained still inside their sockets as she

stared at the back of Mags' head, whose white knit cap revealed pockets of dark hair, but her mind roamed everywhere else except her present location.

Why did she think they would find sites as elaborate as the underground compound where she'd been taken in Boston? If what Truth said was true about how a Triad worked, then the three women didn't even have to know each other, much less congregate in the same building. There only needed to be one who chose the victims, one to decide on the mode of execution, and one who'd be called on to perform the killing. Everything could be done with emails or texts for goodness sake.

Charlotte rubbed her fingertips against her temples. A dull throb had begun inside her skull. She wanted nothing more than to stay in Moscow, rent a hotel room, and run away from the world.

The thought gave her pause. It wasn't like her to not want to deal with her problems. And why stay here? She missed her own apartment, her own bed. And she missed her job as Chief Medical Examiner. So, what made her want to stay here?

Two situations floated to mind that would greet her after this final flight to Boston: the trial and Sean.

She wasn't sure which scared her more.

Running around the world and chasing possible killers had served as a fantastic distraction from her life. The truth was, the previous year had changed her. When the Spider case first fell into her lap, she'd been more than excited, she'd been elated. Her first real case where no one else could solve it. And she'd helped to do just that. Her findings led to the clues which helped Sean and his police team crack the case.

Or had they?

Uncertainty had crept into her head over the past few months like a slow-moving disease. She felt infected by it, tainted. She didn't like feeling. . .wrong.

The truth was she *hadn't* helped. Yes, she'd discovered the link to help solve Spider's motive, but if Truth hadn't called Sean with the whereabouts to their compound, would she and Detective Tay and Mags ever have been found at all?

On top of all that, she herself had been kidnapped. Charlotte had felt so foolish when she'd awakened in the hospital after the whole ordeal. Grateful, of course, that she still lived, but so foolish. How could she not have suspected she'd be a target? How could she have let Truth walk into her workplace at all?

Then there'd been Sean. On the outside he seemed like a normal, albeit attractive, Boston cop. Arrogant at times and just there to do his job. But the passion she saw in him to catch Spider intrigued her. The ease which she felt around him surprised her. And the thought of wanting to spend more and more time with him scared her.

He seemed so *normal*. She didn't like that she'd found herself attracted to normal. And she didn't like how arrogant that made *her* sound.

"Hey, Charlotte," Mags said, returning her from her thoughts. "Can you believe our luck? The whole Miss Russia pack is causing a backup." Mags pointed across the terminal and sure enough, a gaggle of beautiful woman stood in full makeup, their sashes placed strategically across their chests. They appeared to be doing a photo op before heading out on a plane. Charlotte overheard one of the women say they'd collected the past ten Miss Russia's together to do a photo shoot outside of the upcoming Miss World event in Australia, celebrating some milestone of the competition. Several cameras snapped pictures while children stood in line to get autographs. Many random men also hung out nearby as well, their eyes barely in their heads.

Normally Charlotte wouldn't care. She never really found herself jealous of other women. Perhaps because she worked so hard at maintaining a healthy and unmarried appearance, or that she'd cultivated her diction and responses with care that she didn't find other women threatening. But at this moment, viewing the ten or so stunning women in front of her, Charlotte's stomach somersaulted.

"Could you imagine being in a contest like that?" Mags continued. "I don't feel this way or that about beauty pageants, but I couldn't *stand* the idea of someone judging me based on how I look. I'd be a wreck all the time."

Charlotte barely heard the words. She couldn't turn her stare from the gorgeous women. Their perfect hair, perfect bodies, perfect smiles. Her stomach shifted again and her knees felt weak.

"I need to. . ." she muttered. She stepped away from the line and headed toward the nearest restroom entrance.

"Charlotte?" Mags called out.

Charlotte didn't stop. She raced through the door and into a stall, narrowly making it before vomiting.

Once she'd emptied her stomach, she sat back on her heels, her body shaking. A thin film of sweat broke out across her forehead. She wiped it away with her sleeve, her arm trembling.

What had just happened?

The sound of footsteps startled her.

"Charlotte?" Mags repeated.

"I am in here," Charlotte answered, waving her hand under the stall door.

"Are you okay?"

"I think so." She forced herself to stand, flushed the toilet, and opened the door. With a few steps she reached the sink and rinsed out her mouth.

"Did you throw up?"

Charlotte gripped the edges of the sink and peered into the mirror. "Yes." The word surprised her. She'd never thrown up in her entire life. Even when sick, she'd never suffered from a stomach flu or food poisoning, just illnesses that made her feel achy and awful everywhere else. The entire process felt odd—painful stomach contractions and a sore throat, yet her body felt better for it.

"Do you think it was something you ate?"

Charlotte shook her head. "No. All I had today was an apple and some water. I prefer eating heavier for lunch."

"Oh." Mags tapped her shoe against the side of the garbage bin. "Do you think you're okay to fly?"

Charlotte closed her eyes for a moment, letting out a sigh. Of course. They still needed to board the plane.

"Yes, I believe I will be able to fly without any further

issues." *I hope,* she thought.

"Okay, well then we better get going. It's fifteen minutes to take off."

Charlotte nodded and followed Mags out. The area appeared clear now that the beauty contestants had boarded their plane.

Handing over her ticket for the final scan, Charlotte's gaze lingered for a moment where the contestants had been standing. Why had their presence affected her so much? They'd merely been a group of lovely women...

Charlotte paused at the thought, a notion striking her.

"Miss?" the check-in attendant said, bringing Charlotte out of her revelation.

"Oh, yes, sorry." She retook her ticket and headed down the tunnel to the plane, her thoughts racing.

She realized why the sight of those women bothered her. They were stunning, nearly perfect. How *could* she trust them? The main purpose of Truth, Violet, and Anya as a Triad had been to target and murder people who weren't physically "perfect" in their eyes. The three of them had each been healthy and gorgeous.

Add in the fact that Charlotte had just been around the world looking for more groups of physically lovely murderers and of course she would feel anxiety around a cluster of beautiful women.

She involuntarily pressed against the right side of her chest again, as if she could feel phantom pain from the knife wound from six months ago.

"Charlotte, come on!" Mags called out.

Charlotte dropped her hand and caught up to Mags at the plane's door. They boarded slowly as other passengers tucked bags into the overhead compartments and shuffled around in their seats. Finally, Charlotte stepped onto the plane. A striking woman, with sleek russet-colored hair and crystal green eyes greeted her.

"*Dobro pozhalovat,*" she said in Russian, her smile bright and wide. Though Charlotte knew a few other languages, she'd only picked up a little Russian, but she understood the "welcome aboard" words. The flight attendant glanced at the ticket stub Charlotte still gripped in her hand. More Russian words exited her mouth, which Charlotte couldn't interpret, but then the woman pointed towards the rear and said in a cadenced English, "Your seat is near the wing. . .Charlotte."

"Thank you," Charlotte mumbled. She found her seat next to Mags, settled in, and went to tuck her ticket into her pocket when she froze.

Her ticket.

The name on her ticket had been covered up by the envelope which held it. Her seat appeared, but her name didn't.

Charlotte paused. She slid the ticket out a bit further until her name showed.

It must have simply slid down into the envelope, she thought. *My name must have shown when the flight attendant saw the ticket.*

Still, a prickle of fear crept up the nape of her neck.

"Mags," she said.

"Yeah?" Mags had already donned a pair of large headphones and was watching some movie on her phone. She pulled the left headphone off her ear.

"Do you see a flight attendant with coppery-red hair?"

Mags scooted up and peered around the plane. "No. But maybe she's in first class?" She plopped back down in her seat. "Why?"

Charlotte paused for a moment then shoved her ticket into her pocket. She squashed down her feelings of unease, attributing them to irrational paranoia.

"No reason."

6

September 27th
7 a.m.

Detective Juliette Tay fixed her shoulder-length red hair for the umpteenth time. Even though she'd been told by the doctor that her prosthetic ear would be an exact match to her other one, she still felt like it looked bigger. No matter how she styled her hair to cover it, she could see a lump in its outline. She swore that didn't happen with her real ear.

Juliette let out a sigh and told herself to be grateful she was even alive. Six months ago she'd had her ear shot off by a bullet which blasted through a door behind her. On top of that, she'd been shot in the gut and nearly bled to death.

Her mum, living in their small town outside London,

had begged her to come home.

"Nothing like that ever happens here, luv," her mother assured her. "The most problems are stolen bikes and lost dogs."

When Juliette refused, saying she liked living in Boston, liked her coworkers, and liked her job, her mum really laid on the guilt.

"And what if next time they don't get to you in time? You expect me and my ol' bag of bones to come cross the ocean for your funeral? I won't even get to bury my own daughter..."

Juliette had listened for several more minutes, placating her mum as best she could, before finally giving in. Instead of returning to work ten weeks ago as scheduled, she took some personal time off and flew to England.

The weeks dripped by. At first, Juliette had been happy to be home, once again in a comfortable environment, with her mother cooing and fussing over every little thing. But after a while, she felt antsy. She missed working her cases and seeing her coworkers. She missed the hustle and bustle of Boston.

Eventually, she had a talk with her mum and explained she was returning to Boston. After two days of tears and reminders that her daughter had almost been killed, Juliette finally told her England would always be her home, but Boston was where her life was, kissed her on the cheek, and left.

A week passed since her return before her mum finally called. Their chat had been rocky at first, with awkward silences and a few tears, but eventually they settled into their normal conversational pattern and by the end, Juliette promised to call at least once a week and that she'd make it home for Christmas.

But standing here now, in the yellow tiled bathroom of her duplex, staring at the mirror, dressed for work, trying to get her hair to cover a prosthetic ear. . . Maybe her mother had been right. She could have died. Easily.

A shudder ran through her. She could still leave. Quit. Move back to England. No one would think less of her. The local law enforcement there would be happy to have such a well-decorated detective on their squad. They'd specifically told her that during her visit.

Juliette's gaze shifted to the envelope on her sink. Unopened mail from Wednesday. She knew what it was. Her partner, Wilt, had called to welcome her home and tell her about the summons for the Spider trial. He told her he'd dropped it into her mailbox.

With a sudden rashness, she ripped open the envelope and read the upcoming date: Friday, October 4 at 9 a.m. One week away.

Heat welled up inside her chest, replacing the anxiety. These women had not only nearly stolen her life, they were now stealing her safety. They tried to kill her and failed. They went up against the Boston P.D. and *failed.*

Juliette's shoulders straightened. Let her hometown figure out who stole Brighton's bike or find Timmy's dog in the well. She was a detective. A bloody great one. She'd helped bring down a serial killer ring. She'd helped save lives. These women had failed.

She grasped the paperwork in her hand, wrinkling it slightly in her grip.

They wanted to blow off her ear? Fine.

They wanted to shoot her in the gut? Bring it on.

Because she wasn't going anywhere. Except to her job to make every killer's life a living hell.

With a fire in her belly, Juliette pulled her hair up into her trademark loose bun and decided yep, both ears looked exactly the same.

7

September 27th
8:45 a.m.

Sean stared at the small, pathetic-looking store-bought chocolate cupcakes and grimaced. It had completely slipped his mind that he'd been told to pick up dessert for Detective Juliette Tay's returning-to-work party. Though Detective Cam Wilt, who'd suggested the party in the first place, had sent a reminder, Sean hadn't received the message until he'd left his apartment, since he had no cell phone reception there. He'd cursed, not as quietly as he should have, and stopped by the local market on his way to work, collecting the small dollops of brown in cupcake wrappers before him.

"Nice," Wilt said around the toothpick in his mouth.

"These look like my dog ate them first."

"Sorry, man. The market I went to didn't exactly have a bakery. I'm sure they'll be fine," Sean said, opening the package and placing them on the table. A short stack of paper plates, napkins, and a printed-out piece of paper with "WELCOME BACK JEWELS!" in bright purple letters completed the look. Sean knew how happy Wilt was that Tay would be returning today. She was an excellent detective and fun to be around. Without her and Mags, the station had felt pretty flat and dull the past few months. And Mags would be in on Monday to solidify their group again.

Sergeant Millan came out of his office and strolled over to the table. "Is she here yet?"

"Not yet," Wilt said. He flicked his toothpick into the nearby garbage can and ran his fingers through his blond hair, which brushed the tops of his ears.

"Excited to see her again?" Sean asked Wilt.

"Very. I don't know how you did it before Payne came. I miss having someone else out there with me."

Sean thought about his current partner versus his previous one. When Sean first arrived after his transfer from Philadelphia, he'd asked to be paired with Tay, but Millan said she was better suited for Wilt. And eventually, Sean agreed. Wilt had struggled a bit as a detective, getting quite angry with cases he couldn't solve or perps he couldn't catch. His anger began filtering into his day-to-day life, especially with his son. As a single dad of a teenage boy, Wilt wrestled to keep control of his kid, butting heads with the boy on a constant basis.

With Tay as his partner, bringing her British wit and

sharp sense of detail, Wilt mellowed out, both at home and on the job. She was a good balance for him and Sean recently heard that Wilt's son had thought of applying for an internship with the police department after high school. Sean, however, always suspected Wilt's son wanted to join more to be around Tay than to be like his father, but he kept the hunch to himself.

Now, Sean was stuck with Payne. The guy never did anything *wrong* on the job per say, except once again being late, but Sean felt a bit of envy towards Wilt right now.

"I think she's coming!" Judy called out from the front desk, having been told to look out for a red-haired woman.

All three men straightened. Wilt picked up the banner and held it in front of him. Sean was forcibly reminded of a chauffeur holding a sign with his client's name on it. The three of them must have looked pretty silly.

"False alarm!" Judy said and they all slumped.

"Sad," a voice said from behind them.

Sean whirled around. He recognized that voice. . .

"Mags!" he called out, then pulled her into a huge hug. He'd buried her face into his chest and couldn't hear her muffled reply. He pulled away. "Where did you come from? Why didn't you tell us you were getting home today? I thought you weren't back until Monday!"

Before she could answer, Wilt and Millan also came over, the first hugging her as well, the second patting her on the shoulder.

"I came in through the back and I didn't want any kind of commotion," she finally said, adjusting her glasses and eyeing the table behind them. "Although it looks like I wouldn't have had to worry about anything big." She let out a snort and they all grinned.

"Besides," she continued, "I'm technically not fully returning to work until after the weekend. I just couldn't wait to see all of you. I'm not even sure what time zone I'm in anymore!"

Sean gave her a quick assessment, noting the deep blue circles under her eyes, her paler-than-normal skin, and her slumped shoulders. She looked like hell.

Sean threw an arm around her shoulder and squeezed, more gently this time. "Well you just made it. Tay is on her way in and it's her first day back, too."

"Oh, I know," Mags said, a twinkle in her eye. "I checked in on her when I could. After what we went through, it kind of bonds people, you know? And I had a feeling she'd need my help with her return-to-work party." She signaled for one of the interns nearby who brought over a stack of food trays, a bouquet of flowers, and some balloons.

Sean let out a sigh of relief. "You're a lifesaver, Mags."

"I know." She grinned.

Sean peeked behind the intern towards the rear entrance.

"She's not here," Mags said.

"Hm?" Sean asked, shifting his gaze to her.

"Charlotte. She's not here. She went straight home from the airport."

"Oh. Sure. I mean, I wasn't looking for her," he lied.

A smirk touched her lips. "Whatever you say."

Sean removed his arm under the guise of helping to set up

the table, but inside, anger stirred. He wasn't quite sure what he felt riled up about. That Charlotte hadn't even contacted him the past couple weeks or told him she was coming home? That she hadn't come to the station with Mags? That Mags had completely seen through his veiled attempt at casually looking for Charlotte?

A different emotion flooded him: guilt. He shouldn't care about Charlotte. Sure, they'd left things open as a possible. . .some kind of relationship he supposed, but then she'd left. At first, they'd messaged each other a few times and talked on the phone, but after a while, Sean got busy and Charlotte seemed. . .distant. Which was saying something seeing as how her nickname had been "Ice Queen" behind her back. But this had been different. Charlotte's responses had been short, almost curt.

He'd tried to talk to Mags about it, but she only said Charlotte was "outfoxed and fried." Even Mags' conversations became fewer and further between, although hitting 16 different countries in three months was enough to rattle anyone's inner workings.

After the second month, Sean sort of gave up. Not intentionally, but he just felt like maybe neither of them wanted to talk to him. He didn't know why. And now that they'd both returned, he wasn't sure he wanted to dredge things up to find out.

Sean sighed. He just wanted a normal relationship, since his last one ended with his ex-fiancée trying to kill him, then dying in his arms.

That reminded him. . .

"Hey Mags, any other news while you were gone? I mean, any luck on the trip?"

Mags blew a breath through her teeth. "No," she said, an edge to the word. "We found nothing. Sixty places and bupkis. I think that's one reason why Charlotte went straight home. She hasn't been. . .taking it very well."

Before he could ask what that meant, Judy called out "Okay, she's *really* on her way now!"

"Can we catch up later?" Mags asked.

Sean nodded. He then turned and snuck a peek at the table and his mouth dropped in surprise. Instead of a sad sign with lumpy cupcakes, a checkered tablecloth covered the break room table, a box of bagels with two tubs of cream cheese next to it sat in the center surrounded by mini muffins, what appeared to be tiny sausages-in-blankets, and two cartons—one OJ, the other apple juice.

Right before the doors opened Sean whispered to Mags, "You're amazing. I missed the hell out of you."

"I did, too. And we really need to talk." Mags squeezed his arm before everyone shouted, "Welcome Back, Tay!"

8

September 27th
5:30 p.m.

The party had been short and sweet, just like Tay. She breached the subject about her ear and let everyone have a look and feel, if they wanted. Sean had been impressed. He'd worried she may not *want* to return after what happened to her. He could relate. He'd never been shot before in the line of duty and returning to work had been both unsettling and relieving.

Mags hadn't stayed long. Her insistence on being tired wasn't necessary, since her yawns and watery eyes spoke volumes for her. Still, seeing her had lifted Sean's spirits.

The biggest surprise though had been when Payne

showed up. He did his normal leer at Tay, then took one look at Mags, went red in the face, mumbled something about paperwork, and went to his desk.

"Do you know him?" Sean had asked Mags.

"I don't think so," Mags replied, her eyebrows furrowed. "I guess I'll ask him on Monday if we've met before." They decided to grab lunch on Sunday, to give Mags a little time first to readjust to this time zone, so they could catch up.

At the end of the day, Sean felt content on his way home. He entered his studio apartment, kicked off his shoes, and slid out of his jacket. Plopping down on the couch, he flicked on the TV, hoping there might be a good action movie on somewhere.

"Yessss," he hissed. He'd only missed the first ten minutes of some sort of car chase movie. He meant to get up to grab a Coke and the remaining bag of chips he'd started a few days ago, but the fatigue from the day settled over him and he promptly fell asleep instead.

A trill sounded on his phone, waking him an hour later.

"What?" he muttered, pulling his cell from his pocket. Through hazy eyes he struggled to read the reminder message.

Dinner with grad student.

Sean rubbed his eyes. The words didn't register at first. Then he remembered his free meal for answering some questions. After yawning, he used the bathroom, ran his fingers through his hair, and patted his grumbling belly. It would be filled soon. After putting on his jacket, he rechecked the name of the restaurant provided by the grad student, some place he'd never heard of, but he never backed down from trying something new. At least once.

Shoving his feet into his shoes, he left his apartment and locked the door. As soon as he exited, his phone beeped. This time it was a message. He gave a frustrated smile. Most people knew to get ahold of him on the landline, since his cell reception sucked inside his apartment, so he'd missed this message from whoever. Looked like it had been sent about an hour ago. He checked the caller ID.

Unknown caller.

Another one, he thought. He'd gotten several messages lately from cold callers doing polls for the upcoming election. He clicked open the message box to delete it.

He froze.

--wil use her wrds against--

The words, oddly misspelled, meant nothing to him. They had no context, no meaning, and yet Sean felt like a centipede that had fallen into an ice bath now climbed up his spine.

Normally, he ignored unfamiliar or unknown numbers unless they messaged again and then he'd tell them they were sending to the wrong person. But for some reason, this message felt off.

--Who is this?-- he messaged in response.

Nothing. The message was bounced back as "Unsent" since it had nowhere to go. It couldn't be directed to an unknown caller.

Shrugging it off, Sean headed down the stairs and to his car. He may be a couple minutes late, but if traffic were light enough, maybe not.

He swung his car door shut and turned on the engine. He pulled his phone from his pocket and placed it in its car holder.

The screen lit up. Another message.

An unknown number again.

--shell know I talked she wants you and her to notbelive. She wins tht way--

Sean reread the message, filling in the strange blanks. "She'll know I talked. She wants you and her to not believe. She wins that way." He immediately sent a message in return, but it got denied again.

Sean logged it away in his mind, but because he didn't understand the message, or if it was even meant for him, the feeling of unease eventually faded as the evening progressed.

9

September 27th
7 p.m.

Charlotte awoke, disoriented. She'd been to multiple countries and time zones in the past three months so she had *no* idea about her current location. The glow from a street-lamp filtered weakly through the slatted blinds, casting striped rays of light across the bed. She glanced over onto the nightstand next to the bed and saw a familiar sight: big blue clock numbers.

She was in her own apartment.

A sigh of relief escaped her lips. Then she realized what the numbers told her. It was 7 p.m.

For a minute, she didn't know what day it was or if she

was supposed to be somewhere and a wave of anxiety flooded her, tightening her chest. She sat up and reached for her phone to check the date. Friday, the 27th. Another sigh of relief. She'd returned home after the last flight that afternoon, slid into some pajamas, and promptly fell asleep. The time difference made her head swim. It would take her quite a while to get used to her schedule here.

Either way, her stomach didn't care. It gurgled with hunger since she hadn't eaten anything all day except a bag of pretzels, which had been all she could manage on the plane ride home. The experience of throwing up at the airport in Moscow had shaken her. She felt uneasy on both connecting flights back to Boston, nervous she may have another bout of anxiety.

She hadn't really felt settled until she'd arrived at her own place—a small studio apartment on the outskirts of Boston. Clean lines, soft furniture, and whites and creams greeted her. The space made her feel like everything she'd gone through had just been some sort of whirlwind bad dream, full of non-existent insane women, muddled travel, and unfulfilled goals.

Charlotte got out of bed, placed her feet into a pair of white slippers, and headed towards her kitchen. A quick look in the empty refrigerator reminded her why she should have stopped at a market on the way from the airport.

Her stomach gurgled again. She gave it a rub to calm it down.

With quick movements she got dressed—a black button-up shirt, long tan skirt, and black flats. Skilled fingers deftly wove her long, dark hair into a braid, which she then hung over her shoulder. She grabbed her jacket, purse, and keys and left her place.

Once in her car, a sporty little silver Subaru, she paused. Logically, she should go to the market, shop, and make something to eat at home. But physically, she wasn't sure she could wait that long. Instead, she decided to go to one of her favorite places to eat, The Elephant Walk, a Cambodian restaurant about 15 minutes away. She could order enough to take home—dinner for tonight and a soup for lunch the next day—then go shopping tomorrow after she popped into work. Even though she didn't officially return until Monday, she wanted to at least stop in and go through some of her emails to catch up.

Decision made, Charlotte started her car, turned the station to NPR, and headed out to satisfy her hunger pangs.

10

September 27th
7:15 p.m.

The scents of ginger and spicy peppers wafted up from Sean's meal. He had no idea how to pronounce the title of the dish in front of him, but the translated description underneath said spicy pork tenderloin and he figured he couldn't go wrong with that. He'd never had Cambodian food before, but the presentation looked a lot like most Chinese restaurants he'd been to, so he didn't feel too out of place.

When he'd arrived, the grad student, Isabella Bertonelli, had already grabbed a table for them and introduced herself, her words tinged with a soft Italian accent. She showed him her school ID and assignment page as proof of her identity.

She seemed a bit nervous and Sean asked her why.

"I was worried you might think I was a reporter," she'd said, tucking the short strands of dark shiny hair behind her ears. "My brother, he did this program before me three years ago, and told me the cop he talked to made him show ID."

"Well not to worry, I believe you are who you say you are," he'd replied.

They'd both ordered and shared some small talk, but their meals came quite quickly as the place wasn't too crowded.

His first bite hit him like a juicy, meaty treat and he grinned.

"Does that mean you like it?" Isabella asked.

Sean dug into his food with a fork, having given up on the chopsticks, and took another bite. "I definitely don't hate it," he said.

She let out a laugh, her face full of light. He had to admit, she was a looker. With short, almost black curls and curves that popped everywhere they should, Isabella stood out in a room. Her eyes sparkled as she told him about her family's Italian restaurant, where she worked on weekends to help pay for school.

Her forwardness intrigued him. Though she seemed nervous at first, once they got past the initial pleasantries, she opened up quite easily. His past two romantic interests, Angellica and Charlotte, had exhibited completely different types of traits towards him. Angellica, though impulsive, always seemed hesitant to propose ideas, instead agreeing with him right away when he suggested something. Charlotte, on the other hand, came off as difficult to predict. Tight with her emotions, he struggled with how to act around her because he never trusted how she might respond.

Not that he'd had much time to think about Isabella as a possible romantic interest, seeing as how within a few minutes of their conversation she'd mentioned her girlfriend. Sean felt a bit relieved. To be honest, he still hadn't gotten Charlotte out of his head and didn't want to think about someone else until he hashed things out with her.

"I didn't even know this place existed," Sean continued. With exposed brick walls, minimal seating, and a dimly lit space, Sean felt quite relaxed here. Some restaurants in Boston felt a bit high end and Sean often felt out of place in them.

"I used to come here all the time when we first moved here," she said. "School takes up a lot of my time now."

"How long have you and your family lived here?"

"A year. I love it, though. It kind of felt like I was just drifting in life back in Italy, but once I got here, I had a purpose, you know? I knew where I was meant to be."

"Boston has definitely grown on me, too."

"You're not from here?" she asked.

"Nope. Philly, uh, in Pennsylvania. Moved here for work. And to get away from an ex."

"Oh yeah. I remember from class when we learned a bit about you. Philadelphia." Isabella rolled her eyes before her next statement. "And I know what it's like to want some distance from an ex."

Sean doubted any previous relationship she'd had would match up to an ex-fiancée who turned out to be a brainwashed killer and was now dead.

Stop thinking about it.

"Well I'm glad you like it here," he said out loud. He also realized he'd been talking *way* too much about his personal life. He hadn't meant to, it was just this woman was easy to talk to. He needed to get them back to the task at hand.

"So, your assignment," he said, then took a swig of cola.

"Right." She put her chop sticks down and pulled a small notebook out of the bag hanging on her chair. "Okay, I basically broke this down into ten questions. I would have just emailed them to you, but the personal interview is part of the assignment. Our professor wanted us to do things this way. He says that interactions for a police officer are one-on-one, so we might as well get used to not relying on technology to do everything for us."

Sean laughed. "Technology has definitely changed things, but yeah, you still have to deal with people in person, so far at least." He gathered up another bite onto his fork. "Your email said you wanted to know about the McDougal case?"

"Yeah. From when you were in Philadelphia. We learned about it in one of my Criminology classes. I thought it was fascinating."

Sean wasn't surprised. The case had made huge headlines in Philly. "Fire away," Sean said before filling his mouth with more food.

"Okay, question one. . ."

Sean didn't hear the question. He'd stopped mid-chew. His eyes locked on the person who'd just entered the restaurant.

Charlotte.

His whole stomach flip-flopped. Either he'd forgotten or blocked out how incredibly gorgeous she was. Before he got a chance to think about whether or not he should get her attention or hope that she didn't see him, she turned and her gaze met his.

Everything from six months ago rushed over him: the night she "vented" at his house, the excitement they both felt about figuring out the case, and the hopefulness he sensed about the possibility of the two of them together.

Charlotte spoke to the person behind the register, then approached their table.

Oh God, he thought. It had been about three weeks since he heard from her last. *What do I say?*

"Detective Trann," Charlotte said, nodding in his direction. Her attention flitted briefly toward Isabella, her eyes narrowing for just a moment, then returned to Sean. "I was unaware that you frequented this restaurant."

"I d-don't," Sean stammered.

Isabella chimed in. "It was my suggestion."

Sean cleared his throat. Years of his mother's habitual hosting behaviors hit him. "Isabella Bertonelli, this is Doctor Charlotte Salla. She's a coworker, kind of. And uh, Isabella here is a grad student at Boston U, studying Criminology."

Isabella snapped her fingers, looking up at Charlotte. "I recognize you. The Spider case. I saw you on the news a few months ago."

Charlotte's eyebrow arched. "Yes. I had a brief interview after I recovered from my injuries."

Isabella let out a low whistle. "We've been following the

case in class. The trial is coming up soon, right?"

Sean gave a weak cough. "Uh, yeah, but we're not supposed to discuss it since the case hasn't officially closed yet."

Isabella blushed. "Oh, sorry. I didn't mean to overstep or anything."

"Curiosity is normal in your field," Charlotte said. "Good luck with your studies." She turned her head towards the bar. "I believe my order is ready."

Sean impulsively reached out and touched her wrist for a moment. A tingly jolt raced through him at the contact. "How are you?" he blurted.

Charlotte briefly placed her hand on her chest. "I am tired, but recovering." Sean wondered at the hand gesture, then realized that had been the spot where she'd gotten a knife thrown at her. He knew she was fully healed, as they'd discussed it previously while she'd been away, so what made her consciously or unconsciously cover her chest? On top of that, even though her words sounded sincere, something else flashed in her eyes, a look Sean couldn't quite decipher. Sadness? Fear?

"Pleasure seeing you again, Detective." Charlotte turned towards Isabella. "Enjoy your meal."

Sean watched her walk to the bar, pick up her bag of food, and head out.

Everything had happened too quickly. She was here, in Boston. He'd seen her. She hadn't said anything about meeting up another time or talking or anything. What had happened? Why was she so standoffish? Well, more than usual. And why couldn't he have said more than a few words to her?

"Wow." Isabella sat back in her chair, a smile tweaking her lips.

Sean returned his attention to her. "Wow, what?"

"You've got it *bad.*"

"What?" Sean shook his head. "Oh no, you've got it all wrong. . ."

Isabella waved her hands in the air, her mouth curving into a full grin. "Look, it's okay. I've been there."

Sean rubbed the nape of his neck. He felt like an idiot.

"Anyway, I guess we'd better finish the interview."

He nodded, answering her absentmindedly, his thoughts half on her questions, half on Charlotte.

Sean and Isabella finished their meal and interview before heading out. Chilled air swirled around them, causing them both to tighten up their jackets. Isabella's fit her like a glove, a long, white wool coat that hugged every curve. He thought her girlfriend must be pretty happy.

They walked in the same direction to their cars. She reached hers first.

Before she got in, Isabella paused, holding the door open.

"Detective, can I ask you something?"

"An interview question you forgot?"

"No. Something else. A favor."

"I guess. What is it?"

"Do you think I could see how things work at the precinct sometime?"

Sean raised his eyebrows.

Isabella scrunched up her face. "Okay, don't laugh, but you know that I'm going to school for Criminology? Well. . . I'd really like to follow you around sometime. Just for like a day or half a day or whatever. Is that something that could happen?"

Sean thought about it. "I don't see why not. I've had other students shadow me when I worked in Philly. I just have to check and see if it's allowed here, for liability purposes."

A smile blossomed across her face. "Well, thanks for looking into it for me. You have my email, so just let me know if it can happen."

"I will. Have a good night, Isabella."

"You too, Detective."

Sean made his way to his own car, happy to see the end of the evening. He had *not* expected any of these events to occur tonight.

New restaurant? Check.

Surprise from an old flame who wasn't actually an old flame? Check.

Have a grad student who wants to shadow you for a day? Check.

Sean unlocked the door to his Jaguar and hopped in, shaking his head.

Yep. Definitely one of the strangest nights he'd had in a while.

11

September 28th
Noon

Charlotte pulled into her parking spot outside the Chief Medical Examiner's Office. Though it was a Saturday and she wasn't scheduled to return to work until Monday, she'd decided to show up for a short while to sort through some of the emails and cases that had piled up over the past three months.

A yawn slipped from her mouth. The previous night had provided a restless sleep. She'd tried to chalk it up to jet lag and different time zones, but she knew a portion had to do with seeing Sean at the Cambodian restaurant the night before on a date.

A date.

The notion bothered her more than she wanted to admit. She wasn't sure what she'd expected. They hadn't really talked much in the past few weeks—especially because she'd lost her phone two weeks ago—and they hadn't decided on anything specific about starting a relationship, so he had technically been free to pursue other romantic interests, but somehow. . . she didn't know. Had she *hoped* he would still be single? That they'd see each other from across a crowded room and be drawn to one another like some cheesy romance movie?

Charlotte had internally scolded herself. He'd moved on. And good for him. She hadn't wanted a romantic entanglement anyway, right? Besides, their whole connection had been based on an intense serial killer case, nothing more.

Still her dreams last night had been filled with Sean kissing beauty pageant queens one at a time as Charlotte judged who'd win the contest for best murderer.

This morning, however, all she wanted to do was go to work. Physically be in her office and get some normalcy back into her life.

Upon entering the building, a sense of relief washed over her. The quiet, slow pace of the weekend coupled with the smell of sterility soothed her. She headed to her office first, to go through backed-up emails and paperwork, but paused, and turned instead towards the stairwell to the autopsy room.

With quick steps she walked down the sets of stairs and slid her keycard through its slot, unlocking the sealed door. Inside lay a cleaned, metallic table for cadavers and rows of sealed storage doors along the wall. She wondered what sorts of cases and bodies had been brought here while she'd been away.

Many people believed her job to be morbid—working with dead bodies all day—but she found it brought her closer to humanity. Dealing with death made dealing with life easier for her. Everyone became the same once they died. But who they were while they lived proved completely different. In about three hours an autopsy could tell her more about a person than what she normally learned after a handful of conversations. Were they a smoker? A drinker? Ever pregnant? Healthy or sick? Work out at the gym? So many questions answered by just looking inside someone.

Charlotte strode into the room, curious to check out the recent additions, when she stopped as if frozen. Her stare rested on the floor next to the autopsy table. The very spot she'd fallen after Truth dosed her with a paralytic agent six months earlier.

Panic seized her throat. She couldn't breathe.

Scrambling for the door, she flung it open, then tore up the stairs and out into the crisp autumn air. Taking in deep breaths from her crouched position, she fought back the urge to vomit. Slowly, she calmed down, stood, and leaned against the side of the building.

What was wrong with her? Why couldn't she get these emotions under control?

"Good morning, Doctor Salla," a voice called out.

Startled, Charlotte whipped her head around, and gave a deep exhale of relief. "Good morning, Doctor Knottes."

"It's good to have you back," he said. His contrasting

features always made him look slightly out of place. With pale blue eyes, dark arched eyebrows, olive-toned skin, and a thin frame, he reminded Charlotte of the Mendel's genetic test problems she had worked on early in college where they had to determine how someone could have possibly gotten the contrasting characteristics they'd inherited genetically.

"I am only here for a couple hours to catch up. My first full day will be Monday."

He hesitated as they entered into the building. "Well, it's still good to see you. And at least you won't have to be here the entire week."

She furrowed her forehead. "Why is that?"

"You haven't been to your office yet?"

She shook her head as they headed in that direction.

"I put the subpoena right on top, to make sure you'd see it first thing." They walked in and she made her way over to her desk, picking up the brown envelope.

"Subpoena?"

"Yes. The County Clerk's office dropped it off earlier this week. I told them when you were returning from your trip and they said it was all right if I gave it to you. Spider's trial starts on Friday. Didn't you get my message? I called you on Wednesday."

"I lost my phone," she muttered. "A couple weeks ago while traveling. I ordered a new one, but it will not arrive until next week. I have not received any messages from anyone." Her thoughts immediately shifted to Sean. Had he tried to contact her, too? Tell her about the subpoena? Ask her when she was coming home?

Of course not, she thought. *He is dating. Why would he contact me?*

Thoughts overlapped each other, causing a moment of disorientation. Charlotte didn't know what she wanted. She'd been so wrapped up in traveling and failing to reveal any other Triads that she. . .

Admit it, she admonished herself. *You stopped messaging him as well. It was you, not him.*

Charlotte cleared her throat and forced herself to focus on the envelope in her hand. She'd been having a lot of self-deprecating thoughts of late. Normally she could shake herself out of them, but during the past two months, they crawled through her head more and more often, stuck on a never-ending roller coaster, twisting around and around until she couldn't seem to get off the damn thing.

She needed to get ahold of herself.

"Yes. The trial. I am surprised it is happening so soon." She flipped the envelope over to open it, but couldn't seem to make her fingers slide under the flap.

"Soon? I guess. It's been six months since her arrest."

Charlotte paused. It *had* been that long. She couldn't believe it. "Murder trials have up to one year before they need to be scheduled," she recited.

"I'd think you'd want it over with."

"I do," she said automatically. "I merely. . ." She shrugged and slit open the envelope, glancing through its contents. It stated that on the following Friday, October 4 at 9 a.m. in the Superior Court of Suffolk County, she would be required to attend to bear witness.

"Thank you, Doctor Knottes," she said.

"Anytime." He paused before leaving her office. "Oh, and you should check your voicemails on the office line. I got a call on our main line from the district attorney yesterday and then had her call your office directly. She had a question for you. It sounded urgent."

"Of course. I will listen to it right away."

He gave her a smile. "Welcome back."

She nodded, not trusting herself to speak.

Charlotte checked her voicemails first and indeed one message came from the DA: a request to meet that very afternoon to go over the trial. Charlotte returned the call, agreed to the meeting, and glanced at the clock. She still had three hours to delve into her work before meeting with the DA.

Into her normal, regular, routine life.

And out of her own head.

12

September 28th
8:30 a.m.

The weekend.

Sean stretched out on his couch and flicked on the TV. He flipped through a few channels before settling on an ESPN show where people threw hand axes at a board for points. For some reason, he became fascinated by it.

Two hours later, his stomach rumbled as the semi-finals ended, won by a burly man who looked like he belonged on a package of paper towels, and he searched his fridge for something to eat.

A knock at his door gave him pause. Frowning, he headed over and called through it, "Who is it?"

"It's Nell, from downstairs."

Sean unlocked and opened his door to find an elderly woman standing there, her white curls pinned tightly to the sides of her head.

"I wanted to let you know the moving truck has arrived."

Sean blinked a few times. Then realization dawned on him. "That's today."

"Yes. And thank you again! I'll see you downstairs shortly." Nell took off at a brisk pace for her, which meant she shuffle-slid instead of shuffle-shuffled.

Sean let out a sigh and closed the door. He'd completely forgotten that last month he'd offered to help his downstairs neighbors pack up their moving truck today. Living directly below him, Gerald and Nell used to be quite bothersome. But after he'd helped when Gerald got food poisoning six months ago, they'd sung a different tune about him. Once every week or two, as a thank you, Nell brought up a "homemade" pie. Sean never had the heart to tell her that she needed to take the price tag off the bottom of the tin to pull off the ruse, not just remove the plastic cover. Besides, free pie was free pie.

When they'd told him last month that the frigid and wet Boston weather was getting too tough for them to take and decided to move to Arizona, Sean felt mixed feelings about the departure. Now that they'd stopped yelling at him any time he got up in the middle of the night, they weren't bad neighbors. On the other hand, they were still responsible for most of the complaints in the building, which resulted in extra rules like, "Please don't submit complaints about the following items: carpets being too squishy in the hallways, people's door hinges being too loud when they open and/or close them, the mail carrier arriving too early in the morning. . ."

So he'd offered to help load up their truck, both sad to see them leave and thankful they'd be gone.

Sean put on his sneakers and threw on a hoodie to protect himself against the crisp breeze outside, then jogged down a flight of stairs to their apartment.

Three hours later, once he realized exactly how many items they *had* stuffed away in their tiny one-bedroom apartment, including a giant mounted buck head, his stomach told him if he didn't eat soon. . .well, it was always an empty threat, but Sean never pushed his luck to see what would happen if he didn't feed the gurgling monster.

Unfortunately, at that moment, his phone alarm went off.

"Shit!" He'd completely forgotten he'd told the district attorney's office he'd stop by at 2 p.m. to go over his testimony for the trial. He'd never had to go over things beforehand, although he'd only testified in two trials before—one assault and one robbery—so maybe murder was different? Either way, he figured the DA wanted to make sure there weren't any surprises going in, especially in such an odd and complicated case. Being more prepared may also help with his dislike of trials in the first place.

Sean took a beat to decide what to do. He had thirty minutes to get to the DA's office. He could either (a) shower and change or (b) eat and change. He didn't have time to do both. His rumbling stomach and sweaty armpits each offered opposing input.

Ultimately, he decided on option (a). If he hurried, he could probably swing by a fast food place on the way and eat in the car.

Sean washed and rinsed himself as quickly as possible, threw on a pair of jeans and a clean black T-shirt under an open black sports jacket, shoved his feet into socks and shoes, and headed for his car. He had seventeen minutes to spare and with a ten-minute drive to the courthouse, plus about three minutes to get through security, he figured grabbing a burger along the way wouldn't make him too late.

Fifteen minutes later, with a satisfied stomach and a parking job that was only a little askew, Sean jogged up the steps into the building. He checked in, showing his badge, and was directed to his destination. He approached the correct office and knocked.

The door opened. Sean wasn't sure what to expect, but the woman in front of him was *not* it. Just below his eye level he could see the top of her head, covered with reddish-blonde hair cut short, framing her face. Her hazel eyes sparkled in the fluorescent glow of the standardized lighting, but somehow it made them seem more alive. Pale, creamy skin complimented her dark green suit, cut to fit her slim body.

Sean realized his immediate sexist assumption—he'd been expecting a man. The name on the subpoena read "District Attorney Jordan Parker."

"Right on time," she said, her words smoothed with a southern drawl. She left the door open for him to follow. "I appreciate you comin' in on a Saturday. We are scramblin' to get this case together and I want to make sure I have every angle covered. I'm dealin' with expert psychiatric witnesses and professional contractors, who will be checkin' over that underground bunker all next week, so I'm glad most of ya'll can come in this weekend."

"Not a problem," Sean said, entering the room and closing the door behind him.

She gestured for him to take the seat across from her desk. He sat, taking in a cursory glance around the standard-looking office, noting the white walls with a large floral print pasted on the wall behind her chair. A few files and a calendar lay on her desk, covered with penned-in names and appointments, but the rest of the surface appeared clear of clutter. He wondered if she was new to her position or just a neat-freak.

"All right, I'll try to make this as quick and painless as possible. I'm just goin' to shoot you a few queries about the events that happened durin' the Spider case. I'm also goin' to dollop out some questions I think the defense may ask to try and trip you up. Shouldn't take us more than an hour or so. Anythin' before we start?"

"I'm good."

The next hour went by pretty easily, though Sean felt caught off guard a couple times. He felt embarrassed at having to reveal his romantic relationship with Angellica—who'd turned out to be Anya, one of the killers. He'd also had a hard time talking about Counselor Eth's death. Even though he hadn't known the man very long, seeing Violet shoot him point blank in front of him had been a new and disturbing experience.

The DA paused the recording device on her desk. "You know, I've been a part of a lot of trials, many of them murder cases, but this. . .? I just transferred here six months ago from Tennessee, two weeks before any of this Spider stuff happened. I'm doin' my best to be prepared, but if someone would'a told me this would be my first major case, I may have said a polite 'no thank ya' and stayed where I was."

"How strongly do you feel about winning it?"

She blinked a few times, as if returning from her own thoughts. "Very strongly, even if it's off the wall. We've got multiple eye witnesses, the murder weapon, and the compound itself. There's just. . .I'm not sure. Somethin' itchin' at me. Like I'm missin' somethin'." She shook her head. "Anywho, you've been a big help. That's all I need from you for now. If anythin' changes, I'll let you know. Otherwise, I'll see you on Friday at nine a.m."

Sean stood and shook her hand. "Glad I could help." As he left, the DA's words swirled through his head. He didn't see how they could possibly lose the case either, but something "itched" at him as well. This whole situation, the way these women worked, they were *beyond* stealthy. Sean couldn't see it, but he felt in his gut that Violet would have something tricky planned. Some way to slither out of her conviction and prison sentence.

Lost in his thoughts, he turned the corner and went down a stair or two before colliding with someone coming up.

Charlotte.

"Hey," he managed, his mouth suddenly feeling dry. Stuck once again by her attractiveness, she looked stunning in a tailored suit jacket and pants, with an elaborate braid hanging over the side of one shoulder. Plus, she smelled really good, like pancakes and honey.

Her eyes widened as she recognized him. "Hello, Detective Trann."

A sharp burst of anger reared up inside of him. He remembered how difficult it had been to get her to even call him Sean in the first place. "It's back to Detective Trann again?" he said, an edge to his words.

Her lips pursed for a moment, then she let out a small sigh. "I would prefer to call you Sean."

Something in his chest purred. He forced himself to ignore it. "Here for the DA?"

She nodded. "My appointment is at three."

"Oh, gotcha. Um, well I won't keep you." *Say something,* he told himself. *Ask her out. Ask her to talk. Ask her* anything! No words formed.

She smiled with the corner of her mouth. "I wish we had more time, but I prefer to be punctual."

You're in! he thought. "Of course. Yeah, I mean, yeah. So maybe a coffee? Sometime?"

"I would enjoy that." She glanced at her watch. "I do need to go."

"I'll call you?"

"I lost my phone two weeks ago. My new one comes on Monday. Same number. Call me then?"

"I will. For sure."

Her smile blossomed, a rarity on her face, and elation filled him. "I look forward to it. There is a lot to tell you. So much. Including an apology." She glanced at her watch again. "Next week, then. Sean."

She continued up the last couple of stairs and rounded the corner.

"Okay, yeah, bye!" Sean whistled on his way out of the building and all the way to his car. She'd lost her phone— that's why she hadn't responded to his messages this past week about the subpoena or about him explaining about Isabella last night.

Either way, he was going to be ready the next time he saw her. And the first place to start? Getting as much info from Mags tomorrow about exactly what happened to those two traveling women.

13

September 29th
11 a.m.

Sean laughed. He couldn't help it. The restaurant he currently sat in, The Friendly Toast, couldn't have been a more perfect place for Mags to choose. It felt like it had been designed for her—quirky and fun. The green walls were covered with random pictures ranging from a ballerina to a white stallion to a scenic beach.

Mags sat across from him now in the crowded restaurant, handing the server her menu after ordering Biscuits and Gravy. Sean felt more like lunch, so he ordered what they called The Pit Burger, topped with smoked bacon, crispy battered onion strips, and swimming in BBQ sauce.

"Feeling any more at home yet?" Sean asked.

Mags nodded, a soft smile on her face. "That jet lag is killer. Yesterday passed by like some sort of weird haze. I made myself stay up the night before, but last night I fell asleep at eight and only woke up an hour ago. Guess I needed the sleep."

Sean noted that she looked less pale and the darkness around her eyes had lessened. "Well I'm glad you're back."

They exchanged a little bit of small talk while they waited for their food. Sean wondered if Mags felt as nervous as he did about digging into some of the bigger topics. With the trial looming and closing in fast, he knew they'd have to bring up Spider and the trip sooner or later.

Sean took in a deep breath. No use delaying any longer.

"I want to talk about your trip."

Her smile fell. "Yeah, I suppose we should." She squirmed in her seat. "Listen, I'm sorry I didn't respond to you very much in the past few weeks. Things got. . .complicated."

"Because you didn't find any Triad groups off the list?"

"No. Because my fiancé and I broke up."

Shock hit him like a dead weight. They'd split? Sean had met her fiancé about a year ago at some police function, right before they'd got engaged. He remembered she told him they'd been together. . .three years or so before that? They seemed happy. Mags hadn't said anything about any problems. Although, he supposed Mags and he weren't exactly best of friends. They had lunch every once in a blue moon and got along great at work, but it wasn't as though they gabbed every night.

Sean was about to ask what had happened when their

server returned, placing their plates in front of them. Wafts of smoked meat and sweet spice filled his nose and his stomach growled. As soon as the server left, he resumed his desire to ask his question, but hesitated. Did she want to talk about it? In public? If it just happened, would it be too painful?

"That sucks," Sean said lamely. He took a huge bite out of his monstrous burger to fill his mouth so he didn't say anything dumb.

"It does," Mags said, pushing her fork around in the gravy.

Sean swallowed, the bite a little too big, and coughed for a second on some bun stuck in his throat. "Do you want to talk about it?" he managed to ask.

She shrugged, then words seemed to spill out of her mouth. "Yeah, I can. I mean, we kind of knew it was coming to an end. We fought a lot before I left, for the trip I mean, after everything that happened with Spider. He didn't want me to go on the trip. I went anyway. We thought it might still be okay, but while I was gone, things just got more and more. . . strained. Eventually he told me he didn't want to see me when I got back." She stopped and poked at her biscuits.

"I'm sorry," Sean said.

"Me too." She let out a long sigh and looked up from her plate. "I didn't really talk to anyone about it, except Juliette. She and I sort of bonded after being kidnapped together, you know?"

Sean nodded and shoved a few fries into his mouth.

"But I just. . .I couldn't talk to anyone else. It's why I was sort of distant with you, too. I started to hate everything that had to do with Spider and yet I was stuck on a failing fact-finding mission revolving around those stupid women." She stabbed at one of her biscuits, which gave out weak *plops* as gravy slid into the new tiny holes.

"You weren't the only one distant," Sean muttered.

"You mean Charlotte?"

Sean nodded again.

"I'm not surprised. She got. . .weird. Well, weird-*er*. At first, I was kind of excited to get to know her on the trip. She is *so* smart and surprisingly easy to talk to, after a while. But once the first couple weeks passed and we didn't find anything Triad-related? It seemed to take a toll on her. She would go to bed early and toss and turn. After the first month, she started to keep to herself, ordering room service and eating at the small table in our hotel room while reading from files or anatomy textbooks and stuff."

Sean took a slurp of cola, avoiding Mags' gaze. "I thought, before you two left, that maybe she and I. . .but when I sort of stopped hearing from her, I thought maybe she didn't. . ."

Mags reached across the table and squeezed his hand. "I don't think it's you. On the contrary. She talked about you a lot at first. Well, maybe two percent of the time. That's a lot for her." She grinned.

Sean couldn't help but smile as well. Then his face dropped. "Do you think I should bother? With her I mean? Maybe anything between us was just from the adrenaline rush of the Spider case?"

"Honestly?" Mags finally stuck a bite of food in her mouth. "I think you two are made for each other."

Sean had taken another slug of his drink and immediately

choked on it. "W-what?" he sputtered.

"I'm serious. I've seen a lot of people from a lot of walks of life. You two may seem really different on the outside, but you're more alike than you know. And I think the way you're different compliments each other. You just each have to get out of your own ways."

"I'm not in my own way," Sean said, defensive. "I'm into her. I'd date her." He paused. "A lot of times she seems so. . . complicated. I want something simple."

"Exactly. And simple isn't good for you. Don't get me wrong. I don't mean you need something messy, just challenging."

"Well after everything that happened with Angellica, can you blame me for wanting something easy?"

"Not at all." She took a big gulp of orange juice and smacked her lips. "And maybe now isn't the best time to get involved with Charlotte. I don't know if she's ready either. All I know is, once you two are ready. . .?" She took both hands and mimed an explosion.

Sean took another bite, taking those words to heart. Could Mags be right? Could he and Charlotte work, but maybe now wasn't the best time? As he chewed, the notion lodged itself somewhere inside his gut, and a tingly warmth traveled through him, having nothing to do with the feeling of happy fullness from his delicious meal.

14

September 30th
9:30 a.m.

Sean's nose twitched. It couldn't be.

He glanced up from his desk. That aroma. That heavenly scent.

Mags' coffee. . .

A groan of pleasure spilled from his lips. "Yes, God, thank you!" He came from behind his desk and met Mags at the entrance to his office, taking the steaming mug from her hands.

"Careful, I just made it!" she warned.

He didn't care. The hot liquid slid into his mouth as its dark roast with some secret ingredient he could never place coated his tongue. The heat caused discomfort, but happily no burn. He swallowed and let out a long sigh.

"I knew you only missed me for my coffee," Mags joked.

"What can I say? I'm a pig." Sean grinned and threw an arm around her shoulders, giving her a squeeze. He let go and gestured to the chair in front of his desk and took his own seat behind it. "So? How is it being back at work?"

"Besides feeling tired because I still don't know what time of the day it is? Not bad." She paused, chewing on her nails.

"But. . .?" he prodded.

"I don't know. I thought things would be. . .different somehow. After everything we went through. That somehow the place would be different. That *we'd* be different." Mags' gaze darted around the room, fairly quiet for a Monday morning. Several officers were already out on calls.

Sean nodded. "I get it. When I first came back, everything seemed so normal. It was hard to believe we'd been dealing with a serial killer in an underground bunker just a few months before."

"Oh good, then it's not just me." She took a drink from her own coffee mug. "Anything new on the Charlotte front?"

Sean clenched his jaw. "I don't know what you mean," he lied.

"Did you talk to her?"

"Not since I saw her on Saturday when she said her new phone would be in this morning and I should call around lunch."

Mags grinned. "I'm sorry. I'll leave you alone about it."

Sean softened. "No, it's fine, really. I feel dumb about it. And nervous."

"You shouldn't. Charlotte is into you, too. She just. . .got messed up on the trip. We both did, in a sense." She fidgeted in her chair. "Did you get your summons for the trial?"

"Yep. Friday. Can't believe that either."

"I know. I'm supposed to meet with the district attorney today after lunch to go over my testimony."

"The DA seems all right. She doesn't seem too arrogant, either, so hopefully that means she'll be cautious with this case. It really is an unusual one."

"Part of me is grateful the trial is so soon and that it'll be over quickly. Another part wishes I never had to deal with any Spider stuff again." She paused. "I still have nightmares about the compound."

"Have you talked to the shrink?"

Mags nodded. "It wasn't mandatory, like with you all as cops, since I'm just a receptionist—"

"You are *not* just a receptionist," Sean interrupted.

She smiled. "Anyway, I saw someone before I left for the trip, for a couple months. Not like clockwork, kind of every two or three weeks, but we talked through a lot of stuff. I have to admit though, going on the trip was sort of nice, being away, being distracted. Now, being back. . ."

"It makes it real again," Sean finished for her. He took another sip of his coffee. Memories from six months earlier flooded into his mind—the arrival of his ex-fiancée, the clues left every month to a fresh murder, the theory that hundreds of thousands of these Triads of woman might exist around the world, killing at their own discretion. . .

"So what can I expect from my meeting with the DA?"

Mags asked, settling into the chair.

"It was pretty painless. She just asked the same sort of questions from when our first statements were taken. And a few more that she thinks the defense may ask, to trip you up. It was helpful to go over it. I feel better about Friday." He nodded over at Millan's office. "I bet he was happy to see you again, too. The temp, Judy, was all right, but I know you two liked to chat on your lunch breaks."

Mags gazed over towards the sergeant's office and a frown turned down the corners of her mouth. "Is he okay? I saw him smoking outside when I came in. I thought he'd quit."

Sean rubbed his forehead. "Ah. That. It's a long story." Before he could continue, Detective Payne sauntered into the bullpen. "Which will have to wait until another time. Also, I'm sorry for the guy you're about to meet."

"Guy? What guy?"

Sean stood up. "Remember that guy from Juliette's welcome home party?"

"Hey Trann!" Payne bellowed from across the room. He headed over. "How's it hang. . ." he trailed off, mid-word, staring at Mags. He just stood there.

"Uh," Mags said. "Hi?"

Sean took a beat then said, "Sorry. Mags, this is Detective Payne, my new partner. Payne, this is Mags, our receptionist. It's her first full day at work after the whole Spider ordeal."

Payne nodded like a bobblehead and stuck out his hand. "Pleasure, Miss," he gushed. "Everyone here has spoken mighty highly of you. I've been looking forward to making your acquaintance."

Sean's mouth actually dropped open. Where the hell was the crude man who had some sort of gross remark for every woman he met?

"Nice to meet you, too," she said, shaking his hand. "Welcome to the team." She stood and addressed Sean. "I'll go check in with Millan. Think we can eat in the break room together for lunch before I head to the DA's?"

"Sounds great," Sean said.

"Yeah!" Payne chimed in. "Lunch sounds great!"

A pregnant pause filled the room.

"Uh, yeah, sure," Mags said slowly. "See you both later then." She gave Sean a look and he shrugged, since Payne's gaze was still firmly locked onto Mags' face. Mags left and Payne let out a low whistle.

Here it comes. Sean braced himself for something crude.

"She's got the prettiest eyes."

Sean coughed. "Yeah, ah, I guess she does."

Payne returned his attention to Sean. "What's on our docket for today? Besides lunch, of course."

"Let me see. . ." Sean peered down at his desk, all the while wondering what exactly just happened with Payne and Mags.

15

September 30th
1 p.m.

"Thursday for dinner sounds wonderful," Charlotte said to Sean through her new cell phone. "I look forward to seeing you." She hung up and smiled. It seemed as though she hadn't completely ruined things with him. He'd explained the situation about Isabella being a grad student there for a school assignment and *not* as a date. A small sigh of relief had escaped her mouth. Though she originally thought she would end any personal interactions with him, seeing him at the restaurant and then again at the district attorney's office over the weekend revitalized the attraction she felt for him.

Charlotte reclined slightly in her chair and resumed

reviewing her emails. She'd been at work since 8 a.m. and had remained in her office. There had been a new body brought in for an autopsy, but she hadn't been able to bring herself to go down into the lab area after her unease over the weekend.

She'd told herself that her feelings were ridiculous. Nothing would happen to her if she went into that room. She wouldn't be kidnapped again. She'd be fine.

But all the will power in the world meant nothing to the tightness in her gut and the quickened breathing that happened when she thought about venturing into the autopsy area.

She kept putting it off all morning. *After I settle in. After my first break. After lunch.* She was running out of day. A body lay waiting for her to return to work, to help put finality to its life.

Without really thinking, she reached out and touched her phone. The back of it still felt a little warm from the last call. The image of Sean's face flashed through her mind. He was handsome, definitely, and smart. Funny and charismatic. But also stubborn and sometimes dumb and didn't always make the best decisions.

Charlotte wished he were here. She didn't quite know why. Then she did something she hadn't done since childhood—she used her imagination. Not that she never used it for creative problem-solving or working through theories, but she hardly ever used her imagination for personal recreation. She'd never really found a need, not since she'd been a child.

Her family had been mostly happy, though a sliver of cloud always hung over them. When Charlotte turned eight, her older brother by three years was killed by a car while crossing the street to return home for her birthday party. His gift for her, a kid's chemistry set, went flying, its contents splayed everywhere across the road.

Charlotte remembered hearing a shriek and running outside, the ribbons in her hair only half tied. Her mother had told her to stop, but Charlotte ran anyway, because the scream had come from her father and she'd never heard him sound like that before. She never forgot the image—her brother's body lying so still, random bits of wrapping paper flapping in the breeze, and a torn box lying near him with plastic beakers and a petri dish scattered across the street.

That night, after her parents explained what happened, their faces red and puffy, she'd sat in bed, staring at her Animal Kingdom poster. She didn't cry. She didn't pout. She didn't do anything except stare. She thought if she just remained still enough, if she didn't move, then somehow time would stop and she wouldn't have to face the next moment, knowing her brother wouldn't be there.

But time continued forward no matter how still she remained. The tiger's face in the poster continued to roar silently, but the moon brightened and cast its glow through her blinds. The bright blue alarm clock numbers changed.

Eventually she laid down, her eyelids heavy, but she didn't want to sleep. Once she slept, he wouldn't be there in the morning. He wouldn't be there for breakfast. He wouldn't be there after school.

She closed her eyes, but not to sleep. She just didn't want to be alone so she imagined him, standing next to her bed. He wasn't doing anything or saying anything. He just existed.

Without ever opening her eyes, she could sense him. Not as a ghost, but there because she needed him. She fell asleep soundly.

Charlotte pulled on that memory and imagined Sean with her now. Not saying anything, not doing anything, just there. She wasn't alone. She could do this.

One step at a time she left her office, headed down the stairs, and entered the autopsy room. One moment at a time she let herself feel uncomfortable, even scared, giving herself permission to leave at any point, and began her work.

16

September 30th
1:15 p.m.

Sean hung up his phone and walked into the precinct's break room. Payne already sat there, straight as a board, his eyes glued to the door.

"Oh, it's you," he said, slumping a bit.

Sean grabbed his lunch from the fridge and put it into the microwave before turning it on. "Mags will be here in a minute."

Payne straightened again as Sean took a seat across from him at the round, black, plastic table. The seconds ticked away. Sean glanced over at the microwave, which still said there was a minute and a half left on his frozen burrito.

Sean narrowed his eyes as his focus returned to Payne. "What's the deal, man?" he blurted.

"With what?" Payne asked, the Texas twang in his voice wobbling each word.

"Mags. I've never seen you act like this around a woman before."

Payne peered at the door again, as if making sure no one was coming. "I honestly don't know. She just. . .struck me." He licked his lips, but more in a nervous way than a sexual one. "What's her tale? I mean, single? Interesting? Smart? Would she date a cop?"

Sean hesitated. Truth be told, he didn't really *want* Payne to have an interest in Mags. As far as he was concerned, Mags stood *way* above Payne's level.

He also didn't know how much of her personal life he should tell. "Mags is great. She's. . .currently unattached. But she doesn't deal with bullshit. She'll call you out. You can't play games with her."

Payne's forehead wrinkled, as if thinking really hard. Then he sunk into his chair. "I don't stand a chance with a girl like that."

Sean blinked. "What?"

"Why do you think I date trashy women? They don't expect anything of me cuz they ain't expecting nothing special."

Sean had no idea what to say. This constituted the most personal conversation they'd ever had between the two of them since they'd partnered up, unless you counted the "personal" nature of their talk where Payne wanted to compare all the sexual positions they'd performed.

With thoughts of Charlotte and the trial and everything else ricocheting around in his mind, Sean decided he really didn't want to get involved.

"Here's the deal. You want a woman like Mags? You have to do the work. Be a better person and stop all your BS. If you're willing to do that, then you'll be worthy of her. If not, I suggest leaving her alone to find someone who can."

At that moment, Mags walked in. Sean heard Payne mutter under his breath "do the work," but he couldn't tell if he said it as a question or a scoff.

17

September 30th
2:30 p.m.

Mags sat across from District Attorney Jordan Parker. She'd just had the oddest lunch. The new detective, Detective Payne, had been...well...strange, for lack of a better word. He seemed giddy and kept trying to join randomly into the conversation, but his comments didn't really seem to fit with what she and Sean discussed. Even before their break time ran out, Payne stood, shook her hand, told her he hoped to get to know her better, and left the room. Sean had just shrugged and kept eating until Mags had to leave for her appointment.

The whole situation reminded her of middle school.

And yet, there had been something endearing about the

way Payne had acted. Mags could tell he found her attractive, but he seemed to be out of his element. Which felt odd because Mags didn't know him to begin with. Still, she thought she might ask around the station and get other people's opinions of him, since they'd already spent a few months with him, before coming to any snap decisions.

On top of everything, she felt angry at herself for thinking about any of this at all. She and her fiancé, Scott, had barely even split. Why was she already thinking about another guy? Maybe her relationship with Scott had been over in her mind for much longer than she'd thought.

Mags shook her head to try and refocus on the situation at hand. The trial.

The district attorney asked another question and Mags answered, not really thinking. A dull ache had started at the front of her skull. She had a feeling a migraine would begin soon. The mind-splitting headaches had been occurring for the past six months or so, not often, maybe five or six times, but since she'd never had them before, she went to see a doctor about it. The doctor had told her it may be a side effect from when she fell and hit her head against the concrete police station parking lot six months ago, before being kidnapped.

"It could also be stress," he said, "lingering from your trauma. A lot of doctors dismiss the severity of what stress and trauma can do to the body, but I've seen enough medical evidence to show how the body internalizes emotional and mental stressors. I suggest keeping track of when the migraines occur and see if any common factors revolve around the pain. And perhaps see a counselor."

Sitting today in the district attorney's office, answering questions about her captivity by murderous women, Mags didn't feel surprised that a migraine would crop up. She glanced at the clock and thought if they didn't wrap up in about ten minutes, she'd asked to be excused for a bathroom break to take one of her pain pills before the migraine gained any traction.

To her relief, Miss Parker said, "We are just about done."

"Really? That's great."

"Just a piece of advice, if you don't mind?"

Intrigued, Mags said, "Not at all."

"When you're on the witness stand, regardless of how you physically feel, can you give your answers with less apathy?"

Mags sat for a moment, confused. "What?"

The district attorney leaned forward, her elbows on her desk, her face cupped in her hands. "I've done this 'interview' thing with a lot of people. Normally, I get some kind of feelin' from them. But you? You seem almost. . .disinterested. Like you don't care. It won't come off well to a jury, because they'll think you weren't negatively affected by what happened to you."

A swirl of rage stirred in her chest. "Not *negatively* affected?" she asked, her words curt.

"I'm not sayin' you weren't, I'm sayin' that's how you come across." She paused. "*Are* you okay?"

A sharp point of pain pierced the middle of her forehead. She closed her eyes briefly, thinking about all the things that had changed in her life, everything she'd gone through. She just wanted this whole ordeal to be over.

"I will be," she said, opening her eyes. "Once Violet is behind bars, I'll feel much better."

The district attorney shifted in her seat. "Well then let's hope she gets put behind bars. Until then, I'll see y'all on Friday at the courthouse."

Mags collected her jacket and bag and left the office, feeling a bit unsettled at the idea of Violet not being in jail. She *had* to be, right?

"As long as nothing else goes wrong," she muttered to herself, pulling a pain pill from her bag, "I'll be just fine."

18

October 1st
9 a.m.

Isabella looked like a kid in a candy shop and Sean couldn't help but grin. They'd decided for her to shadow him today, since he figured it would be better for her to come before the trial started on Friday. She blended in well, open and outspoken, asking interesting questions about his normal day to day routine, and quickly became engrossed in his current case: the murder of Serena Watkins.

Sean would have bet the boyfriend had been involved in the murder, and he had, but not fully. The young man, Jerry, confessed to conspiring with a friend to murder Serena, but that he hadn't done the actual killing. When pressed, though,

Jerry refused to give up the name of his friend and his appointed lawyer stepped in and halted the line of questioning at that point.

Sean and Payne were scheduled to do some recon about Jerry's friends, find out who might have been the accomplice, and go ask questions. It'd be a good day to be shadowed.

The two of them had narrowed the suspect list down to four of Jerry's friends: three boys and one girl. They'd just driven away from the second boy's house and were headed towards the third when Isabella asked, "Is it hard when you don't catch a killer?"

Payne started to talk right away—he had no trouble opening up to such a pretty woman—and told her about how difficult it could be to know a murderer was running around free and clear. Sean simply continued to drive, thinking about the answer.

"What about you, Detective Trann?" she asked.

Sean waited a few beats before answering. "I learned a long time ago that if I felt bad about every killer I didn't catch, it would drive me crazy. It almost did once, back in Philly. I had to convince myself I did my job the best I could and let the rest go. I don't forget about the unresolved cases, I just won't hold on to them anymore."

"Does that hold true for a criminal you caught that doesn't get convicted?"

Sean could see Payne scowl out of the corner of his eye.

"That's the worst, honey," Payne said. "We work so hard to catch these jerks and the courts can't keep 'em locked up."

"But it's tough for everyone," Sean added. "No one likes

to see a criminal go free, including the prosecutor."

Isabella tapped on her tablet, taking notes. "Does that leave animosity between the police department and the DA's office?"

"Not really," Sean said. "We know they are doing their jobs, too. We get angry in general at the system, not the lawyers. Unless they screw up. But even then, sometimes cops don't do everything right either."

"It's not a perfect system," Payne added, "but it's the only one we got right now."

"I don't know if I could handle that," she said, her voice quiet. "Knowing these criminals were still free, especially knowing they are guilty?" Sean saw her shake her head in his rearview mirror.

"If you aren't okay with it, this job may not be the best fit. Sometimes we don't win and the bad guys go free. We aren't superheroes."

"Or vigilantes," Payne chimed in. "I hate those guys."

Sean kept quiet. Payne was a by-the-book cop, which seemed ironic because of his attitude towards the rest of life. But Sean didn't know how he felt about someone who decided to make the world better, even if it broke the law. The problem was, those people always got greedy, and the line of what constitutes a "bad" person for a vigilante to go after becomes more and more blurred. Was it only killers who'd be targeted? Or rapists? What about someone who assaulted others? Or child molesters? Thieves? Drug dealers? Drug users? Prostitutes? Indecent exposure? Loitering? Any so-called vigilantes he'd ever dealt with always felt justified, but in the end, they decided to put themselves above others.

In a sense, they thought they were better than other humans.

They wanted to be gods.

Sean's mind flashed to the Spider case. These women had used the words in a book as the basis to murder millions of people over the years because. . .what? Someone wasn't physically "perfect?" That definition was so vague that *anyone* could be a target, no matter what was wrong with them.

"What about you, Detective Trann?" Isabella asked, butting into Sean's thoughts. "Do you think vigilantes are ever justified in what they do?"

He turned the wheel to the left and they pulled up in front of a small, light green house. A woman and her dog played inside the forest green fenced-in front yard. She had no idea they were coming to ask if her son had planned and possibly committed a murder.

It wasn't fair. . .

"Vigilantes are always justified," Sean said, turning off the car, "in their own minds. But justification is never enough to satisfy them, so eventually they become the criminal they fought so hard to stop in the first place."

19

October 1ˢᵗ
5:30 p.m.

Sean blew a breath through his teeth. It whistled softly in the small room.

"I don't know," he finally said.

"It's not an easy question," Dr. Carla Moria said, tapping her pen on her notebook, "so I'm not surprised you don't have an answer right away."

"But it should be an easy question to answer. The answer should be 'yes,' plain and simple."

Sean leaned back on the small loveseat, the fake leather squeaking underneath him. This was his second-to-last session with the counselor and they'd talked about nothing except for the upcoming trial. Sean began the session by saying he felt like a trial gives him closure for a case. At that point, the case was out of his hands. If the perp didn't get convicted, then Sean would keep an eye out in the future to see if he could catch the criminal again, but he never held onto a case anymore once it went to the courts. He'd learned that the hard way after a case in Philly.

But then Carla had asked if he felt like he'd have closure after this case, regardless of the verdict.

He immediately wanted to say yes, but the word wouldn't come. How could he feel like anything revolving around Spider was "over" when there could be hundreds of thousands of women around the world still murdering people? How was he supposed to wrap his head around that fact?

"Okay," she said, "let's try a different track. Why is this case different from others?"

Sean rubbed a hand across his mouth and chin. "Well. . . Spider went after people I know."

"So it's more personal?"

"I suppose."

"Do you think these other possible women out there will also target people you know? Is that why you feel like you can't get closure?"

Sean's forehead crinkled. "Surprisingly enough, no. I don't think these women would go after someone I know. At least, not intentionally. It really does seem like I was targeted only by this specific Triad."

"Then why won't this case feel like you're getting closure

when the trial ends?"

"I don't know. I mean. . .this case. It screwed everybody up. Me. Charlotte. Mags. Juliette. We're all so different now. Cases can do that sometimes, really mess with you, but this one? Three of us almost died. And Officer Eth *did* die. Right in front of us."

"Because of you." Carla's words hung in the air. They weren't accusatory, but her tone held a sense of responsibility.

"Yeah. . ." Sean said slowly. "Because of me." The guilt and pressure settled onto his chest like a bag of wet sand. "If Spider hadn't been focused on me, no one in my life would have been affected. They'd all have been safe."

"Bullshit."

Caught off guard by the abruptness of the word, Sean shook his head. "Whoa. . .what?"

Carla put her notebook down on her table and folded her hands on her lap. "I'm not going to trivialize what you went through, but you aren't the first cop to be the focus of a killer. In all honesty, you aren't even close to the first *person* to have to deal with this. Women who've been stalked, authors who get copycatted, celebrities who get fixated on. . .I've talked with a lot of different types of clients. There is also one root that digs deepest and is the toughest to get out: 'somehow it's my fault that they focused on me and did what they did.' People feel responsible when they are attacked, when their houses are vandalized, when their families or loved ones are targeted. 'If only I'd had a security system. If only I had a bodyguard. If only I hadn't done this or that to provoke them.' We are trained to think it's somehow our responsibility to prevent these things from happening."

Carla paused to catch her breath, shifting her crossed legs to face the other direction. "My point is, you have choices in life, all the time. They may not be good: do I quit my job or deal with a *cabrón* boss? But it's a choice. Well, the killers have choices, too. 'If you don't do what I say I'll kill your friend.' It's not *your* fault they pull the trigger, no matter what you say. You are not responsible for their actions—they are."

She picked up her notebook and jotted something down. "So, the question is, can you let what these women did to you and those you love be *their* responsibility and know you did your job to the best of your ability? Can you let the trial give you closure on this case?"

Sean sat there, silent, his mind swirling with thoughts.

Carla nodded at the clock. "Our session is up. I hope you can think about what I said as you move forward this week. I look forward to talking to you next week for our last session and to hear how things went after your testimony. Take care, Sean."

20

October 2nd
10 a.m.

Charlotte stared at the Italian woman in front of her, wondering how she'd agreed to this situation. It had happened so fast.

Doctor Knottes came into her office that morning, begging her to do him a favor. It seemed he'd made an appointment today with a grad student to shadow him and he'd completely forgotten he already had a consult appointment with a doctor on a case one county over. With a puckered face and wide eyes, he'd pleaded with her to help him out and take on the grad student, promising the young woman would only be here until lunchtime. Charlotte, knowing that Knottes had taken on extra work while she'd been traveling the past three months, agreed, and he'd shaken her hand vigorously before sweeping out of her office.

The entire scene had taken all of ten minutes.

And now Charlotte stood with the grad student in front of her. She'd recognized the woman immediately as Isabella, the one who'd been on a date with Sean the previous weekend.

It was not a date, she reminded herself. Even if it had been, Charlotte was a professional, and would treat this woman with courtesy and respect.

After the first hour, Charlotte found she didn't have to try very hard. The woman, Isabella, was quite bright. Her insightful questions seemed above those of a standard Anatomy 101 class and Charlotte soon found herself settling easily into their conversation.

They'd just been discussing some details of a recent autopsy procedure when Charlotte's watch pinged.

"Lunch break," she said, surprised that two hours had already passed.

Isabella's mouth gave the slightest frown. "Already?"

Charlotte concurred. She had enjoyed the woman's company.

"Well I appreciate your time, Doctor Salla. This is going to help immensely with my upcoming project." Isabella looked at her notes. "Oh no! I got so distracted about the procedure stuff I forgot to ask you my ethics questions."

Charlotte paused. "Would you care to join me for lunch? I would be happy to continue our discussion."

Isabella's cheeks flushed. "That would be incredible.

Thank you! I'll just grab my lunch from my car. Should I meet you in your office?"

Charlotte nodded and the two of them exited the room, went up the stairs, and parted ways in the hall. With brisk steps, Charlotte continued to the break room, retrieved her lunch, and brought it to her office, musing at the situation. She hadn't felt this at ease with another woman in a long time. On her trip with Mags, she'd been so disappointed that they hadn't blended as well as she would have liked.

Charlotte thought about that notion. Perhaps she'd been too hard on Mags. Perhaps the trip had been too hard on both of them. She decided to make a better effort towards the spunky woman in the future.

Isabella appeared in the doorway, a grin on her face. Charlotte gestured for her to enter.

"I appreciate you taking the extra time," Isabella said, sitting across from Charlotte at the desk. "I promise to make this as quick as possible."

"I am scheduled for a half hour break. You have plenty of time. Please, begin when you are ready."

After the first few questions, revolving around how Charlotte dealt with privacy and religious views of the deceased, she asked a question that made Charlotte think.

"Can you clarify your question?" Charlotte asked.

Isabella finished chewing her mouthful of pasta salad before speaking. "What I mean is, if you found evidence on a body, after the fact, and it led you to the killer, what do you do about that?"

"As in a false arrest?"

"Just the opposite. If you found evidence that would convict someone who had already been released by the courts, what do you do with it?"

"If I can apply the evidence to reopen the case, I would do so."

"What if you can't reopen the case? What if you know that the killer got set free?"

A prickly sensation began in Charlotte's underarms. She cricked her neck to the side and adjusted her collar. Had the heat been turned up for some reason?

"If the case cannot be reopened, it remains closed. No amount of evidence on my end would change that verdict."

"That must be difficult."

Charlotte frowned. "Difficult? How so?"

"To know you found a murderer and there's nothing you can do about it. I mean, I get it as a cop. You do your job and then it's up to the courts, but when the courts screw up? That must be. . .difficult."

A sense of pressure began building in Charlotte's chest. She found her breath coming quicker and forced herself to slow down her breathing. She glanced at the clock, realizing she only had a few minutes left of her lunch break.

You can make it through the next few minutes and then Isabella will leave and you will feel fine.

Charlotte pushed aside her unfinished lunch—the tightness in her gut making her suddenly no longer hungry.

"Have you ever had a case like that happen to you?" Isabella asked.

Charlotte shook her head. *Not a case. But a hit-and-run*

killer went free once. . .

"Well that's good. When I spoke to Detective Trann, he said it was hard for him to let that go, but that he had learned to do so."

A flutter rippled through her at Sean's name. "I would imagine it would be upsetting to discover you could do something to stop a murderer and not be allowed to. The feeling of helplessness. . .

She flashed to the image of her brother's body, lying motionless in the street. . .

. . .would be difficult indeed."

Isabella wiped her mouth with her napkin and closed up her lunch tote. "Thank you again, Charlotte. I know I'm going to ace my assignment. And who knows? Maybe we'll work together someday once I graduate!"

Charlotte shook the woman's hand absentmindedly and hardly realized Isabella had left. She sat for several minutes, staring into nothingness, wondering what she *would* do if she knew who a killer was and no one else could do anything about it. . .

21

October 3ʳᵈ
6:15 p.m.

Her eyes opened. They tried to take in their surroundings, but everything looked gray and hazy. Her head throbbed.

She placed her hand to her forehead to still the pain. Something came with her hand. Something in her palm. Black. Plastic. Cold.

A phone.

She tapped on it. Nothing happened.

Her eyelids fluttered. She could fall asleep, right now. Everything would be okay if she fell asleep.

She dropped the phone and it slid across the floor. The

noise disrupted her thoughts.

What was she doing?

She reached down to grab the phone, her body swaying. Her stomach swaying.

She pulled the phone back onto her lap. Up onto the table. She sat at a table. It was plain, with nothing on it.

She flipped open the phone. Was this hers? Someone else's?

The screen lit up and showed two recent outgoing messages to someone named DST. Her fingertips pressed the screen. Something changed. She could see the messages.

A sense of clarity returned to her. Yes, she remembered now. She had to warn him, to tell him.

She wasn't supposed to. *She* wouldn't want her to tell him anything. *She* would find out.

With deliberate yet sloppy taps, she typed out another message and hit *send*. Then she heard a *clack clack clack* noise like a roller coaster starting up. A voice called to her from across the room.

"You've been keeping something from me."

The tone sent both shivers of fear and hope down her spine.

Someone moved forward. *Her.* The woman snatched the phone from the table.

"I see," the woman said. "You sent messages to *him*." The contempt in that one word spoke volumes of the hatred towards DST. She felt sorry for whoever he was. He was no match for *her*.

"This changes everything," the woman said. "I can't

depend on you. It's my own fault. I thought I could do it. But I can't. Let *her* take the fall." The woman took a seat across from her. "It's time for another session, your last one. Not that you'll remember this. . ."

With a nod, she let her hands drop. No sense fighting. Not against the beat.

Then it started. *Tap Tap Tap Tap.* Pause. *Tap Tap Tap Tap.* Pause. Always the same. No change in volume, in speed, in anything.

"You will do nothing but listen to my voice," the woman said. "You will do nothing but what I tell you."

She sat there, motionless. She shouldn't nod. She shouldn't blink. She shouldn't speak. Not until the woman told her what to do. . .

22

October 3rd
5:45 p.m.

Sean ran his hand through his hair again. He had to quit doing that as he knew it would eventually make his hair look oily, but he had a hard time stopping the nervous habit. He'd arrived 15 minutes early for his dinner date with Charlotte at an Indian restaurant called *Mela*. Sheer raspberry-colored curtains filtered in the remaining outside light while large glowing ball-shaped lights hung from the ceiling, reflecting off the bronze metallic wall behind the bar.

Though he'd been here several times before, Sean shifted in his chair, still feeling uncertain. Was it a date? Or, just dinner? Dinner *meeting*? He wasn't quite sure what this meal represented.

The week had flown by. Between being shadowed by Isabella, his therapy session, and the complications to the Watkins murder, he'd hardly had time to think what he might say to Charlotte.

She *had* said she wanted to apologize when he'd seen her outside the DA's office last weekend, so that had to be good, right? Unless it was something like "I'm sorry I ever thought you could be anything but a *good friend.*" Kiss of death, that phrase.

A server came up to the table and Sean ordered a beer. He hoped the drink would settle his nerves a bit.

Of course, the other part affecting his nerves revolved around the fact that in a little over 12 hours the Spider trial would begin. He'd have to see Violet again—the woman who murdered Counselor Eth, who'd almost killed Charlotte, Tay, and himself, and was responsible for terrorizing Sean and the Boston P.D. for months with psychotic clues and elaborate deaths for her victims.

When Sean first returned to work after three months of medical leave, he'd been obsessed with learning everything about the case—especially with Charlotte going on her trip to search for other sects of murderous women. He felt convinced he'd find something to aid her during her travels, some vital clue or revelation to help her track down these other Triads. After all, he was a good cop. A really good cop. He often figured out things no one else could.

But there had been nothing.

Oh, he'd looked through the evidence first, thumbed

through the photocopies of pages from the "Book" that supposedly revealed why these women killed people, but the text was in some sort of ancient language and the translations made his head spin. All the words felt more like riddles which circled over themselves.

He'd also checked out the underground bunker, sure to find files or a secret door or something, but the place was pretty straightforward and organized. The compound had been massive, over 20,000 square feet, two floors, and 15 rooms. He rechecked the place, but everything was accounted for: the eating area where he'd found Charlotte when she'd been stabbed, a room with two chairs and a non-functional fireplace, a greenhouse area, eight single rooms, most of which were being used as personal living spaces, (one in which Mags and Juliette had been held), an office, a waste, storage and workshop area, a giant washroom, and a library.

The basic construction had apparently been there for over a century. According to one of the women who lived in the bunker, she'd been told that the compound had been first built by Martin Milmore in 1862. Sean had looked up the name and yes, he'd been the sculptor for the Soldiers and Sailors statue, but no information existed regarding the creation of the bunker. Although, since it had been secret, there wouldn't be information out there about it.

"Most people don't know this," one of the women had said when Sean questioned her in jail, "but Milmore didn't join the Civil War, not because he didn't want to fight, but because he'd been creating this bunker to help hide supplies and soldiers. When the war ended, Milmore didn't trust that things wouldn't ever escalate again, so he asked the city to commission him to sculpt a statue. He planned to place it above the entryway to the bunker. It took him five years of sculpting to make sure he got the mechanics right for the secret entrance to open." According to the woman, the underground bunker was discovered thirty years later and used to house Triad members, some from other Triads, some new recruits, some who just wanted to stay on and help, until the 1990's.

"Why stop then?" Sean had asked the woman.

"The internet, of course. We couldn't keep that many recruits together anymore."

Sean had never gotten any other type of answer from any of the women. They simply said the internet changed things.

"But when Truth became in charge three years ago, she decided to start using the bunker again. To restore things to the way they were." What that meant also stayed a tight-lipped secret.

The inventiveness of the inner aspects of the bunker for this small group of extremely intelligent and creative women was evident. They seemed to have thought of everything to not only live in the bunker for years at a time without needing to leave, but also to make their environment comfortable and inviting.

The supply of electricity had been illegally splinted off from a neighboring corporate building, whose company never even noticed the slight increase in their monthly bills. When checked against the accountants' documents, the police determined the Triad women had been siphoning electricity for about three years, which coincided with how long the bunker appeared to be in use again.

An electric greenhouse had been installed in one of the rooms, which grew a variety of plants, including spinach, tomatoes, beans, carrots, potatoes, mushrooms, and broccoli. There was even an herb garden. Berry bushes sat in another corner, as well as a few fruit trees. The watering system had been interesting—they'd apparently tapped a local plumbing line that went to a different corporate building, so they were able to sustain themselves year-round for irrigation, cleaning, and drinking water.

An air filtration system had been installed, with piping that let out into various areas of the park, and an imaginative waste-management system had been implemented, which actually converted human waste into reusable fertilizer to feed their very own plants.

Detective Wilt, who'd been in charge of the case, had traced through the past three years as to how and when these items were most likely brought inside the bunker. The first time, three years ago, the Soldiers and Sailors statue area had been partitioned off for "construction" and the second time, last year, the same area had been closed for "statue upkeep." Wilt had confirmed with the remaining women in the compound that the first time had been to move everything inside, including furniture, appliances, a generator, containers, soil, tile, brick, etc. and the second had been to update their supplies, including food, backup equipment, and medical. They'd planned to be able to last for eight more years before ever needing to replenish anything.

An unscheduled delivery, though, had been made about two weeks before Violet had been arrested. One of the women noticed that Truth disappeared for a few days, and returned with a vast quantity of new supplies, including yeasts for bread, fruit, and spices for sauces. She said she was expecting a special guest. Sean deduced that it must have been a set up for Charlotte, to impress her.

Anything inside the compound had been crafted by hand. Each of the women learned how to tile, lay brick, create items from wood or fabric, and they formed their own environment. Truth, according to the women, had been a botanist and geneticist, and had done a lot of work in her home country on combining and splicing genes. She brought her talents to the compound and they were able to have a variety of items no one else on Earth had ever dreamed of, based off of her years of previous lab work.

As for the remaining women, out of the 13 found in the compound, only 8 remained alive: Truth and Angellica were dead, Juliette and Mags killed two of their captors while escaping, and Violet was in custody. Of those who still lived, they were all scientists who'd been brought into the group over the decades. Most of them had been naked when the compound was raided by the police, and when asked about this, they said they were comfortable that way.

"There aren't any men, there isn't any competition, and there's a level of comfort I've never felt anywhere else," one of the women said. "I've never felt such peace and safety as I did these past three years."

Psychologists were brought in to test these women and

their sanity. They were all proclaimed sane. There seemed to be no brainwashing or manipulation techniques used on them to get them to stay in the compound or help the Triad continue on with its work. Because of this, they were all currently in jail, having been tried and convicted as accessories after the fact, since none of them ever attempted to report the crimes they knew were orchestrated by Truth.

The general consensus of these women was, "The Book makes sense. I'd rather live in this kind of world than the one I lived in before I knew about the Book."

Sean shook his head. He couldn't imagine finding something in a book that would change you so much you'd give up your whole life for it. But then again, he'd dealt with enough religious fanatics in his line of work to know it was a real and true thing. One book could change everything. . .

Sean glanced up and all his thoughts about Spider, the trial, and the rest of the world vanished.

Charlotte arrived.

She looked incredible.

Though still modest in her attire, the slim black pants and low-buttoned, fitted men's blue dress shirt accentuated everything it should on her. Her long, dark hair, usually tied up in a bun or braid, hung in long waves over her shoulders. A blue pendant hung on her chest, reflecting off the restaurant lights.

She took a seat and smiled. A full smile, with teeth and shining eyes and everything.

Sean thought his heart might jump out of his chest.

"Hello Sean," she said.

"Hey," he managed. "You look. . .I don't even have a good enough word."

"Thank you," she said. "I am not complaining about my view either."

Sean grinned.

Charlotte picked up her menu. "Have you ordered yet?"

"Just a drink." At that moment the waiter put down his beer. "Didn't know what you'd want."

"Water is fine," she said to the server. When he returned a minute later, the two of them ordered. Sean asked for the Tandoori Chicken while Charlotte ordered something that sounded like a sneeze followed by a cough to him, Achoo Coal-ey or something like that. He'd been to this place on several occasions and loved the food and atmosphere, but had a tendency to order the same thing every time. Maybe he should try something new someday.

Charlotte began the conversation once the server left. "I have never been the best at small talk, so I want to start by apologizing."

"You said that outside the DA's office. What exactly are you apologizing for?"

"Our lack of communication during my travels."

Relief washed over Sean so strongly he almost sank into his chair. "It *is* something I wanted to ask you about. What happened? I thought maybe we were on the same page. About us, I mean. Was I wrong?"

Charlotte took a sip of water. "On the contrary. I enjoyed staying in touch with you, in the beginning."

"Then what happened?"

"The trip became. . .difficult."

Sean waited a few beats before he realized she didn't plan on saying anything else. "That's it? Difficult?"

Before Charlotte could respond, a different server walked past, tripped, and spilled half of whatever brown spiced dish she carried onto Sean's chest and shoulder.

"Damnit!" Sean cried out, pushing back his chair and standing. He began to wipe gobs of lumpy brown liquid off his shirt.

The server, a young blonde girl who couldn't have been more than 18, blushed furiously. She stuttered several apologies, tossed him her serving towel, then burst into tears and ran from the room.

Sean used the towel to wipe what he could from his shirt, his anger abating a bit at the girl's outburst. "I didn't mean for her to cry," he said. He looked over at Charlotte. "Are you all right?"

"A few flecks, but otherwise yes. It appears you received the bulk of the meal." She sniffed. "At least it smells delicious. Perhaps I should change my order."

Despite the situation, Sean couldn't help but laugh. "Maybe I can squeeze enough out of my shirt and into a bowl for you to try."

Charlotte reached over with one finger, scooped a touch of the sauce from the back of his hand, and tasted it. "Not too bad. But I think I will stick with what I ordered."

Sean stood there. The gesture had been so quick, but so. . . *sexy.* For a few moments, he forgot he was dripping brown sauce onto the floor and thought about her licking her finger.

"Uh. . ." he muttered, bringing himself back to the present. "I'll go wash up."

"I will be waiting," she said.

Another flush rushed through him as he headed towards the men's room.

Once there, Sean did his best to rinse off his shirt, but truthfully, it was pretty well covered with sauce. Luckily it was already a dark grey, so he hoped he'd just be able to wash it when he got home and no one would be able to see any stains.

He decided he might as well use the restroom as well and while at the urinal, his phone buzzed in his jeans pocket. Finishing quickly, he washed his hands and pulled his phone out, checking the message.

Unknown number.

--if yu andshe testfy you wil loose—

Sean gripped the phone in his still slightly damp hand. What the hell was going on? He'd put the previous messages out of his mind, what with everything happening lately, but now he couldn't ignore them. Someone had gotten his number and was messaging him about the trial.

With a furrowed forehead, Sean returned to the table, deep in thought. He rechecked the previous messages and put them together in a circling stream:

--will use your her words against--

-- She'll know I talked. She wants you and her to not believe. She wins that way--

--If you and she testify, you will lose--

Who could be sending these? Was it a prank? A friend? An enemy? Someone he knew?

Sean returned at the table, their meals having arrived while he'd been gone, and saw the concern in Charlotte's eyes.

"Is everything all right?" she asked.

"I'm not sure." He took a seat.

"Was there a problem in the restroom?"

He shook his head, already having forgotten about his wet shirt. "No, that was fine. I mean, it's not clean, but I'm sure it'll be fine, until I get home."

"What is it then?"

Sean took a breath. "I got a message. On my phone. Just now."

"Clearly it upset you. Bad news from work?"

"I don't know. I don't know what it is." He took a few moments to explain the messages he'd received, showing her his phone. She stared at it, tapping back and forth between the messages, reading them a couple times each.

"This is definitely odd," she said, returning the phone to him.

"It is, but I don't know if it's actually a real thing. I mean, after the press got hold of the case, we had multiple crank calls and letters, ranging from Spider Triad sightings to claims that they, themselves, were targeted by a Triad. Some were from people who thought their neighbors might be sleeper agents or they themselves might be. I even got a few notes like the 'clues' from the case. We followed up, but they all led no-where. One of them directed us to a plain brown box which, after the bomb squad got there and inspected it, ended up having a note inside that said "Fuck Off Pigs!" We took everything seriously, but I haven't really gotten anything specific in weeks, months maybe."

"Perhaps with the trial starting tomorrow a new influx is occurring?"

"Maybe." A wave of weariness washed over him. "But no one has ever sent something to my phone before. They were always to my job. Well, a couple were sent to my apartment, I guess." He let out a sigh. "I'll just add it to the file at work tomorrow."

"That may not be possible."

Sean paused. "Why not?"

"The trial? You may be gone the entire day."

Sean slapped a hand to his forehead. "Oh, yeah." He glanced at the messages one last time. "Do you think what they're saying could be true? That something in my testimony will keep Violet from being convicted? And who is the 'she' besides me? You? Mags? Tay? Violet herself?"

"I am not sure. Your testimony should be crucial in condemning her. You witnessed her interaction with Counselor Eth. She killed him in cold blood in front of you and Mags and Detective Tay."

Sean rubbed the back of his neck. An ache had started there. "Yeah. I asked Millan if he thought she could get out of it. Violet I mean. He says he's worried they are going to try to plead self-defense and get her to be found not guilty."

Charlotte's eyebrow raised. "How so?"

"Because Eth killed Angellica right before, so Millan thinks the defense will claim Violet felt 'threatened' by Eth and that's why she killed him."

"A bit farfetched from my point of view."

"Unfortunately, that's a lawyer's job. They just have to prove reasonable doubt, not innocence."

Sean realized he hadn't touched any of his food and his stomach felt a bit too upset to eat anything. On top of that, his shirt still smelled and had begun to itch against his skin. "I hate to say this, but I think tonight's a wash. Between smelling and feeling sticky and the trial tomorrow and this stupid message, I just want to shower and get some sleep." Suddenly he realized Charlotte may think he didn't want to spend time with her. "It's not you, you know," he blurted.

The edges of her lips raised. "I understand, Sean. In all honesty, I feel the same way. I have not been sleeping well since I returned from the trip."

"How come?"

She paused, as if hesitating, and Sean recognized the body language from dealing with suspects. She was deciding if she wanted to lie.

"I want to blame it on jet lag," she began slowly, her gaze cast downward, "but I am not sure I can."

"Is there another reason?"

"I do not remember them, but I believe I have been having dreams. Possibly nightmares."

"What makes you think that, if you can't remember them?"

She shifted in her chair. Sean hadn't seen her this uneasy since the night she stopped by his place and "vented" about her frustrations revolving around the Spider case.

"I have woken up often during the night, feeling ill at ease. I also rarely feel as awake as I believe I should after a night's rest."

"That sucks." He paused. "What did the shrink have to say?"

She cocked her head. "Shrink?"

"Yeah, you know, the therapist. The one you had to see after everything happened."

"I was not required to see a therapist."

Realization kicked in. "Oh, yeah, of course. You're not a cop. I guess it wasn't a requirement for you to see someone." This time Sean shifted in *his* seat, but not because he felt uneasy. It was because his damp shirt now felt chilly and the smell of the brown sauce was starting to get to him.

Charlotte must have noticed because she said, "I forgot. You wanted to go clean up."

"Yeah, but I also don't want to leave." He put as much emphasis into the words as he could. Once again, he found it surprising that even though they hadn't really spoken in weeks, his nervousness had disappeared once they'd starting talking.

"Sean, I would like to be up front."

"Are you ever not?" he joked.

The corner of her mouth raised on one side. "The truth is, I originally intended to come here to dinner and tell you we should remain friends, and only friends."

Happiness leeched out of him like a deflating car tire.

"However," she continued, "once I arrived and saw you, once we began our conversation. . ." she hesitated. "I thought our shared experiences six months ago were responsible for my attraction to you. I was wrong. I believe there may be something between us, something beyond friendship. I would like to explore that." She nodded at his shirt. "Though, another night perhaps?"

Happiness rushed right back in. "I would love that."

She smiled again, a true full smile. "Wonderful."

Sean's car was parked in the back lot and Charlotte had parked right near the front of the restaurant, so after dinner— in which the manager comped them for the mess— and their to-go bags were packed, they said goodbye at the table, that they would see each other in the morning at the trial, and went in separate directions.

When Sean got into his car, he left a message for Millan on his office phone about the cryptic messages he'd received. Millan hadn't been a witness for the Spider case and wasn't subpoenaed to testify tomorrow, so perhaps he could come up with some ideas on what the messages might mean, if anything, while Sean gave his testimony. He hoped the two of them could connect later and chat about it.

Once home and after a hot shower, Sean lay in bed, his thoughts drifting from the quietness of the empty apartment below him, to the craziness of what they'd all gone through, and finally settling on the idea of starting a relationship with Charlotte. He peered over to the left side of his bed, wondering what it would be like to see her laying there next to him. The idea definitely stirred him, emotionally and physically. He then thought about her struggling to sleep in her own bed. He hoped she could get some decent rest tonight.

The trial will be good for her, he thought. *Once it's over and Violet is behind bars, she can put this whole mess behind her. We both can.*

23

October 4ᵗʰ
8:45 a.m.

Sean arrived at the courthouse 15 minutes early. The media hoarded around the main doorway, but Sean merely kept his head low and moved through the pelting questions. He headed inside, went through the arrival and check-in process, and made his way to the courtroom where the trial would be held.

Upon entering, Sean had the strangest feeling of walking into a squashed church. The wooden benches reminded him of pews, with a huge desk up front, similar to an altar. The main difference being an American flag hung behind the desk instead of a crucifix.

He supposed the law had that aspect of religion—to judge and punish those who've stepped out of line, according to the rules put upon them by a "higher" authority. Except these authorities were only people, trying to do their best in a mixed-up world. Or screwing it up even worse, depending on the verdict.

Stationary cameras sat in separate corners, set up beforehand with their lidless black eyes constantly watching, to broadcast the trial on the news. Sean didn't feel as nervous as on previous trials, due mostly, he assumed, to his prep work with the district attorney, but the hugeness of this event did make his stomach quiver a little. There hadn't been a case of this magnitude where people were personally scared for their own lives since the Boston Strangler, and the press devoured any tidbits they could get their hands on. Even, in Sean's mind, the Boston Marathon bombing hadn't created such an influx of fear and panic from the public as individuals.

Sean found a seat on one of the benches. Juliette and Mags planned to ride together, as Mags didn't have a car. He figured they'd get there soon and left some space for them next to him.

"May I join you?"

Sean looked up and smiled at Charlotte standing beside him. The judge had decided the witnesses didn't need to be sequestered for the trial, to which Sean felt grateful. He knew they could all use each other's support.

"Of course," he said, scooting over. The day would consist of opening statements and then witness examinations, so he, Charlotte, Mags, and Tay would all testify. Beginning

Monday and throughout the following week, the court would listen to Wilt's testimony, as the lead detective on the case, then expert witness testimonies, cross-examinations, and finally closing statements.

Sean noticed the DA already had herself set up at one of the front tables, but the defense hadn't come into the courtroom yet. He knew the suspect wouldn't be brought in until the last moment.

As he settled in, the DA surprised him by coming over to where he sat.

"Detective Trann," she said, holding out her hand. "A word?"

He shook it. "What's going on?"

"I haven't seen Detective Wilt yet. He was supposed to bring the evidence this morning before the trial started."

As the lead detective, Wilt was charged with bringing in any physical evidence from the evidence locker at the police station. "I can try to call him for you, if you'd like. . .?" Sean trailed off as Wilt entered the courtroom, his hair a bit ruffled, his face flushed.

"Thank goodness," the DA said, marching over to him. She stopped abruptly. "Where is the evidence?"

Sean then realized Wilt didn't have anything in his hands.

Wilt shook his head. "I just got sideswiped. The Book and the guns are gone."

Sean jumped from his seat, with Charlotte close behind.

"What do you mean they're *gone*?" the DA asked.

"Sideswiped?" Sean asked at the same time.

"Are you injured?" Charlotte chimed in on the heels of Sean's question.

Wilt took a breath, leaning against one of the benches. He addressed each of them in turn. "Someone smashed the passenger window and grabbed my duffle bag containing the evidence out of my car," he said to the DA, "after they ran into me at an intersection two blocks away from here," he answered Sean. "And yeah, I'm all right. Just rattled. Thanks, Doc," he said to Charlotte.

Wilt ran a shaky hand through his hair. "Please don't tell me I ruined this case. My first huge murder case, serial killers no less, and I botched it. Why did I have to get assigned this screwed-up piece of garbage!"

Sean turned toward the DA. "Is it a bust? Without the evidence?" Sean watched her eyes flit back and forth, as if mentally scanning all the information she needed to assess the situation.

"No," she said finally. "No, I don't think so. We have copies of the pages from the Book and the murder weapons were confirmed by ballistics as belonging to yourself and Officer Eth. I really only wanted to show the Book to the jury."

"Why show them?"

"It symbolizes the reason why the suspect killed people. Just like in a case about a religious zealot, it's proof that she took the law into her own hands, following her own type of 'religion' you might say. It would have made her look unsympathetic and above the law."

The DA's face appeared strained, but she put on a smile

and patted Wilt on the shoulder. "It'll be all right. We can still get her. She'll be found guilty." She walked away, her posture rigid, and returned to her table at the front.

After she'd left, Sean wondered about her statement. It was the only thing he'd been worried about, that the defense might try to plead not guilty by reason of insanity. He didn't know if they could get her off—brainwashing cases were notoriously hard to prove—but there was always a first time for everything.

Sean turned towards Wilt. "Did you report the accident?"

"Of course," Wilt said, his shoulders sagging. "Millan told me to come in here and let the DA know what happened. I gotta go and deal with my car. It's wrecked."

"What *exactly* happened?"

"I left the station about a half hour ago to bring in the evidence early before the trial started. I was driving through an intersection, two blocks up. A car, a red Jeep, T-boned me on the passenger's side. It pinned me against the streetlight post on the other side. Someone exited the Jeep, came over, bashed in the passenger window with a black baton or maybe a dark steel bar, grabbed the duffle with the evidence, got back in their vehicle, and took off."

"What did the assailant look like?"

"Hard to say. Medium height. Black trench coat. Black boots. Black motorcycle helmet. Couldn't give you race or gender even. It happened so fast. Whoever it was knew how to pin me and to just smash and dash. They wanted that bag, man."

"Okay. Don't worry about it now. Go get yourself and your car dealt with. We'll touch base later."

Wilt stood, running his hand through his hair again. "I'm really sorry."

"It's not your fault. Just go." Sean saw Tay and Mags enter the courtroom. It was almost 9 a.m. "Don't worry. I'll fill them in." Sean sunk down on the bench, sensing Charlotte doing the same thing next to him.

Wilt nodded a thanks, gave Tay a shoulder pat and a head shake, then left. Sean and Charlotte scooted down to make room for Tay and Mags to join them on the bench. They all said their morning introductions.

"What was all that with Wilt?" Tay asked.

Sean quickly and quietly filled her in, then he nodded up at the front. The proceedings were about to begin.

Before the suspect entered, Charlotte leaned over. "Sean... I wonder about Wilt's assault. If someone wanted to help Violet escape from a sentence, stealing the evidence would not do that."

"I know," he whispered back. "So why do it?"

"Someone wanted the evidence. Not because it *was* evidence, but because of what it *is*."

Sean paused at her words. Someone specifically wanted either the guns or...

...the Book.

At that moment, the defense lawyer walked in from a side room, followed by Violet.

A stream of anger bubbled up unexpectedly inside Sean. His body shook at the sight of her. He hardly even noticed that Charlotte had put her hand on his arm. Glancing over at it, he thought it was to comfort him, but her own face appeared rigid as stone. Her nails dug a bit into his arm, as if she wanted to anchor herself to him so she didn't storm across the room and attack the woman who tried to kill her.

Sean's own anger abated a bit. Even though he'd almost been killed by the same woman, suddenly all he cared about was how Charlotte had almost died. He covered her hand with his and squeezed. The motion seemed to break her stare and she glanced over at him, giving him the tiniest nod, and squeezing his hand in return.

Once all the players were in their place, the judge came in, everyone stood for a moment, and the proceedings began. There had apparently been a delay with jury selection the day before, so opening statements still had to be made.

The DA began first. Her speech sounded pretty standard: she planned to prove the defendant's guilt, without a reasonable doubt, based on eye witness testimony, ballistic reports, and motive. She then took a seat and the defense attorney stood.

The woman approached the judge first, adjusted her gray suit jacket, and turned towards the jury.

Sean immediately noted her beauty. With bronzed olive-toned skin and cascading brown curls to her waist, she looked like a Greek goddess fantasy from an art history class Sean had taken in college as an elective credit. He wondered if she'd been picked specifically to defend Violet, who, despite being a psycho killer, was quite beautiful as well. Sean thought that the jury might see Violet as "too perfect" compared to a frumpier woman. He shook his head at the intricacies and details put into the courtroom process. Lawyers were always trying to skew things in their favor.

"Ladies and gentlemen of the jury," the defense attorney began. "This case will seem out of the ordinary, and you may very well be part of history in the making." Sean noted the hints of a New York accent in her words. They cut into the rhythm, giving it a sharp, yet curled quality. He'd heard the accent quite a bit in Boston, as many New Yorkers lived here and commuted, but she made her words sound couture, and he could tell why they'd chosen her. She made you feel important, like you were going to help shape the world through this case.

"The prosecution," the defense continued, "will attempt to claim that my client is guilty beyond a reasonable doubt. But there is no way this can be true."

A murmur swept through the courtroom.

"What is her angle?" Charlotte whispered.

Sean shrugged. "Insanity?" he whispered in response. It had to be. The defense would claim Violet wasn't in her right mind or was influenced by others.

"A woman *did* commit those crimes. But not my client. She should not be held responsible. And you, as the jury, will get to decide that. It's time to bring those responsible for corrupting innocent people to justice. It's time to stop blaming those who have no control over their actions."

The defense attorney swept her arm around, indicating Violet. "The woman sitting there is a wonderful person. She's competent, bright, and organized. She runs an animal shelter in Boston. She owns two dogs, a Ford truck, pays her taxes on time, and loves spaghetti and meatballs. And her name is Veronica Chasis. She's never killed anyone.

"Think about this," she continued. "If you were asleep and had nightmares of being chased by a killer and shot them in self-defense, only to wake up and discover you actually pulled the trigger on a gun and killed someone by mistake, should you be jailed for the rest of your life? If someone came into your home and made you drink alcohol until you blacked out and you woke up the next morning to find you'd killed someone, should you spend the rest of your life in prison? When you aren't in control of yourself by the hand of another, are you to blame? If someone kidnapped you and experimented on your brain, should you be punished, or should they?"

This time everyone in the courtroom started talking, even the jurors. The judge banged her gavel several times.

"Order!" she cried out. Her dark skin stood out against the white collar of her shirt beneath her black robe. "Order, now!"

The room stilled.

The defense attorney smiled. Not the creepy lawyer smile that oozed with sleaze, but a sad little smile that spoke of tiredness and pity. "The woman sitting here committed no crimes. She just wants to go home. This case will finally put the blame where it belongs—on those that take advantage of others. It's up to you to make sure an innocent woman gets the help she needs to return to her life. Thank you." She took her seat.

The judge cleared her throat. "We will proceed. Prosecution, please call your first witness."

The DA stood up. "I call Detective Sean Trann to the stand."

Sean stood up, slid past Mags and Tay, and headed up to the witness box. He took his oath to tell the truth and peered out across the courtroom.

He noted the jury first. It seemed a fairly random lot, as usual. He never felt very good at gauging how best to select a jury. That was a lawyer's job.

But one juror stood out. He counted. . .Juror #6. A woman. A stunning woman.

The hair on his arms rose. Why had this woman jumped out at him? Just because she was physically attractive? Then he realized he'd been noticing that pattern a *lot* lately, but not necessarily in a sexual or appealing way. He glanced around the courtroom again. Yes, he'd noticed the DA when he'd met with her and the defense attorney just now. Both beautiful. And then this juror. Why? Why were attractive women jumping out at him?

Suddenly he thought about what Charlotte had told him about the Triads, that they believed in physical perfection above all else. Would their members only be attractive, healthy women?

Could members of other Triads be here right now? Watching this case? A *part* of this case? Planted this woman in the jury box? Sean glanced at the judge. Even *she* was lovely, with dark mocha skin and springy hair. And one of the reporters in the back. And a woman sitting on the furthest bench, watching the proceedings.

But did they have to be physically attractive to be part of a Triad?

He cleared his thoughts; they wouldn't do him any good right now. There were too many variables and not enough information. He logged his observations away and planned to talk to Charlotte about them later. At this moment, he had to focus on his testimony.

The DA approached him and began her line of questioning—all things they'd rehearsed the past weekend. He spoke of his involvement in the case, his transfer from Philly, and how he witnessed the suspect in question murder Officer Eth.

"Yes," he said, re-explaining the situation. "Violet had Eth's gun and held him at gunpoint in front of her. I told her to lower her weapon. She did not do so. She claimed she only wanted to leave. I flipped my weapon so it was not pointed at her, though I still kept it in my hand. She then proceeded to fire the gun into the back of Officer Eth's head, killing him." His gaze flickered over to the jury. Several faces had furrowed brows, like they were angry—a good sign. Juror #6, however, remained neutral.

His eyes moved away from them and he looked across the room again, finally falling onto Violet.

Shock coursed through him.

He just realized he actually hadn't seen her face when she'd entered the courtroom. She looked completely different from the woman he'd seen that night in the compound. This woman's stature was hunched, she had wide, terrified eyes, and her normally caramel-toned skin looked almost yellow with illness.

Could it be? Could Violet have triggered her alternate persona and an innocent woman was going to take the fall for crimes she didn't commit?

Sean mentally scolded himself. He wasn't here to judge the woman in the chair. If her alternate persona did exist, she could switch into Violet at any moment. She could also be faking, like Anya had, trying to convince Sean that she'd returned to her persona of Angellica. It wasn't his problem anymore. His only concern had to be giving his testimony.

"Then what happened?" the DA asked.

Sean realized he'd lulled in his story. "Sorry. It's. . .it's not easy to talk about."

"I understand. Seeing a fellow officer murdered. . . Please continue when you can."

Sean nodded and finished his story, about how Violet chased them upstairs, firing at him, Tay, and Mags. About how she shot Tay and himself and how he finally subdued her by knocking her unconscious.

"Thank you, Detective." She paused. "One last question. Is that the woman who you witnessed killing Officer Eth?" She pointed over at Violet.

"Let the record state the prosecution is pointing at the suspect in question," the judge said out loud.

Sean looked over at Violet, her eyes wide, her face slack with exhaustion.

What if it isn't her anymore? Sean asked himself. *What if she's like Angellica, a totally different person now?* Sean would be condemning an innocent woman.

That's not my job, he answered his own thoughts. *The woman in that body killed Eth, tried to kill me and Tay and Charlotte and Mags. I have to say what I saw.*

"Yes," Sean said, though he hoped he was the only one who heard the slight waver in the word.

Violet burst into tears and dropped her head to the table.

"I have no more questions, your honor." The DA took a seat.

"You may step down," the judge said to Sean.

He nodded, swallowing hard.

As he walked by the defendant's table, he could hear Violet muttering to herself, "Why is this happening to me?"

24

October 4th
11:30 a.m.

Charlotte left the courtroom, followed closely by Sean, Tay, and Mags. Charlotte had given her testimony, confirming how she'd discovered the connection between the victims in the case, how she'd been kidnapped by Truth, and how Violet had thrown a knife into her chest to prove that she would die. The whole ordeal had gone easier than she'd thought, although she did find that she couldn't make herself look at Violet. In the one moment she did by accident, a feeling stole through her like the rumblings of an earthquake: hatred.

Charlotte had always considered herself a tolerable person. Though she wasn't always the easiest person to get along with, she found other people to be irritating or annoying more than disliking them. But the one glimpse of that woman's face had been enough. Charlotte had flashed back to standing inside the compound, seeing the grin on Violet's face, the flick of her hand, and hearing the *thud* when the knife entered Charlotte's chest.

Yes, hatred definitely festered inside her.

After Charlotte finished her testimony, the judge ordered a lunch break, and the courtroom cleared. Mags and Tay still had to be called to the stand when court resumed. For now, Sean, Mags, and Tay decided to have lunch together before Sean returned to work.

"Want to join us?" Sean asked Charlotte.

Charlotte felt tempted, but something inside her squirmed. She didn't want to be near the courtroom anymore. She didn't want to be around any of them, because they'd all been together when it happened. She just wanted this whole ordeal to be over. "I am very behind at work. I really need the time to catch up." She nodded at Mags and Tay. "I hope your testimonies go well."

"Good to see you again, Doctor Salla," Tay said.

"Yeah," Mags said more slowly, "hope you're taking care..."

Charlotte gave a weak smile. "Of course. Merely busy."

The two women sauntered off down the street towards the restaurant where they planned to have lunch. Sean hesitated for a minute. "Can I call you? I'd like to see you this weekend."

"I would enjoy that."

"Great." He reached out and squeezed her hand. "Have a good rest of your day."

"You as well."

Charlotte turned and headed towards her car, which sat parked in the opposite direction from where the others headed. The sun blazed overhead, hotter than she thought it would be for an October day. Her shadow strode in front of her, long and dark on the sidewalk as she walked with her gaze towards the ground. She was *really* getting tired of feeling uncomfortable all the time. And that feeling of hatred towards Violet? It left a bad taste in her mouth.

She wanted to return to her normal life.

"Doctor Charlotte Salla? Can I have a word?"

Charlotte swung around, finding herself face-to-face with a makeup-heavy blonde woman holding a microphone. A man carrying a camera followed closely behind. The lens reminded her of a fully dilated eye, staring at her.

Charlotte didn't have time to say anything before the journalist launched into her question.

"Do you think the defendant should be given life in prison for something she doesn't even remember doing?"

"No comment," Charlotte said, turning back around. Her face felt hot as she started walking away.

The reporter caught up with her, walking backwards to face her. "What about these *mysterious* Triads everyone is talking about. Seems a bit farfetched, doesn't it? I mean thousands of women killing people all around the world? And nobody has ever seen any proof?"

"I said 'no comment,'" Charlotte repeated, the heat in her

body evident in her voice.

"And isn't it true you failed to find any proof of these so-called Triads? That you spent the past three months running around the world and have no evidence to show for it? Doesn't it make more sense that the defendant is simply insane?"

Charlotte stopped for a moment, flabbergasted. How did this woman know about her trip? She hadn't talked about it in the courtroom. She hadn't discussed it in any interviews.

"Get out of my way," Charlotte snarled, storming away from them. She could see her car and took off in a fast stride, pulling her keys from her inside coat pocket.

"Thank you for your time, Doctor Salla. I'll be in touch," the reporter called out after her.

Charlotte opened her car door, slammed it shut, and started the engine. She peeled away from the curb, barely looking to make sure no one was in the street, and forced her ragged breathing to slow.

That reporter had only been doing her job. She had contacts. They all had contacts and sources. That was all.

Charlotte took a left towards her office, traffic forcing her to ease up on the gas. Her heartbeat slowed. Her shoulders relaxed. Media was to be expected. She just couldn't let them get to her.

It was at that moment something on the floor of the front passenger seat caught her eye. She stopped at a stoplight and peered over for a better look.

A note lay on the floor.

In a white envelope.

With the name "Charlotte Salla" typed on the front. Charlotte's blood ran cold.

25

October 4th
11:45 a.m.

Sean checked his ringing phone. "It's Charlotte," he said across the table to Mags and Tay. They'd just arrived and had sat down at the Ashburton Café, a cafeteria-style restaurant across the street from the courthouse. He answered the call.

"Hey, Charlotte! Did you change your mind about joining us?" He paused, listening to her shaky voice and quick words. He frowned. "Okay, don't touch anything and head to the station. I'll meet you there." Sean hung up and called Millan.

"What's going on?" Tay asked.

"Hold on. . .Millan? It's Trann. I just sent Charlotte your

way. She found something in her car we need to look at. I'll be there shortly." He hung up.

"Trann?" Tay asked. The tone of concern in her voice came from her years as a police officer. He knew she could recognize something was amiss.

"Charlotte found a note in her car, a typed note. I'm going to meet her at the station and find out if it's anything."

"A typed note? Like the ones Violet used to leave as clues?" Tay began to stand. "I'll go with—"

"You can't," Sean said, cutting her off. "You have to go back to the courthouse to finish your testimony." He shrugged his jacket on, looked with both longing and a tight stomach at his just-plated burrito, and pushed his chair under the table. "Don't worry, I'll fill you in when you're done." He nodded to Mags whose eyes had gone wide. "It's probably nothing," he said. He wasn't sure if he was trying to reassure her or himself.

"Good luck," Mags said. "I'll bring the rest of your burrito and leave it in the break room for you back at the precinct."

"Thanks." Sean left, jogged to his car, and drove to the station. He found Charlotte's silver car parked in the lot. Millan and Wilt stood outside it, checking the vehicle itself, the passenger side door open. Charlotte waited behind them, staring, as if her car was a threatening, alien creature.

"You all right?" Sean asked, sprinting over to her.

"Embarrassed, but fine," she replied, her mouth turning into a tight line. "The envelope may have only been from a file or leftover from work and fell out in my car. I did not want to touch it, in case."

"Better safe than sorry," he said.

"Trann?" Millan called out.

"Yeah?"

"You should see this."

Sean headed over. Millan, wearing blue latex gloves, held up the already opened envelope. He'd pulled out a single sheet of white paper, which he kept shielded from Charlotte.

Typed were the words: YOU ARE NOTHING. THE TRIADS ARE FOREVER.

Sean looked back at Charlotte, whose almond-shaped eyes were narrowed, as if trying to read the letter through them.

Millan looked over at Wilt. "You know what to do."

Wilt nodded, took the evidence with his own gloved hands, and brought it inside the building.

"Doctor Salla?" Millan asked, motioning her to come forward.

"Yes, Sergeant?"

"It appears as though the perpetrator pulled the window down just far enough to slip the note inside. There are a few small scratches along the edge of the glass. Probably used something like a screwdriver.

"I don't want to alarm you," he continued. "In fact, the note may be nothing. Trann, myself, and the department have all received cryptic notes from all this 'Triad-related' nonsense, ever since the case leaked to the press. But I want to be thorough. Would you mind coming inside the precinct for a few minutes? I'd like to ask you some questions."

"Of course." She didn't move.

"Is there a problem?"

"What did the note say?"

"I'll tell you about it inside." He coughed and waved her forward. "We can set up in my office."

Sean walked in with her, giving her a nod of encouragement. The three of them entered the precinct, headed towards Millan's office—the scent of stale cigarettes lingering in the air—and took a seat. Wilt joined them shortly.

Sean remembered the first time he'd gotten a creepy note from someone after a case. It had been in Philly, when he'd caught and arrested a suspect for drug dealing. Two days later, a rock with a note tied to it sailed through his car window— this was before he'd gotten the Jag from his almost in-laws. The note said he'd better watch his back and that the man he'd arrested had friends in "high places" who would cause problems if the suspect went to jail.

Sean had been terrified, of course, as he'd never been threatened like that before. Luckily, nothing ever came of the threats. The suspect was convicted and sentenced to three years in prison. They'd also found fingerprints on the note thrown through his car window and matched them to some low-life. They'd booked him for vandalism and threatening a police officer. While under arrest, the man apologized and cried, saying he was just mad that his brother was going to jail.

Since then, Sean had dealt with a few crank calls and hostile notes, but not all of his coworkers had been that lucky, so officers always took a threatening note seriously. Better a dead end then a dead cop.

After the Spider case, he and the station could barely keep up with the antics from the public, and the precinct had an outpouring of notes, letters, and threats, anywhere from fake Triad members to enraged citizens. Everything got stored in a file in the station. Sean had been more aware of his surroundings, especially after the first few weeks when the murders went public, but found it difficult to constantly keep up that level of alertness. After a while, when things slowed down and none of the notes or letters led anywhere, he basically returned to his job, as did the other officers.

A glance at the note made Sean think this was just another phony crackpot who wanted some attention, but since it had gone to Charlotte, he didn't want to take any chances. She'd already been through enough.

Millan asked a few basic questions: have you noticed anyone following you, any phone calls you can't explain, any exes or people in your life who would want to hurt or scare you? Charlotte answered politely that no, she had not noticed anything out of the ordinary.

"So, what does the note say?" Charlotte asked again.

Millan cleared his throat. "It says: 'You are nothing. The Triads are forever.' It isn't signed, not that we would expect it to be."

Charlotte's eyes widened, but she looked more curious than anything else. "What do you think the note means?"

"I think it means someone is playing a sick joke on you," Millan answered. "We've gotten dozens of notes of this type when the case first broke. None of them led to anything. Just rantings."

"It really doesn't seem to fit the Triad's style to send a note like this," Sean said. "It seems like nonsense."

"Their *style?*" Charlotte asked, a note of disdain in her voice. "If everything Truth told me was correct, there is no way to determine how any of the other Triads function. Violet and Anya were not supposed to deviate from their orders and send notes in the first place, but they did. Leaving any clue would have been considered outside of their *style*."

Sean swallowed. He wasn't sure what to say. He hadn't meant to upset her, but clearly Charlotte appeared agitated.

Millan looked over at Wilt. "Will you bring in the Spider follow-up file?" Wilt gave a nod and returned a few minutes later, holding a box. He placed it on the table. Millan gestured to the contents. "Doctor Salla, this is *full* of fake notes, threatening letters, complaints, and the like related to what happened with Spider. We investigate each one, but most lead nowhere and not one of them has turned into anything else. It's probably nothing."

He nodded at Wilt who removed the box. "However, we do take them seriously. We'll run the envelope and paper for prints and see if we get lucky. In the meantime, keep your eyes open and let us know if anything else happens."

Charlotte gave a tight smile. "Thank you, Sergeant." She nodded curtly at Wilt and glanced at Sean. "I better get back to work." She stood and left.

"Wait!" Sean called out, catching up to her. His forehead furrowed with concern. "I'm sorry about in there. Are you okay?"

They paused at the doors.

She let out a short rush of air. "No, Sean, I am not. I am tired, I am scared, I am. . ." She let out a longer sigh this time. "I just want to return to work and finish the day."

"Okay," he said. "Do you still want to meet up this weekend?"

Charlotte rubbed at the spot between her eyes. "I would like to, but I will have to see how I feel."

"All right. I'll call you?"

She nodded. "Have a good rest of your day, Sean."

With that, she left.

26

October 5th
3 p.m.

Sean decided not to call Charlotte until Saturday afternoon. He kept himself busy with a workout, consisting of push-ups, sit-ups, and a five-mile run. After working up a sweat, he took a quick shower then plopped himself in front of his TV, happy to watch a *Weekend at Bernie's* marathon.

Finally, he got up the nerve to give her a call on his landline. Charlotte answered after the third ring.

"Hello?"

"Hey. It's Sean."

A few crackles sounded on the other end. "Oh. Good morning."

"It's, uh, afternoon actually. Like three."

A pause. "Oh. You are right. Afternoon then."

Sean hesitated. "Did I wake you up?"

"It appears so. I still have not quite recovered from my travels. And I did not sleep well again last night."

"Sorry to hear that." He waited a few beats. "Should I let you go?"

"No. Yes. I mean, can I call you in about half an hour? I would like to shower and brush my teeth. Also my stomach is telling me it is empty."

"Yeah, of course. Take your time." He felt a little deflated. He'd been looking forward to seeing her.

There was another pause and some rustling, like maybe she was pushing away the covers. "If you would prefer, you could stop by in about forty-five minutes and we could head somewhere for a late lunch?"

Sean grinned. "I'd love that. But only if you're feeling up for it?"

"I am. Just tired. I would like to see you."

"Good. I mean me, too. See you, I mean." Sean thought about how often he'd been going out for food lately. They'd have to find someplace a little cheaper if he planned to keep dining out. "What restaurant did you have in mind?"

"How about The Elephant Walk? The place where I saw you at dinner the night I returned from my trip. It is a place I enjoy quite a bit."

"Sounds good. That place was great."

They said their goodbyes and Sean hung up. He sniffed under his arms and figured he smelled decent enough, but thought another swipe or two of deodorant wouldn't hurt. He strode towards his cell phone, which sat plugged into an outlet beneath his window. With a few taps, he pulled up some music, and began to hum. While heading to the bathroom, his phone beeped that he'd received a message. Surprised, but happy to think that maybe he'd found a spot where he actually got cell reception in his place, he did a quick turn, then side-stepped the corner of the bed he often hit his foot on, and let out a sigh of relief before picking up the phone.

I gotta put it here more often. Maybe I can get messages from now on.

He glanced at the screen.

Unknown Caller.

Sean had completely forgotten about the cryptic messages in all the chaos of the trial and Charlotte's note. He quickly read the message.

--the drm,mng hurts—

Sean's forehead wrinkled in thought. He sounded out the words. "The dorm. . .dram. . .drumming? The drumming hurts." He tapped his knuckles against his bottom lip. He had no idea what these messages were about.

He replaced the phone towards the window and saw one bar on his reception waver in and out. The phone beeped once more.

Unknown Caller.

--she wnts char they all want chrltte—

"She wants Char. . .they all want. . ." Sean trailed off, scared to finish saying it out loud.

They all want Charlotte.

Someone wanted Charlotte. Or was someone *after* Charlotte?

Sean dashed over to his landline phone and dialed Charlotte's number. No answer. Panic constricted his chest.

"She's probably in the shower," he told himself. But the logic meant nothing.

Without thinking about deodorant or food or if he looked okay for a date, Sean grabbed his keys, cell, wallet, and jacket and took off out of his apartment.

27

October 5th
3:15 p.m.

Charlotte stepped out of the shower. She rolled her shoulders back and sucked in a deep breath of steam from the fogged-up bathroom. It may have been a cliché, but hot showers were one of her favorite things. Something about heat and feeling clean and fresh sated her.

She reached for her towel, fluffy and dark steely blue, like the ocean right before a storm, and dried off. The ocean on the East Coast appeared so different than the one she'd sit out in front of in Hawaii during grad school. Here the water looked darker and colder, almost like a giant lake, as opposed to the island's signature dark blues or greens with crashing waves. She used to visit the ocean every week in Hawaii, but rarely had done so since she'd moved to Boston. Maybe she and Sean could take a day trip sometime and have a picnic.

Notes resonated through her closed lips as she hummed, and she felt better already, excited to see Sean. She flipped her head over and wrapped her wet hair up in a towel before righting herself. The humming turned to soft words and she lightly sang a tune from some musical she'd seen years before. She didn't even remember the name of it.

Leaving her bathroom, the change from hot and humid to the coolness of her bedroom sent a shiver through her. She headed for her closet, opened the door to it, and stared inside at its contents.

What. . .to. . .wear. . .

A brisk knock at her front door startled her. She glanced over at the clock. It had only been fifteen minutes since she'd spoken to Sean. It wouldn't be him yet.

Another knock, this one more persistent.

Charlotte snatched her robe from the hook inside the closet door and slipped it on, heading towards the front entrance. "Who is it?" she called out. A sudden flush of fear ripped through her when she remembered the note in her car. Was someone here for her?

"It's me!" the voice called through the door. "Sean!"

The fear eased. "Sean?" she said, heading towards the door. Right before she grabbed the doorknob, she slipped on something on the floor she hadn't noticed, which blended in with her white carpet.

Another envelope.

28

October 5th
3:20 p.m.

Sean heard a shriek from the other side of the door.

"Charlotte!" he yelled, trying the door handle. It remained locked. He banged on the door again, terror gripping his chest.

After a few moments, the door unlocked from the inside and Charlotte stood there as it swung open.

"Are you all right?" Sean said, rushing in. He grabbed her by the shoulders, did a quick glance to make sure she wasn't bleeding or hurt, and then surveyed the room. Nothing appeared out of place. He didn't see any broken glass or a shadowy figure or anything amiss.

Sean could hear his heartbeat pounding in his ears.

"I am all right," Charlotte said, clutching him for a moment before composing herself. "There is another note. On the floor. I stepped on it." She pointed to the envelope on the floor and backed away, lifting her foot slightly as if she'd stepped in something sticky or toxic.

Sean dashed out to the hallway, but he knew no one would be there. He would have seen them when he came upstairs. He'd been lucky—a woman had been exiting the building and held the door open. . .for. . .him. . .

"I think I might have walked right past the woman who left this letter."

"What?" Charlotte's voice cracked.

"A woman was leaving the building. She held the door open for me."

"What did she look like?"

Sean forced his "police brain" as he called it, to work, dredging up any detail from that moment. "Short. Stocky. With brown hair in. . .curlers I think? Glasses."

Charlotte shook her head. "That is Mrs. McDowen. She and her husband live in the apartment on the first level. She is notorious for letting people in the building and has been reprimanded about it several times." With measured steps, Charlotte headed towards her bed and sunk down onto it, knees drawn together, feet on tiptoe. "She likes to sit outside the door and smoke, as if her husband does not know. It makes her feel helpful to let people in." Charlotte raised a hand to her mouth. Even from across the room, Sean could see it shook.

"I'll take care of this," he said, pointing to the envelope. "I'll call the station and get whoever is on duty this weekend to come by and pick it up. First thing Monday morning, I'll ask for a rush job on the fingerprints from the first envelope, and this one too, if there are any."

"Monday," she muttered. "Two whole days away. I cannot outrun these women." Charlotte seemed to be talking more to herself than to Sean.

He crossed the room and sat next to her on the bed. With slow movements, he put his arms around her. She collapsed into him and shook. He couldn't tell if she were actually crying or just reacting to her adrenaline dropping, but whatever she'd been dealing with seemed too much right now.

Not that he could blame her. As a cop, in some ways you know what you're signing up for. Not that you ever expect to be kidnapped or almost killed, but at least you know it's a possibility in your line of work. But Charlotte? A coroner? Nobody cared about them. They dealt with victims *after* the crimes. They were usually nameless and faceless and weren't important to anyone for anything, except autopsy reports.

Now Charlotte had been targeted, a bullseye on her from the possibly thousands of murderous women around the world.

Sean mentally chided himself. This line of thought wasn't helping things.

One thing he did realize was that in all the movies he'd seen, this was supposed to be the "vulnerable" moment for a girl and a guy to get together physically. But Sean hated the idea of being with Charlotte like this. He wanted to be with her because it felt good, not because she was scared to death and he happened to be there.

As if sensing his thoughts, Charlotte slowly pulled away. Her eyes were rimmed with tears, but her face remained dry. She still looked stunning. He could love to see that face every day.

"Any better?" he asked.

She nodded and sniffed. "I am all right. How about you call the precinct while I get dressed?"

Sean registered the black bathrobe and lopsided towel on her head. He swallowed hard, forcing himself to focus on the situation. "That sounds like a plan."

While she headed towards the bathroom, Sean glanced over at the envelope. He frowned.

"Hey, Charlotte?"

She turned and paused. "Yes?"

"Your name. It's handwritten on the envelope." He glanced at her. "Wasn't the other one in your car typed?"

Her eyes narrowed slightly. "Yes. . ." she began.

Sean grabbed a tissue from her nightstand and carefully picked up the envelope. It wasn't even sealed.

"What the. . ." he said. He gently lifted the edge of the flap and could read a few of the typed words. A sigh of relief slid from his lips.

"What?" Charlotte asked. She'd approached behind him and peeked over his shoulder.

He dropped the tissue away and handed her the envelope. "It's all right. It's from your landlord."

Charlotte took the envelope gingerly and slid out its contents. Her eyes flicked back and forth as she skimmed its subject matter.

"Changes to my upcoming lease renewal," she said. She let out a shaky laugh. "I forgot my landlord said he would drop off the paperwork today. I must have been in the shower when he knocked so he slipped it under the door." She brought her hands to her face, the envelope covering her cheeks and mouth. "I am *so* embarrassed."

Sean patted her on the arm. "It's okay. Hey, I thought it was another note, too." He nodded towards the bathroom. "Why don't you finish getting dressed and we can still grab a bite to eat. If you're up for it?"

She nodded. "That sounds perfect."

As she walked away, Sean took a seat at her kitchen table, glancing around her apartment. A studio, like his, but other than that, the spaces looked completely different. Covered in whites and creams, with cool blue and green accents, he felt a bit like he sat in the middle of a magazine shoot. The place appeared beautiful, but hardly felt lived in. Granted, she'd just returned from traveling for three months, but Sean had a feeling her place always looked like this.

He thought of his own messy apartment and the time she'd visited him. She must have been disgusted by his place.

Sean scratched the back of his head. It wasn't like him to second-guess himself and the way he lived. But Charlotte just seemed. . .

In a different league? he thought.

Sean let out a grunt. They hadn't even really started dating yet and he was already thinking he didn't measure up. He'd had this problem in previous relationships as well. That's why Angellica had been so easy to be with—she just went along with whatever he wanted to do, so he always felt like he was good enough.

But Charlotte? What was he thinking? They didn't match at all.

He remembered Mags' words from the lunch the previous weekend: *Simple isn't good for you.* Except he thought of himself as a "simple" kind of guy. He didn't want to deal with someone high-maintenance or having to make sure he put a coaster on the table or worry about spilling beer on the floor. Not that he wouldn't clean up after himself, but he didn't want to be afraid to relax in the place where he lived. He wasn't sure he could relax in Charlotte's apartment—he'd be too afraid he'd stain her carpet or something.

Charlotte emerged from the bathroom, her tousled wet hair hanging loosely over one shoulder, dressed in a slim, green dress which stood out in the white and cream surroundings.

"I am ready," she said.

He grinned. All thoughts about what their relationship could or couldn't be were wiped away in his mind. The only thing he cared about right now was taking this gorgeous creature out for some good food.

After driving her home, Sean pulled over in front of Charlotte's apartment building. They'd decided to take one car to the restaurant. The meal had gone better than Sean could have hoped. No awkward silences. No strange questions. And no talk about work. That was the kicker. Any time in the past he'd dated someone in his line of work, or relating to it, they always talked about cases.

He'd learned so much about her, not only stuff he assumed she must have cared about, but because he always saw her as this aloof out-of-touch Vulcan, he didn't realize she'd care about other things like movies and books and music.

And not just cultured stuff like classical music and black and white films. She may not have had a huge interest in blood and guts, but she seemed to enjoy a good kung-fu action film or thriller. She had other interests too, like she enjoyed watching tennis and she used to play volleyball in college. No siblings, though he thought she'd mentioned something about playing with a brother when she'd been little, and her parents were still together, still living in Portland, OR.

All in all, a pretty decent official first date.

Now they sat in the car, finishing their discussion on their thoughts about which ocean they liked better: East Coast or West Coast.

After they both agreed that it depended on what you wanted *from* the ocean—the sunset/sunrise, swimming, sailing, surfing, relaxing on the beach, etc., they decided the Pacific Northwest was the best to live near, Southern California had the best for recreational use, and the Southeastern coast lent itself most to relaxation. Charlotte did suggest that perhaps they hadn't given the Boston coastline enough credit and proposed that someday the two of them could spend some time at Carson Beach, to give it a fair shot. Sean had hurriedly agreed.

"Thank you, Sean," Charlotte said, in reference to their current outing. "I needed something to take my mind off my life right now."

"Glad I could help."

"I would like to do this again sometime."

"Me too." He grinned. His eyes kept flickering to her mouth. Should he kiss her?

She unbuckled her seatbelt. "Enjoy the rest of your weekend."

"You too." She turned to face him. *Go for it!*

He leaned forward a bit, so she could see his intent, but be able to pull away if she wasn't interested.

The smallest trace of a smile touched her mouth and she leaned in towards him as well.

He closed his eyes right before their lips met. Her lips were so soft, completely unlike the Ice Queen he'd once thought of. He was just about to pull away when she parted her mouth just a bit and pressed in harder. A sensation, like the feeling of a stretch that makes your body shudder, surged through him. He'd never felt anything like that before.

Charlotte eventually broke contact, her eyes still closed for a few moments.

He cleared his throat. "Uh," he managed.

"Same," she whispered. "Good night, Sean."

With that, she slipped out of his car. He watched her walk up to her door, turn, and give him a brief wave before heading inside.

Finally, he registered that he should probably turn on his car and head home, but it took him several moments to make the blood flow to the correct body parts needed to do just that.

29

October 7th
8:45 a.m.

Juliette raced out of her house, skidding down the wet concrete stairs.

"Bloody hell," she cursed. She managed to grip the edge of the hand rail, but it, too, was slick, so her hand slid and she twisted it against the edge of the bar. Shaking off the pain, she hurried to her car parked in the driveway, since it wouldn't fit in her crammed-full-of-items garage. A silent prayer went from her mind to the powers-that-be to give her minimal traffic. Otherwise she'd be late for work.

With a glance at her car she cursed again, noticing her back bumper hanging over the sidewalk. She had a bad habit of not pulling far enough into her driveway when her mind was preoccupied. She'd even gotten a ticket once, no doubt tattled on by one of her "perfect" suburban neighbors.

With quick movements she got into her vehicle and shut the door, shaking the rain from her hair. Keys in hand, she started up the car—still a little uneasy with, in her mind, the fact that the steering wheel sat on the wrong side. Her trip home to England hadn't helped, as she now had to realign her brain again to switch sides of the street on which to drive.

Juliette turned on the car and paused for a few moments, rubbing her sore wrist. Being distracted was a surefire way to get herself killed in a car collision. She'd just been so scattered the past few days since she'd delivered her testimony at the trial.

All the previous week had gone well. She felt good about returning to work and comfortable starting new cases. She felt like she'd returned home after a really long bad dream.

But sitting on the stand, recounting what had happened to her...

That night, while she slept, she'd returned to the scene where she'd been kidnapped. Nightmares of endless corridors, women hiding in her room to grab her, and always, *always* having to kill someone to get out of the situation.

On Friday night she'd woken at 2 a.m. in a cold sweat and immediately started to sob. She never managed to fall asleep again. On Saturday, fear kept her from wanting to go to bed, so she'd called Mags and invited her over for a "Girl's Night." They'd watched movies, eaten popcorn, and drunk copious amounts of wine coolers. Juliette had passed out more so than fallen asleep, but she at least didn't remember her dreams.

Last night though, no such luck. She even had a few drinks—Mags had left the remaining two wine coolers in the fridge—but Juliette hadn't drifted off until nearly 5 a.m, at which point she began to dream about being captured by hordes of women. When her alarm went off an hour later for work, she'd slept through the incessant beeping until 7 a.m., her mind incorporating the sound of the alarm into a dream as a warning to the women who'd captured her that she'd escaped from the facility. She spent the whole dream running and hiding and fighting. She'd awakened with a scream on her lips and a fist in the air.

These things are to be expected, the counselor had told her when they'd first started their sessions six months ago. *As we work through what happened to you, the dreams will dissipate. I promise.* Her dreams had been just as bad six months ago and Dr. Moria had prescribed sleeping pills and anti-anxiety medication to help her sleep. But the good doctor's advice rang true. After a few weeks, the dreams did lessen. She reduced and then got off the meds and could sleep soundly once again. That was when she'd decided to visit England.

Juliette let out one more sigh. She still had one session left with Dr. Moria this coming week. Perhaps she could get on the medication again for a little bit to help her sleep, just to take the edge off until the trial ended.

Feeling like she had a plan of action, Juliette turned on the front and back windshield wipers and adjusted her rearview mirror. When she returned her attention to the front, she noticed a piece of paper sliding up and down, caught under one of the wipers.

"Just perfect," she muttered. "A bloody ticket." Grimacing at the heavy raindrops, she got out, grabbed the piece of paper as it skated towards her, then popped again into her car.

"I'll deal with you later," she said to the culprit. She plopped the envelope onto the front seat and took off towards work.

30

October 7th
9:05 a.m.

Sean lifted his gaze from his desk at the precinct doors opening. He watched a drenched Detective Tay walk through the entrance. The rain had barely started coming down when he'd left for work a half hour ago, but he could tell by her sopping clothing that it had picked up since then.

"Morning Tay," he called out. He'd just returned from Millan's office, having told him about the cryptic messages on his phone and the envelope that was "not an envelope" at Charlotte's. Millan had offered to put in a request for a court order to get the number traced.

Now, once again in his office, Sean watched as Tay

stalked over to her own space, smashed her bag and papers on top of the desk, and started pulling off her coat. Finally, she plunked down into her chair.

"Bad morning?" Sean asked, moving closer so he could keep his voice down.

"Something like that," she answered. "I dropped my bag in a giant puddle on the way in and on top of that," she said, holding up a piece of paper, "I got a ticket on my car."

Sean grimaced. "Sorry." He glanced at the paper in her hand. She still held it up while she sorted through some other things on her desk.

Sean's eyes widened. "Hey, Tay?"

"Hey, what?"

Sean strode across the room, his gaze never leaving the paper. Except it wasn't a paper. It was an envelope.

And though wet, he could still see her name across the front.

Typed.

There wasn't much use in searching for fingerprints and the like, since the envelope had been soaked through, so Sean took it to Millan's office with Tay trailing behind and the three of them carefully peeled apart the pages, hoping to see if they could salvage any words.

Sean glanced over at Tay, her freckled skin pale and ashen. She looked like she hadn't slept in weeks.

"What does it say?" she asked Millan.

Millan grunted, then mumbled something under his

breath, then appeared to be reading without speaking.

"Millan," Tay demanded.

"I hear you, Detective," Millan said, raising his eyes to look at her. "I'm still working on it."

"Sorry," she muttered. She sank down in the chair across from him.

"I can't read all of it," he said finally, "but if I fill in some of the soggy blurs, it looks like it says: 'You are nothing. The Triads are forever.' Sound familiar, Trann?"

Sean nodded. "Same thing for Charlotte." He turned towards Tay. "They cracked open her car window and slid the envelope in." He narrowed his eyes at the soggy mess. "Why under the windshield for yours? Maybe they didn't have time to get your window open, or they couldn't, or your car was too exposed? Leaving it on your windshield is pretty sloppy. This could have been completely unreadable."

Millan said, "We'll put a rush on Charlotte's envelope and see if we can get any prints." He called out for Wilt.

"He's not here," Sean said. "Remember? He's testifying today."

"Oh right, I forgot," Millan said. "I'll have him add this to the 'Spider box' if he comes in today. Otherwise we'll add it in tomorrow." He paused. "We should keep it separate though," Millan continued, "in its own folder with the other one. This is the first note that isn't a solo act, having gotten more than one from the same person." He nodded at them. "Go ahead with your day. Tay, I don't need to tell you to be careful and watch your back. This could be nothing, but if they targeted two of you, it could be more than an idle threat."

"Smashing," Tay said, laying sarcasm on the word.

Sean and Tay left the office.

"Doctor Salla got one, too?' Tay asked.

"Yeah. On Friday afternoon, remember? When we all left the trial and went to lunch?"

Tay let out a sigh and her shoulders relaxed. "That's right. I completely forgot."

Sean's forehead furrowed. "Does that make you feel better, knowing she got one, too?"

"Surprisingly enough, it does. Doctor Salla and Mags spent the last three months trying to prove there are other Triads out there, with no luck. Mags has been feeling really down about it lately. Honestly, if she hadn't actually been in the compound, she said she felt like she wouldn't even believe the Triads existed at all. But this proves they are still out there. Still trying to mess with us. Which means we can find them and stop them." Tay nodded sharply then sat at her desk, shoulders hunched.

Sean returned to his own office, thinking about what Tay had said. He wasn't sure this proved the Triads existed. To be honest, he felt like the delivery was a bit chaotic compared to what Truth and her group had done. However, from what Charlotte told him before, the Triads were autonomous, which meant some of them may not have been as well structured.

Sean shook his head. Too many wild speculations and once again, not enough proof. All they could hope for was that one of the envelopes provided some DNA or a fingerprint. Then maybe they could go from there, find another one of these "Triads."

Taking a seat at his desk, Sean looked towards the entrance of the precinct, happy to see the back of Mags' head once again at the front.

A thought slashed through his mind. Tay had said all three of them, she, Charlotte, and Mags, had been kidnapped.

If Charlotte and Tay had gotten notes. . .

Sean made his way to the front. "Hey Mags?"

She swiveled in her chair. "What's up?"

"Did you get any note or envelope or anything on your car or at your apartment today?"

She frowned. "No. But I don't have a car, remember? Should I have gotten something?"

Sean raked his fingers through his hair. "I thought maybe. . . nah, never mind. A hunch."

Mags crossed her arms. "What aren't you telling me?"

Sean waited a few beats. "Charlotte and Tay both received notes."

"You mean like the one Charlotte got on Friday? Juliette got one, too?"

Sean nodded.

Her eyes widened. "You think I might get one?"

"It's a theory. Both of them got it in or on their car, though. Since you don't have one, maybe it's fine."

At that moment the doors opened and a delivery person entered. "Mornin'!" she called out. She smacked her gum and smiled. "Got a letter here for a 'Margaret Stinton.' Is she here?"

"That's me," Mags whispered, her eyes wide.

The deliverer handed over a sealed envelope, got a signature from Mags, and left. Mags opened it with shaking hands. She peeked inside and expelled a breath.

"It's just an invoice from the office supply company. Their systems have been down so they said they were going to snail mail me a copy of it instead." Mags pushed Sean in the chest.

"What was that for?" he asked.

"You scared the *crap* out of me!"

"Sorry. I didn't know. . ." he trailed off. "It was just a hunch."

"I have enough going on at home already not to deal with 'note' things," she said, shuffling some papers on her desk.

Sean cleared his throat. "How's all that stuff going? You know, at home?"

"Hard." She looked at him, blinked a few times, then returned her gaze to her desk. "Scott moved out over the weekend. To his brother's. Until we get things sorted out. With our stuff, I mean, like what we own."

Sean shifted between his feet, wondering if he should ask more or return to his desk. "That sucks," he finally said. He felt like he said that a lot lately, especially because he didn't know what else to say.

"It is what it is," she replied, her voice oddly flat. When she didn't say anything more, Sean turned away.

He glanced around the room. People had enough to deal with in life already. And then Spider had messed with everyone's heads. Mags with her ex-fiancé, Millan with his responsibility for killing someone on the job, Juliette with her healed injuries, Charlotte with her near-death experience. He couldn't forget about himself either—his ex had turned out to be a serial killer.

Sort of.

Sean sat back down at his desk and rubbed his face, trying to clear away his thoughts—focus once again on work. But the trial kept popping into his mind. He felt like he was living in a dream. The whole situation seemed ridiculous, and yet he'd seen it with his own eyes. The compound, the bodies, the notes. It had been real.

And it kept affecting them all.

As soon as Violet is behind bars, all of this will be over, he thought. But he wasn't so sure. If she and Angellica and Truth had been the only women behind these murders, then it would end with Violet.

But if there really were other women out there, killing, would it ever end?

Sean had a fleeting thought, something so secretive he almost didn't like that it popped into his head.

If this Spider stuff blows over, I don't care how many other Triads are out there. Let someone else deal with them. We've done enough.

He didn't like feeling that he wouldn't want to help stop any other murderous women, but the toll it had taken on both him and those in his life? He didn't know if any of them, including himself, could handle going through a process like this all over again.

Sean glanced up at this moment to see Payne race through the door, huffing and puffing.

"Am I late?" he asked, glancing up at the clock.

Sean gave a soft chuckle. "Yeah, but barely."

"I swear I tried." He slicked his hair back. "Damn truck wouldn't start. I could use a coffee though. Want one?"

Sean stuttered. "Uh, sure. Black is fine." He saw Payne's eyes flicker over towards Mags and realized the reason for his sudden generosity.

Except she wasn't looking in their direction.

"Great. I'll be back in a few. Gotta ditch my stuff, first."

Sean felt a sudden surge of hopefulness. If someone like Payne could make an effort to be more decent, maybe the whole world wasn't as lost as he'd thought.

31

October 8th
11 a.m.

"We got a match!" Wilt came running over to Sean's desk, waving a piece of paper in the air and holding a file. Several other officers perked up at his announcement.

"A match for what?"

"A print from the envelope left in Doctor Salla's car!" A grin stretched across his face.

Sean stood up and snatched the paper from Wilt's hand. "Who is it?" he asked, skimming the fingerprint results.

"A guy named Bruno Zido. We busted him a couple years ago for stealing a car, which was the first thing we could catch him on. He didn't do anything with the car, just a joyride and abandon, so nothing really came from the case, but tell me can we nail this guy on something now?" Wilt laid the file open on Sean's desk.

Sean stared at the results before glancing at the rap sheet of the suspect. "Huh."

Wilt sucked on his toothpick. "What is it?"

"I don't know. I guess I thought it'd be a woman who left the envelopes."

"Well either way, I'm heading over to his last known address now. I talked to Judge Hawkins right away this morning and got a search warrant. This Spider case may be crazy, but everyone is taking it really seriously. You and Payne want to come with? Tay's coming, too. We don't want to make any mistakes."

"Yeah. Payne's in the bathroom. I'll let him know when he's done."

Wilt pumped his hand in the air. "Finally, a break!"

Sean couldn't blame the guy for his enthusiasm. As lead detective on the case since its inception over two years ago, Wilt had this hanging over his head for a long time. Sean knew the guy must be exceedingly stressed out about the trial results. And now possibly a man related to the "Spider" women? Sean had a few unsolved cases on his own docket, but something this big? Wilt deserved a break.

Although Sean still wasn't sure if this was *actually* a break.

He saw Payne returning from the bathroom and waved him over.

Only one way to find out.

* * *

An hour later, Sean, Payne, Wilt, and Tay pulled up in two cars to a rather ordinary yellow house. A patrol car followed them. White shutters complimented the white window boxes. The lawn looked neatly trimmed, the hedges all level. Fluffy clouds floated overhead, casting cheerful shadows across the lawn. It looked like something from an old 1950's TV show. Sean almost expected to see 2.5 children and a dog playing in the yard.

They all exited their vehicles and followed Wilt's lead. He motioned for Tay to head around the back, in case anyone tried to flee. Once she was in position, he took a deep breath and pounded on the door.

"Police! Open up!" A few moments later he heard the clicks of the locks release.

A stocky man, about 5'8", opened the door. His eyes looked bloodshot, as if he'd been drinking heavily the night before, or perhaps already this morning. A grease stain smeared his white undershirt. He reeked of fish.

"I ain't done nothin', why are you here?" he said, his words slightly slurred.

"Bruno Zido?"

"Yeah? I ain't done nothin'!" he repeated. "I been home for an hour from my job on the docks. Check with my parole officer."

Wilt walked into the doorway. "You're under arrest for sending threatening letters," he said, pulling out his handcuffs.

Bruno's eyes widened. "What?"

Wilt took care of the arrest and Miranda rights, letting

Bruno know they had a search warrant to inspect his house. He then nodded to Payne. "Will you take him to the officers outside?"

"Sure thing," Payne said, escorting the suspect out. Bruno apparently didn't care about his option to stay silent. He bellowed all the way to the car, claiming his innocence and his distaste for pigs.

By this point, Tay had returned to the front and joined Sean and Wilt inside the house.

"Well," she said, "let's take a look around."

They spent the next half hour searching the place. The messy, yet mostly empty interior did *not* reflect the neatness outside. Empty beer cans littered the floor, the bed had no sheets on it, and the garbage can overflowed with dirty take-out containers and paper plates. Although furnished, plastic covered the couch and two recliners, the lamps had all been taken down off their respective side tables and placed in a corner, and the rugs had been rolled up in the corners. There were no pictures, knick-knacks, or personal items of almost any kind, except for some large yellow-flower bouquet paintings on the wall behind the couch.

Sean paused in his futile search through an empty dresser in one of the bedrooms. "I would say Bruno would be in the middle of a move, but everything feels haphazardly scattered around, like someone just wanted things out of the way. This feels more like he's squatting here. What the hell is going on?"

Tay came from the bathroom across the hall and popped her head into the bedroom. "I don't know. This does feel off, though."

"Guys! Come down here!" Wilt called out to them from the floor below.

Tay and Sean thundered down the stairs.

"You gotta see this," he said. He led them down another flight into the basement. "It's like something straight out of a horror flick." He gestured towards one of the far corners, which was lit up by a single bulb hanging above it.

"Bloody hell," Tay whispered. She moved nearer to the corner, her face pale.

It looked like a shrine. Three unlit candles sat in a triangle around a short wooden crate. On the crate lay a red cloth, sprinkled with newspaper clippings. Sean followed close behind Tay and glimpsed at the clippings—they were all about the Spider case and trial. His gaze traveled up the wall. Four pictures were tacked onto it—three in a triangle surrounding a central picture. The three photos were of Charlotte, Tay, and Mags. The image in the middle was of Violet, sitting at the trial.

"Looks like we found our guy," Wilt said.

32

October 8th
6 p.m.

Sean flopped onto his couch, an open beer bottle in his hand. Earlier that afternoon, right after they processed Bruno Zido, Sean had messaged Charlotte, letting her know they caught the guy who'd sent the notes. He decided to keep quiet on the "shrine" in the basement, figuring all it would do would be to scare her even more. He hadn't heard from her yet, but she often didn't keep her cell turned on at work. She'd be getting done with her day soon and he figured he'd hear from her shortly.

He'd also received a summons from the defense attorney, ordering him to report for court Thursday morning as a witness for cross-examination. The DA had warned him this would most likely happen, especially after the insanity plea, suggesting that the defense would try to prove Violet was not in her right mind during the shooting. He wasn't quite sure how he could be helpful for the defense, seeing as how he only ever saw Violet as Violet, and she seemed pretty in control of her actions, but he figured he'd find out in two days.

The itch for a snack reached him and he dragged himself off his couch, searching his counter for the half-eaten bag of ridged potato chips before settling back down. He flicked on the TV, hoping the ax-throwing finals were still on. Surprisingly enough, he'd gotten hooked on the sport and wanted to see if the burly guy won in the end. He paused while fishing for his first salty treat when he stumbled past a news network and saw his own face briefly on the screen.

Sean pursed his lips, then turned up the volume. A female voice spoke over the images of Sean and Charlotte.

"The 'Spider Triad Trial,' as it's been named, has taken a strange twist. After testimony last week from Detective Sean Trann and Medical Examiner Doctor Charlotte Salla, the case seemed fairly straightforward. Two witnesses testified to seeing the accused suspect killing a police officer in an underground bunker below a statue in Boston Common.

"But the strange testimony today has caused a backlash in the streets."

The images changed over to what appeared to be looting and rioting near the courthouse.

"Crowds have gathered to support both sides: one claims the suspect is responsible for the death of Officer Eth six months ago. The other claims the suspect was brainwashed by a cult, called a Triad, and coerced into killing—to save her own life and the life of the other women held in the compound."

Sean sat up. "What?" he said to the TV.

The television camera switched to images of the women who the police had found in the bunker. The pictures showed the women testifying at the trial and then photos of them from what appeared to be their past—at baseball games, a Fourth of July party, a graduation, etc.

"The most striking testimony came from two of these captive women, Monica Sarris and Brigitta Karlsson, who'd been inside the compound for three years. Their strange words have led many of the public to believe they suffered coercion, and possibly torture, under their captors. Saying things such as 'Killing makes sense,' and 'The Triads are forever' has led to the notion that they are unable to tell right from wrong and have been psychologically damaged by the Spider Triad. Speculations have arisen that perhaps the woman currently on trial also underwent the same damage. Chants can be heard from some of the protestors, stating that Veronica Chasis should not be held responsible for the crimes she committed."

Sean's heartbeat raced. Then it skipped a beat when

another image showed up on the screen: Angellica's parents standing next to another couple.

"These are the parents of Veronica and the parents of another woman, Angellica Neros, who'd been killed in the compound six months ago. According to Detective Trann's own testimony, he and Miss Neros were engaged the previous year. He claims he knew nothing of any illegal dealings she may have been involved with concerning the Spider Triad. If this is the truth, could she have also been a victim, like Veronica Chasis?"

Angellica's mother then spoke, her eyes red and watery.

"These monsters took away our baby. She just wanted a normal life. To find love. To have friends. They turned her into a killer. And now she's. . ." She turned away and sobbed into her husband's shoulder.

"The woman truly responsible is dead," the other woman said. With the same skin tone and dark hair, Sean could see the similarities between her and her daughter, Violet. . .or Veronica. *"The woman who called herself 'Truth' is gone. But there may be others out there, hurting our daughters, forcing them to kill, and the police aren't doing anything about it. The courts need to stop condemning the victims and find the women responsible for corrupting our girls!"*

The image returned to the TV anchor.

"It seems the community is divided about this case. We will be monitoring the trial as it proceeds, bringing you up-to-date infor—"

Sean turned off the television. His stomach turned. Suddenly the thought of salty chips made him queasy.

He hadn't thought about Angellica's parents. Not once. He hadn't been the one to call them and let them know their daughter had been killed. Or that she was a killer. A different police officer had performed this duty because Sean had been in the hospital at the time.

Now they were here, in town. Their daughter was dead because. . .because why? She *did* kill people. Well, that was the claim. In all honesty, no one from the police department actually saw Angellica kill anyone or had proof she'd killed anyone in the past. According to Truth, who was now dead, Angellica had been the executioner of their group during any Triad activity. Violet had only chosen the method of death, until the end, when Violet wanted more, and started involving herself in the kills as well.

Sean had discussed all of this with his therapist months ago—how to deal with the aspects of Angellica compared to her alter ego, Anya. They'd talked about if he should see them as two different people, or a split personality. Did he think Angellica was to blame for Anya's wrongdoings? Did he think, if she'd lived, they should have put Angellica in prison?

It had been a terrible few sessions. He'd had to attach thoughts of murdering people to a woman he'd almost married. How was he supposed to deal with that? Especially since, according to what Charlotte said Truth told her, Angellica wasn't even a real person. Anya was. The Triads had simply created Angellica to live a normal life, to hide Anya in plain sight. So, was Angellica just a construct and not a real person? Had everything he'd experienced with her been a fabrication of someone who didn't truly exist?

With help from Dr. Moria, he'd slowly come to some realizations, especially that he didn't know if he could ever be sure, since Angellica had died. For his own sake, he divided them in his head: Angellica was the person he had a relationship with and Anya was the killer. He would never know absolutely if they weren't really the same person, but it was the only way, at least for now, for him to sanely handle the situation.

What about Violet? Or Veronica, if you called her by her other persona. He'd seen her shoot Officer Eth point blank. She tried to kill his friends and himself.

But was it really her?

The words of Violet's parents rang through his mind:

"There are others out there, hurting our daughters, forcing them to kill..."

Sean would never in a million years have thought he wouldn't think someone was guilty when he watched them kill someone in front of him. But a strange memory surfaced in his mind. He remembered once how he'd lied to his cousin. When he'd been six, and his cousin nine, his cousin pinned him down, twisting his arm up, and wrenching it. Sean had shrieked in pain.

"Tell me you're a fat piggy," his cousin said, laughing.

Sean resisted as long as he could, but eventually, he gave in. For a year his cousin did this, every time they saw each other. Finally it stopped, but only because his cousin's family moved to another state.

Sean never forgot how much shame he felt for giving in. He felt like he wasn't strong enough or good enough to resist the pain. And worse than that, it affected him through middle school and high school. He always worked out, stayed fit. He never liked the idea of becoming fat. Of becoming the lie he'd been forced to repeat over and over again.

Because after a while, on some deep secret level, he almost believed it.

Had this happened to Angellica and Veronica? Had they been convinced they were someone else, just so they could be used to kill?

33

October 9th
8:30 a.m.

"Excuse you!" Mags said, clinging to the steel bar above her. Someone had shoved into her from behind on the bus, knocking her off her feet and into the person who sat in a seat near her. Usually Mags took the earlier bus, which was less crowded, but she'd been running a little late that morning. She and Scott had been on the phone until past midnight, so she'd overslept.

Mags could hardly believe how much had to be taken care of to end their relationship. The lease on the apartment was hard enough, but dividing their things, wondering about which friends would side with whom, and the idea of being on her own in such an expensive city crept into her dreams during the night, causing a fitful and restless sleep.

Packed full of bodies on the bus like sardines in a tin, she had done her best to avoid sticking her face in the underarm of the large man who stood in front of her. But whoever had needed to get to the rear didn't care about plowing into her and she'd gotten a face full of fuzzy wool.

Wiping at the tiny threads in her teeth with her free hand, she held tighter onto the handrail.

Only two more stops, she thought, replanting her feet.

After ten more minutes, Mags signaled for her stop, slid between two high school-aged girls and a pregnant woman, and exited. She picked up her pace and walked quickly to the precinct, a cold wind biting into her exposed face and hands. Their last remnants of warm autumn weather had taken a fast turn the night before. Temperatures had dropped fifteen degrees overnight and Mags hadn't switched over to her heavier coat.

A ring sounded from her left, distracting her from the chill. She yanked her purse over, which was really more like a large bag, and unzipped it. Without looking, she reached down to fish out her phone. When she did, she felt something in the way of her hand.

"What the. . .?" Mags peeked into her bag.

An envelope lay across the contents.

Her name was typed neatly across the front.

34

October 9th
9 a.m.

Sean grimaced at the sound of a large purse smacking against the edge of his desk.

"Morning?" he said to Mags.

"Technically," she said. "Guess what I got?" She held the bag open and tipped it towards him. He hesitated, having learned the hard way from a girlfriend in high school that men should *never* look in a woman's purse, but when Mags shook it, he peered inside.

He saw an envelope.

"You've got to be kidding me."

"I wish I was,'" she said, her face neutral.

"But. . .Bruno is in a holding cell."

"Yep," she said, the "p" popping off her lips.

"Fuck. That means he didn't put this in your purse."

"Yep again."

Sean didn't have time for this. He and Payne had been told to bring in the other killer in their Watkins case. The first kid, Jerry, had finally given up his friend, in hopes of a lighter sentence.

"Are you okay?" Sean asked.

She took a seat across from him, pushing her glasses up the bridge of her nose. "Physically, yeah. But every other way? I don't know. I guess I'm all right. I really thought this wouldn't happen. I can't believe it did."

"When do you think someone put it in there?"

She scrunched up her face. "I'm not sure. Except. . ." her face lit up with realization. "It must have been someone on the bus. I mean, the envelope wasn't there this morning when I put my stuff in my purse for work."

"Do you remember seeing anyone suspicious on the bus?"

Mags shrugged. "Not really. It was packed full. I remember a guy's armpit." She wrinkled her nose.

"Would you give this to Wilt and let him and Millan know what happened? They'll send it down to evidence, but we can probably guess what it's going to say."

"Yeah. 'You are nothing. The Triads are forever.'" Mags got up to leave, her words monotone. She looked defeated.

"I'm sorry, Mags."

"It's not your fault."

"I know. I'm just sorry."

She gave a weak grin. "Thanks."

Sean leaned back in his chair. With Bruno currently in a holding cell, someone else must have put the letter in her purse. But if his fingerprint had been on the first envelope, he had to have been a part of it, right? Or at least touched the envelope that was used?

Sean tapped his fingertips against the edge of his desk. Something was missing. He stood up, left his office, and went over to Wilt's desk, who'd just returned from Millan's office. Mags strode by, heading to the front desk. "Hey," he said to Wilt, "can I see your notes on the Bruno interrogation?"

"Sure," Wilt said, shuffling through his files. "What's up?"

"I'm not sure. But I think we missed something."

"Agreed," Wilt said. "Bruno couldn't have put the envelope in her purse."

"Exactly."

The two of them spent the next several minutes looking at the report.

Wilt spoke first. "He denied the whole thing. Said the only thing he knew about Spider was what he'd seen on the TV."

"Which brings me to another question. How could he afford to pay the bills on that house?"

"Uh," Wilt said, flipping to the next page. "Ah. Here. He said it is his brother and sister-in-law's house. He said the brother had gone to Spain for four months for work and the sister-in-law moved out into her mother's house, who is ill. The sister-in-law apparently comes by every week or so to collect the mail and clean up, but she usually comes during the day, while he's at the docks for work. They also have a landscaping service that comes once a month. Bruno said his brother told him he could stay in the house, rent free, during the four months, to keep up appearances of someone being there. Bruno said he's been living there for about three months. He had to file the address with his parole officer, which is why it came up in our system."

"Have we gotten ahold of the brother?"

"Not yet. There didn't seem a reason to."

Sean thought of the messy state of the place. "What about the sister-in-law? If she was coming to clean, it looked like she hadn't been there for a couple weeks, at least."

Wilt frowned. "You think something happened to her?"

"I don't know. If Bruno is crazy and made that shrine, she might not be safe. But if it's not him. . .? I don't know. It doesn't add up."

"Tay and I can track down the sister-in-law and follow-up."

Sean nodded to Wilt, then glanced up at Payne, who had just sauntered over.

"I heard we get to arrest the real killer in the Watkins case?" Payne said.

"Yeah," Sean answered. He motioned to the Bruno files. "At least we can close one case."

Payne retracted his arm, as if to punch Sean, then swung it limply at his side. "You ready?"

Sean eyed him, then shrugged and said, "Let's go." He nodded to Wilt. "Let me know how it goes with the sister-in-law."

"I will."

35

October 9th
6 p.m.

Dr. Carla Moria stared at Sean, tapping her pencil on a steno pad. Sean had just spent the last half hour spewing everything that had happened over the past week, including testifying at the trial, seeing Violet again, his date with Charlotte, the envelopes, and the strange text messages he'd received.

"That's quite a lot in one week," she finally said with a sympathetic smile.

"You're telling me." He took a swig of soda from a can he'd brought with him. As this was their last mandatory session, he wanted to make sure he got everything out and dealt with to have the final "all clear" on his report.

Carla let out a sigh. "Let's start with the trial. When you saw Violet, you said you felt conflicted. Do you believe her to be innocent?"

"No," he said immediately. He paused. "I think she did it. I mean, I *saw* her do it. Kill Officer Eth."

"But. . .?"

"But I don't know. When you and I worked through my issues about Angellica versus Anya, I saw her as two people. If I could do that for her, should I do that for Violet and this Veronica persona she claims to be?"

Sean recalled how difficult those sessions had been. After Angellica's death, Sean felt perplexed about some of the things she'd mentioned during her final minutes. She'd told him she had a chip in her arm, which she could push and make her change from the Anya personality to being Angellica, and that Truth had found her in a psychiatric ward after murdering her entire family, except Sean had met her parents on several occasions, including his "almost" wedding. Needing answers, and some sense of closure, Sean explored Angellica's past.

After recovering from his injuries, he investigated, along with a bit of help from Mags when red tape stopped him. What he learned made the therapy sessions all the more difficult.

The first claim had been easy to check: Angellica's autopsy revealed no chip in her arm, so that had been a lie.

The second claim, about killing her family, got complicated.

Sean discovered that at seven years of age, Angellica's

house caught on fire in the middle of the night. When the firefighters showed up, Angellica was standing alone in the middle of the street, muttering to herself that she'd just wanted to light a candle. When they extinguished the fire, they found the bodies of Angellica's older brother and sister, dead. Her parents were still alive, but had been badly burned, and rushed to the hospital.

Angellica's aunt had taken her niece in, but didn't let Angellica go to the hospital, believing her parents' injuries to be too scary for a small child to deal with. The aunt later told Angellilca's parents that her niece had terrible nightmares during that time, screaming when she'd wake up that her whole family was dead and that she'd killed them. No matter how many times her aunt reassured her, Angellica had been convinced her parents were dead.

A couple weeks later, Angellica was reunited with her parents, but denied any nightmares or self-blame that her aunt suggested.

Thirteen years later, at the age of 20, Angellica apparently took some hallucinogenic drugs with a couple friends of hers in college and when she returned home, she told her parents they weren't really there, that they had never been there, that she'd killed them and they were imposters.

Concerned for their daughter, they convinced her to check into a psychiatric facility the next day. Angelica remained as an inpatient for several weeks, talking with a counselor, and according to the doctors, dealing with her trauma.

Five weeks after her admittance, she checked herself out,

claiming she'd gotten better and wanted to return to her life.

The doctors and counselors touched base with her over the next few months, but they all agreed, she was like a completely different woman: charming, helpful, generous, and kind. She never shied away from talking about her past, but they saw no traces of disassociation or suppressed triggers. Eventually, she got a clean bill of health.

That had been three and a half years ago, when Truth first became the head of the Triad, and a year before she and Sean ever met.

Sean searched for clues to show that Truth had met with her at the facility, but there'd been no record of anyone named "Truth" as a visitor; however the hospital staff couldn't guarantee that no one meeting Truth's description hadn't at one point come to see Angellica.

"She had a lot of friends," a nurse there told Sean. "She was real well liked, I remember that much. Just troubled."

So the second claim Angellica had made seemed to contain some partial reality, as well as some distortions. Because of the lack of hard facts, Sean found it difficult to understand who Angellica really had been.

Dr. Moria currently shifted in her seat, the chair creaking, which brought Sean out of his thoughts. "We worked on you keeping Angellica and Anya separate for your sanity. We never looked at it related to the law or the responsibility of her crimes."

"I guess not." Sean sat forward in the loveseat, hands clasped between his legs. As much as he felt like a more stable person having had these sessions, he never enjoyed them.

Talking about himself was hard. The notion sounded cliché in his head, but it was the truth.

"Then let me ask you this," Dr. Moria continued. "Based on the testimony given at the trial from the prosecution's psychologist, do you believe the techniques used by the Triad are real? Do you believe Angellica really was two people somehow?"

Sean frowned. "I didn't listen to the psychologist. What did they say?"

"That there were no known techniques proven to create an alternate persona inside another person. Though brainwashing tactics and torture could have created a separate personality, the individual would be using a coping mechanism to commit the crimes. Therefore, it is basically a rationalized version of the same person and they should be culpable."

Sean took a few minutes to sort through her words. "Wow. So even if they were a split personality, they created the split themselves, to cope?"

"Yes."

"So, it's still them doing what they're doing?"

"Does that change things in your mind?"

"If it's not possible to have a new persona, then yeah. It means Violet is guilty."

"That means Angellica would be as well."

"I guess so," he said slowly.

"How do you feel about that?"

The notion bothered him less than he thought it would. The idea that Angellica's personality was just a coping mechanism to cover up a killer? It may not have been Angellica's fault, exactly, but if she was just a component of Anya, then it was still Anya the whole time. Like a puppeteer behind a marionette. It's not the puppet's fault, but they aren't really real to begin with.

"Honestly? It makes me feel like I understand it better."

Carla made a few notes then switched subjects. "What about the envelopes?"

"Wilt and Tay are following up on that. We caught the guy whose fingerprint was on one of the envelopes, but it still feels a little sloppy. I'm sure they'll figure it out."

"What feels 'sloppy' about it?"

"I don't know. Just the notes themselves. I've worked a couple stalker cases and though they are usually men, the notes don't feel. . .masculine."

"How so?"

Sean leaned back in the loveseat. "Without sounding sexist?"

"I understand the uses of profiling. No judgement here."

"Men are usually more aggressive. They want an object or person and convince themselves that force is the best way to get it. Their notes are to the point. These ones? They feel like a message, like a personal connection, or the culprit *thinks* they have a personal connection. But they aren't *wanting* in the note. They are telling. Putting Charlotte and Mags and Tay down. Like they are competition. Which is more of a feminine response to other women."

"What did the notes say?"

"They said 'You are nothing. The Triads are forever.'"

Carla's pen stopped scratching. "That seems unusual for a stalker note."

"Exactly." Something stirred at the back of his mind. The words from the note. He'd heard them before.

Carla must have noticed his pause. "Is there something else?"

"Yeah. That phrase: 'The Triads are forever.' I think I've heard it somewhere before. I mean, besides in the notes."

The room fell silent while Sean thought. He could hear the hiss of heat blast through the vent near his feet. He could see Carla shift slightly out of the corner of his eye, reaching down to get her purse.

"That's it!" he said, remembering.

Carla finished her motion, retrieving a pack of breath mints from her bag. "Yes?"

"On the news. One of the witnesses we found in the bunker, she said that line in her testimony."

"What did she mean by it?"

"I don't know," he said, a shot of adrenaline coursing through him. "But it can't be a coincidence. I can check out the transcripts, see what the context was."

"Sounds like an excellent idea." Carla glanced up at the clock. "We have a little time left. I'm happy to say you seem able to deal with your situations well after your encounter six months ago. I will reflect that in my report."

"Thanks Doc. Truth is, these sessions did help."

"Don't worry. I won't tell anyone you said that," she said with a grin. "I have one more question for you."

"Shoot."

"These Triads that Truth told Charlotte about. What do you think about them? I mean, it's one thing to put blame on Violet or Truth or Anya, but do you believe other Triads exist?"

"I honestly don't know. Six months ago, I wouldn't have doubted it at all, but I think after Charlotte and Mags returned empty-handed from their search around the world and there hadn't been any evidence that other Triads are out there. . .it just doesn't seem very likely."

Carla nodded, made another quick note, and put down her pen. "As far as I'm concerned, we're finished here. It was a pleasure meeting you, Sean. I'm here in the future if you ever want someone to talk to." She held out her hand.

His first reaction was to say "Thanks, but no thanks," but he waited a beat instead.

He then took her hand and shook it. "I will."

36

October 10th

9 a.m.

Sean found himself once again sitting in the Suffolk County Superior Courthouse. The media crews outside had been relentless, pressing microphones and cameras in his direction as he walked, shouting different questions. He'd sidestepped them as best he could, but he couldn't keep the annoyance off his face.

Once inside the courtroom, he'd spotted Charlotte on one of the wooden benches and took a seat next to her. His annoyance dissipated.

"Hey," he said, giving her hand a squeeze.

"Good morning." Charlotte paused and Sean noticed her

swallow hard before she continued. "Anything new about the suspect, Bruno Zido?" she asked.

Sean shook his head. "Sorry, not yet. Wilt and Tay found the address of the sister-in-law's mother, where the sister-in-law is staying. They are heading over there today. I'll let you know if I hear anything new."

"And you feel confident Bruno is not behind the envelopes?"

"All we know is that his fingerprint was only on the one left for you, and though we found the shrine-thing in the house he's staying at, the envelope in Mags' purse was delivered while Bruno sat in a holding cell. Bruno may have someone working with him or somehow planted the envelope earlier and Mags didn't notice it, but that seems unlikely. She sounded pretty certain of the timing."

"I am sure you will find whoever is responsible." Charlotte's eyes narrowed as the officers led Violet into the courtroom. "The sooner this is over, the sooner we can get back to our lives," she said softly.

"I'm with you."

A few people testified before Sean was called to the stand, including the psychologist the DA had originally brought forth, the one Sean's therapist quoted to him in their session. Sean paid attention to the cross-examination with much interest.

"You stated that there are currently no known techniques that would allow a separate personality construct to be built inside a person's mind, correct?" the defense attorney asked. Today she'd donned a slim-fitting black suit with a bright pink shirt underneath, which made her skin seem to glow. Her hair had been pinned up in a neat bun.

"Correct." The psychologist, by contrast, had flyaway hairs coming out of her tight ponytail, sported a wet spot on her greenish sweater, and constantly twisted her fingers in her hands. Sean felt bad for the woman, as she seemed quite uncomfortable on the stand.

"Do you believe, however, that the human brain can be altered through drugs?"

"What do you mean?"

"For example, an anti-depressant changes the chemical imbalance in someone's brain, so that they feel differently than they usually do?"

"Yes."

"This goes for illegal drugs as well, correct? The influence of PCP or cocaine changes a person's brain and their behavior?"

"Yes. But it's still the same person."

The defense attorney paused. "I didn't ask if they were the same person. I asked if a drug could change someone's brain, so that they'd act differently than normal." Sean noted that a couple jurors smiled at the defense attorney's statements. The words should have sounded accusatory, but instead, they made the psychologist seem dumb for not realizing what was being asked. Sean had to hand it to the defense attorney—she knew her stuff.

The psychologist shifted in the seat. "Yes."

"Thank you. Now, you said that brainwashing and torture techniques can also change brain chemistry, correct?"

"Yes."

"Creating what you called in previous testimony a 'split personality.'"

"Yes."

"Because of this, you claimed a person is still responsible for their actions because in the instance of brainwashing or torture, a separate personality is still an aspect of the same person, correct?"

"Yes."

The defense sauntered over towards the jury box. "If I told a depressed person to 'feel less sad,' could they do it?"

The psychologist frowned. "I'm not sure what you mean."

"I mean, there is a reason you provide medication as an option. The patient cannot change their brain patterns on their own. They need something else to help them, correct?"

"I guess so, yes."

"Once they are on the medication, and assuming it's working properly, could you tell them to be depressed again and have them do it?"

The psychologist scoffed. "No. The medication affects the neurotransmitters in the brain, altering how and what they transmit."

The defense attorney folded her hands in front of her. "How much of a person's brain chemistry would you have to change before they aren't themselves anymore?"

"I..uh..I don't understand the question." The psychologist wiped her brow.

"What if someone *created* the chemical imbalance in someone's brain to make them act differently? To make them more aggressive. Less empathetic. More depressed. Less trusting." She paused and faced the jury for a moment, then returned to the psychologist. "We are conditioned for a response to things, correct? Like if someone eats too much, their stomach aches. If they touch fire, signals to the brain tell them they're are in pain and to stop touching the fire."

"Yes,"

"Well if someone uses drugs and medication to change those responses in their brain, can they be held accountable for their reaction to them?"

"If it's killing someone, yes."

"Ah. So, there is a level. If my brain chemistry were changed to make me *more* anxious, it's okay that I *act* anxious, as long as I don't kill anyone? I could hide in my house and never leave or yell at the mail carrier to go away or think my phone is being tapped or lash out at someone who grabs me from behind because I think they might be attacking me?"

"Well, yes, I suppose. But those are either non-violent, or it's self-defense."

"Even if it's someone you *know* who grabs you from behind? Say, because they are trying to get your attention?"

"Well, I guess, no, but—"

"What about hallucinations?" the defense attorney said, abruptly asking the new question and walking towards the psychologist.

"What about them?"

"If I'm taking a drug that makes me hallucinate, am I responsible for what happens when I see something?"

"If you took it on purpose, you should be responsible."

"What if someone slipped it in my drink without my knowledge? How about then?"

"No. I mean, you didn't decide to take the drug, so you wouldn't be in your right mind once *on* the drug."

"Exactly." The defense attorney strode back towards her table. "If something out of my control is making me do something against my will, how can I be responsible for my actions?"

"But not murder," the psychologist chimed in.

"What if I hallucinated that my mail carrier had a knife? What if when he raised his arm to wave hello I thought he meant to throw that imaginary knife at me? What if I struck out to defend myself? What if I accidentally killed him in the process?"

The judge chimed in. "Counselor, I think you're getting off topic."

"Apologies. I just want to establish a baseline of when it's someone's fault when they hurt someone and when it isn't." She turned her attention once again to the psychologist. "If someone did enough damage to a person's mind, using drugs and behavioral torture tactics, and that person's brain was changed enough that they weren't responding to their surroundings as themselves anymore, should they be held responsible for their actions?"

The psychologist shot a desperate glance at the DA's table. "Yes!" she squeaked, strain in her voice.

"Interesting." The defense held up two files. "I have here two cases in which you were called upon for your expertise, doctor. One involved a woman who had mixed medications and attempted to free all the animals from the zoo and another of a man who'd been given the wrong medication, had a side-effect reaction, and punched his best friend and his best friend's wife in the face because he thought they were, quote. . ." she flipped through the pages and then read ". . . 'aliens coming to steal his son's lunch money,' end quote. You recommended that both these individuals *not* be held accountable for criminal charges in a court of law because they were acting under the influence of improper medication, correct?"

"Ye. . .yes."

"Well how can this be? How can *they* not be responsible when my client was subjected to drug usage, behavioral modifications, and torture?"

A murmur rumbled through the courtroom. Sean watched the jury all glance around, shift in their chairs, or whisper to each other.

The judge slammed her gavel a few times. "Order!" she called out. The room settled.

"One last question," the defense said, staring straight at the psychologist. "Did you recommend for these two previous cases that there should be no judicial action taken against the defendants?"

During the last question, the psychologist had sunk down into the chair. "Yes," she said, her voice barely a whisper.

"I'm sorry. I couldn't hear you."

"Yes."

"Thank you. No further questions." The defense attorney glanced at the jury, then took a seat. The psychologist left the stand, her gaze downward.

The judge banged her gavel. "I will call a short recess. We will reconvene in twenty minutes."

The judge left and the room bustled. Sean leaned over toward Charlotte. "What'd you think of all that?"

"I am. . .unsure."

Sean understood. He'd felt so certain yesterday, when he'd spoken to his therapist, about the guilt of Violet. But now that the very same psychologist had spoken out for other individuals who had committed crimes, saying that they didn't deserve jail time, he didn't feel as confident. If Violet *had* been given drugs and tortured, did she deserve to go to jail? Or did she just need help?

Twenty minutes later, Sean was called to the stand.

"Good luck," mouthed Charlotte.

They began with all the formalities, reminding him he was still under oath, and he took a seat. The defense attorney approached him.

"I only have a few questions," she began. "My first has to be, did you have any idea your ex-fiancée was a serial killer?"

"Objection!" the DA said, standing up.

"Sustained," the judge said. "We are not holding a trial for anyone except the defendant and there is no evidence that anyone else committed a murder."

"My apologies," the defense said. "I'll rephrase. Detective Trann, you were romantically involved with Angellica Neros, correct?"

He'd been briefed by the DA that the defense may come at him about Angellica, so the response came methodically. "Yes. We were engaged, she broke off the engagement. I didn't see her again until six months ago. We became briefly involved again romantically until it was discovered that she was linked with the defendant in criminal activity."

"That's quite a lot for a yes," the defense said.

Sean bristled. "I already said all this for the prosecution. I'd like the trial to move as quickly as possible, so that justice can be served."

"Very well, I'll get to my point. Detective Trann, you witnessed the death of Miss Neros in the underground compound discovered by yourself and another officer, Officer Eth, correct?"

"Yes."

"Can you tell us what happened?"

"Miss Neros spoke to me at some length. We agreed that I would put her under arrest. She moved toward me. Officer Eth entered the room behind us, saw she had a weapon, and fired his sidearm. The bullet killed Miss Neros. He saved my life," he added at the end, a catch in his throat.

"You say Miss Neros moved towards you. Was it a hostile movement?"

He hesitated. "Not exactly."

"What type of movement was it?"

"She gave me a hug."

A murmur swept across the room.

"Order," the judge warned.

"A hug." The defense attorney paused. "Tell me, Detective, is it your policy as an officer to hug suspects you are about to arrest?"

"No." *What was this woman driving at? The DA didn't prepare me for these kinds of questions.*

"Then why were you hugging her?"

"I wasn't. She hugged me."

"Do most suspects who are about to be arrested hug the arresting officer?"

A few snickers echoed in the quiet room.

"No."

"Seems like *unusual* behavior then." The defense attorney walked towards the jury box. "No further questions."

Sean stepped down, still unsure of what the defense attorney had gotten from her cross-examination, but at this moment, he didn't care. He was in the clear.

The judge pounded her gavel. "One hour recess for lunch."

Everyone stood up to leave. Sean caught up with Charlotte.

"Guess you're going to testify later this afternoon," he told her. He pulled out his phone and turned it on, as it had been silenced during the proceedings.

"Seems so."

"Mine wasn't as bad as I thought. I don't think she really got anything out of me."

"I believe it is a setup, for me," she said quietly as they left the courtroom.

"Really? How so?"

"There were items found during Angellica's autopsy that may reveal—"

She stopped mid-sentence as the two of them turned a corner and ran into a woman coming up the stairs.

"Excuse us," Sean said. "We didn't—"

THWACK!

Sean's head recoiled at the violent slap across his face.

"How *dare* you!" A voice hissed.

Sean turned towards his attacker. Angellica's mother stood before him, her face pinched in anger.

"Ma'am," Charlotte began, stepping forward. "Control yourself."

Angellica's father, who'd apparently just returned from the restroom, hurried over.

"Melinda? What's going on?"

Melinda shook a finger in Sean's face. "You got our baby girl killed!" she said, tears forming in her eyes.

"What?" Sean asked, stunned, rubbing his cheek.

"If she'd never met you, she wouldn't have gotten involved with those horrible women!" Melinda's words rose to a screech at the end. Several other people in the building turned to view the commotion.

"That's not true," Sean said, immediately defensive.

"Come on, Melinda," Angellica's father said, pulling her away.

"Thank you, sir," Sean said to the father.

Angellica's father stopped in his tracks. "Don't thank me.

Don't ever speak to me, you asshole. You ruined our lives." He guided Melinda away, who'd now broken into sobs, and led her down the stairs.

Sean just stood there in shock. He felt a hand touch his arm.

"Ignore them," Charlotte said. "They are grieving."

"How could they think. . .?" he muttered. "If Angellica *had* killed people, according to Truth, she'd been doing it before we even met! What do I have to do with anything?"

"You were there, Sean, when she died," Charlotte said. "They need to place their anger on someone. They obviously do not want to place any blame on their daughter."

Sean barely had time to process anything when his phone rang. It was Wilt.

"Hold on," he said, grateful for the distraction. "I gotta take this." He answered. "Wilt? What's up?"

"We just got back from visiting the sister-in-law of Bruno," Wilt told him over the sound of a car door slamming and wind blowing across the microphone.

"And?"

"She confirmed his story, about him living there, and about how she comes in every week to get the mail. She said she hadn't been to the house in two weeks or so, that she'd been feeling ill, having dizzy spells or something, because she'd been missing sleep taking care of her mother. She said she didn't know anything about the pictures in the basement or of Bruno sending any notes."

"Okay, well if it's not her, it has to still be him somehow, even if he was in holding when Mags got her note. We must be missing something. We should check out the house again."

"My thoughts exactly. You done in court? Thought we could go this afternoon."

Sean looked at Charlotte. "Hold on a sec." He muted the call. "Do you want me to stay while you testify?"

Charlotte raised an eyebrow. "No. I mean, I did not expect you would."

"I mean, I can. If you want me to."

Charlotte nodded to the phone. "Do you have work to do?"

"Potentially. It's about the Bruno case."

"I would rather you securely conclude the case than stay for me. I would like to *not* get any more mysterious notes delivered. And I trust that you can make that happen."

Sean loved that she believed in him so much. "All right, sounds good." He returned to the call. "Wilt, I'll be there in about an hour, around twelve thirty. Just wrapping up here." He hung up.

"An hour?" Charlotte asked.

"I thought we could still have lunch before you have to return to court."

She smiled. "That sounds wonderful."

37

October 10ᵗʰ
1 p.m.

Juliette scratched at her real ear. Something didn't add up.

She'd returned with Wilt, Trann, and Payne to Bruno's house. They'd found nothing out of the ordinary. No new fingerprints, besides Bruno's, the sister-in-law's, and what they assumed to be the brother's.

The sister-in-law, Jasmine, had been very helpful. A lovely woman with dark skin, long braided hair, and dimples. When they'd entered her mother's house, Jasmine showed them around—the guest room had been filled with knick-knacks and pictures, which Jasmine said she'd taken from her own house to feel more comfortable. That explained why they'd been absent from her home. She spoke about missing her out-of-the-country husband, about taking care of her ill mother, who was improving after her stroke, and about how she felt ready to return to her own place in a month.

What didn't add up was the odd feeling Juliette got when Jasmine looked at her. There had been something when they first met, a glimmer in her eyes. Recognition perhaps? Juliette sometimes got that because she'd been splayed on the news a few times in the past six months regarding the trial—her grocer and a random woman in a retail shop both mentioned they'd recalled seeing her on TV —but this felt different.

Juliette brushed it off after a while until they showed Jasmine copies of the pictures that had been on the basement wall. Jasmine denied having ever seen them, but for one tiny moment, her gaze flickered over towards Juliette and she'd felt the look contained. . .anger. Hatred almost.

The look disappeared instantly, but Juliette kept thinking about it. She'd only seen that glare once, in her brother's eyes, when they'd been young. He'd developed an intense fever, spiking up to 104 degrees, and had been hallucinating. He'd been lying on the couch, then peered over at her and said, "I hate you. I wish you'd never been born." His gaze burned into her, like the fire in his head had spread to his eyes. He'd then immediately returned to watching TV, as if nothing had happened.

Juliette didn't understand until a year later, when she'd turned seven, and her parents sat her down and told her about her brother's illness. They told her he sometimes had "episodes" where he wasn't going to act or talk the same as he normally would. They assured her that he had medication to help, and it worked wonders.

When she grew older and researched these "episodes," she learned he had a dissociative disorder. She realized how lucky her family had been that her brother responded so well to the medication. He only had three other "episodes" that she could remember over the years, none of them ever towards her, but she never forgot the intensity of his eyes and voice in that fever-induced moment.

It was like he was two different people, she thought.

That look in Jasmine's eyes. . .it felt the same.

Something is wrong with her, Juliette realized.

"Tay!" Wilt called from upstairs. "You ready?"

"Yeah," she said slowly. "I'll be up in a mo'." Juliette leaned over. She'd been staring at the wall in the basement, where the pictures had been. A piece of duct tape lay across a random section near the area. Using her nail, she picked away at the corner, peeling it away slowly.

Ice seemed to creep its way up her spine. She straightened up.

"Wilt? Trann? Payne? You gotta come see this."

Underneath the duct tape, carved into the wall, were the words: *THE TRIADS ARE FOREVER.*

38

October 10th
4:45 p.m.

Charlotte couldn't shake the shiver running through her as she left the courtroom. She felt sick to her stomach. The cross-examination had gone horribly wrong.

As soon as they finished Sean's questioning, she knew she was in trouble. And still, she'd felt terrible about the answers she'd given:

"Yes, there were drugs found in the body of Angellica Neros during her autopsy."

"Yes, these drugs are known for their uses in the treatment of mental illness."

"*Yes, they contained a 'time-release' element that could keep the drug active for several weeks at a time.*"

"*Yes, if used improperly, they could cause behavioral problems in the patient.*"

Then she'd been asked about her time in the compound.

"*Yes, I spoke to the woman who claimed she was their leader.*"

"*Yes, I suggested that Detective Juliette Tay and Margaret Stinson be brought into the compound.*"

"*Yes, I heard Angellica Neros get angry when everyone thought she was someone else.*"

And finally, her lack of proof:

"*No, I did not find any proof that other Triads exist.*"

"*No, to my knowledge, no other autopsies I have performed outside of this case have been the result of a Triad murder.*"

"*I do not currently have enough facts to conclude either way if other Triads exist.*"

The defense attorney had then turned to the jury, tutted, and said:

"*So, the woman responsible is dead, another victim just like my client was drugged, and there is no proof of other Triads. Let me remind the jury that similar drugs were found in the system of Veronica when she was processed for her arrest. No further questions."*

Charlotte suddenly wished Sean was there. She wanted someone to talk to, to *vent* to as they'd determined several months ago. He would most likely be finished with work soon. Perhaps they could meet up for dinner.

Her stomach lurched in protest at the thought.

Or maybe they could do something else, like a movie.

Pulling her jacket tighter around her body against the chilled air, Charlotte strode to her car, parked in a nearby parking garage. Fat raindrops plunked all around her and on top of her head. She quickened her pace, hunching down, as if the gesture would help minimize the rain hitting her.

Finally, she arrived at the structure. She raced inside, shook some of the wetness from her head and body, and jogged up the stairs to the second level. Her flats pounded on the cement floor as she rustled in her bag for her keys.

She just wanted to get away from this place, from this whole case. Her head swum with thoughts. The woman sitting behind the defense table had thrown a knife at her six months ago. She'd wanted Charlotte dead. And yet. . .what if it *hadn't* been Violet's fault?

Charlotte's chest constricted and her breathing came in tight wheezes. This type of sensation had happened twice since she'd returned home. With a medical degree and background in science, she logically knew it must be the beginnings of a panic attack. After it happened at her work the first day she'd returned, she'd looked up ways to stop the attacks when she'd gotten home. There were several very helpful suggestions about breathing, visualizing a "safe space," grounding oneself, and telling yourself STOP to racing thoughts.

Charlotte employed each of these tactics. The thought that the attack wouldn't end crept into her mind and a feeling like electricity stole through her body. Her heartbeat increased and her breathing became even shallower.

Stepping sideways, Charlotte grabbed the edge of a random car as her vision dimmed then brightened.

You are going to die here! her mind threatened her.

Charlotte forced in a deep breath then let it out. She did it again.

I am all right, she thought, countering her out-of-control allegation.

Another breath.

This will pass.

Gradually, each moment feeling like an eternity, her breathing returned to normal. Her heartbeat slowed. Her shakiness diminished and her body felt stable again.

"Are you okay?"

Charlotte let out a shriek.

"I'm sorry!" the woman said, holding up her hands defensively. "I didn't mean to frighten you."

"It is all right," Charlotte said, grasping her chest, but putting on a smile. "I was unaware anyone else was in the area."

The woman gave a soft smile in return, dimples forming in her dark cheeks. "Okay. Just wanted to make sure you're all right."

"I am."

The woman nodded, swung her scarf around her neck,

and walked away.

Charlotte continued on to her car. She needed to get herself under control. These "attacks" were inconvenient. She would do more research when she got home, figure out new and better ways to combat them.

"Oh, Miss?"

Charlotte turned around to face the woman. "Yes?"

"I think you dropped this."

The woman stepped right up to Charlotte and, before she could react, she felt something hard and cold slide into her, near her shoulder blade. Pain lanced through her back.

"You are *nothing*," the woman hissed. "The Triads are forever." The woman ran off, laughing.

Charlotte fell to the ground, her head bouncing against the concrete. The smell of oil and car fumes filled her nose as she huffed in and out, the feeling of fire racing through her. Each movement caused a fresh slice of pain in her back and a dizziness in her head, but she managed to reach her purse, pull out her cell, and dial 911.

"This is 911, what is your emergency?"

"I've been stabbed. . ." she managed. "Parking garage. . . courthouse. . ."

The woman on the other end asked another question, but darkness called to Charlotte and she gave in, sinking into the void, her phone clattering on the ground as it fell from her limp hand.

39

October 10th
4:58 p.m.

Sean peered up at the clock: almost done with work for the day. He wanted to check in with Charlotte and see how her cross-examination had gone. Also, he wanted to update her on what they found at the "Bruno House."

After Juliette told them about how she'd felt when Jasmine looked at her and the message found carved into the wall about the Triads, the four of them, he, Tay, Wilt, and Payne, had returned to the sister-in-law's mother's house to bring Jasmine in for questioning. When they'd arrived, though, the mother said Jasmine had been gone all afternoon and wasn't sure when she'd be home. They asked the mother to call when Jasmine returned.

"Sean!"

Sean perked up at the sound of Mags' frantic voice.

"What's up?"

Mags rushed into his office, her eyes wide. "I just heard through dispatch. A 911 call came through. A woman said she'd been stabbed in the back in a parking garage near the courthouse. Sean, the ambulance showed up and took her to the hospital, and the EMT's description of the victim sounded a lot like Charlotte."

Sean's stomach dropped. "What?" He stood up, accidentally knocking his chair over. "What hospital? Is she okay?"

"Mass General."

"I'm heading over there." He grabbed his jacket. "Will you let Millan know where I'm going?"

"Sure. Call me as soon as you see her."

"I will."

Sean raced to the hospital, flashed his badge at the desk, and asked for information on the woman just brought in with a knife wound.

The nurse checked his computer. He looked extremely tan and Sean wondered briefly if he'd just been on vacation or did the whole "tan-in-a-can" thing. *What the hell does it matter?* Sean thought. It amazed him the things that went through his head when in a panic.

"Ah, here," the nurse finally replied. "Doctor Charlotte

Salla. She was moved to Recovery."

"Is she okay?"

"It looks like the knife didn't do any permanent damage. Five stitches. She may have suffered a concussion from when she hit the ground. Have a seat and I'll have a doctor escort you there and fill you in on the rest."

After several minutes of pacing and *not* sitting, a doctor approached Sean. Dark bags hung below his eyes.

"Detective?" the doctor asked, his papery skin wrinkled like discarded origami.

Sean stood up. "Yes."

"I'll bring you to Doctor Salla's room. She's just waking up. She may be a bit groggy from the painkillers we gave her."

"I understand."

They walked through a few halls and found the room, the doctor jabbering the whole way about a bus accident that had just occurred. "I was supposed to be done with my shift three hours ago," he muttered.

Sean kept quiet, focused solely on seeing Charlotte.

After a quiet knock, they entered. "I'll ask you to keep it brief," the doctor said, rubbing his hand across his five-o'clock shadow. "She needs to rest. I'll be back shortly, got to deal with something else first, and then I'll update you on her situation."

"Thanks, Doc."

The doctor walked away, already bombarded by another nurse, and Sean stood still for several moments, his stare fixated on her blanketed body. Flashbacks of six months ago flickered through his mind. He'd seen her the last time she'd been in a hospital. Also a knife wound. But that time, she'd almost died.

Charlotte blinked slowly as she seemed to register his presence. "Sean?" she asked, the word elongated.

"Yeah, it's me." He sat next to her on the bed and took her hand. "How are you feeling?"

"Like a tortoise."

Sean's forehead furrowed. Had the concussion damaged her brain? "What?"

She licked her lips. "Slow. Like a tortoise."

Sean smiled. "Ah. I get it now." He brushed a strand of hair from her forehead. "The doc said you're going to be fine. Just some stitches and a bumped head."

"Strange. She seemed so helpful."

Sean peered out the doorway, expecting to see a nurse. "Who?"

"The woman who stabbed me."

Sean's gut tightened and tried to keep the excitement from his voice. "You saw her?"

Charlotte nodded, then winced, raising a hand to her shoulder as if she'd pulled something. "Dark skin. Long braids. Dimples. Pretty dimples. She wore a jogging suit. Purple, I think. Or pinkish."

Sean froze, a buzz floating around in his ears. He recognized the description.

Bruno's sister-in-law.

Jasmine.

"We are going to get her," he said.

"How?"

"We already know who she is."

Charlotte's eyes widened. "You do? That was fast."

Sean laughed. "Sorry. I mean, we've already met her. She's Bruno's sister-in-law. It fits. She's the one who's after you, not Bruno."

"No," Charlotte said, her voice syrupy.

"No?"

The doctor stuck his head in the room. "Detective?"

"Yeah?" Sean called over his shoulder, pulling his focus away from Charlotte.

The doctor gabbed Charlotte's chart and motioned for Sean to join him. "Like I said, the knife wound was fairly superficial, but we want to monitor her for a concussion. We also gave her some painkillers for her wound and since she told us she lives alone, we'd like to keep her overnight for observation."

Sean wanted to say that he'd watch her, but he knew he needed to return to the precinct and work on trying to find Jasmine. "I can pick her up tomorrow. Time?"

"Early afternoon should be fine."

"Thanks, Doc. In the meantime, I'm going to station an officer at her door."

The doctor paused. "Is she dangerous?"

"Not at all. A. . .stalker did this to her. We just want to make sure she's safe."

"All right. Have them check in at the front desk when they arrive."

"Will do."

The doctor left and shortly thereafter the nurse entered,

his white teeth practically glowing next to his overly tanned skin. "Sorry to interrupt, but visiting hours are over."

"Okay," Sean said, waving him away. "I'll be just a minute."

The nurse frowned, but his gaze flickered onto Sean's badge and he popped out of the room.

"Charlotte? What did you mean by 'no' when I said Jasmine is the one after you?"

"Not just me." Her head lolled to the side.

"Not just you. . ." The meaning clicked into place. "She's not after *just* you," he said.

Charlotte's eyelids fluttered closed.

"Rest. I'll come pick you up tomorrow."

She answered with the sound of deep, even breathing.

Sean kissed her forehead, pulled the covers up a little bit, and left the room.

He had to find this Jasmine woman, and fast. But first, he had to get an officer here to protect Charlotte and needed to alert Juliette and Mags that they could be the next targets. . .

40

October 10th
5:30 p.m.

Juliette stretched across her dark blue couch, catching a sleeve on her coffee mug, and spilling its contents across the tan carpet.

"Bollocks," she cursed and got up to grab a towel and sponge. On the way, her phone rang. She swung back around to the couch, grabbed her phone, answered it, and continued to the kitchen.

Halfway there, she halted, listening to Sean's words about Charlotte's attack.

"I can meet you at Jasmine's mother's house shortly," she said. "I just got home from work."

"No," Sean's voice said through the phone. "I don't want you anywhere near this woman."

Juliette frowned, but she understood. "Fine. Just. . .make sure you get her, all right?"

"We will. I'll call you as soon as I have something new."

She hung up and slipped her phone onto the end table next to her. After cleaning up the spill as best she could, she sunk back onto the couch, drew her feet up underneath her, and grabbed the remote. A moment before she unmuted the TV, she felt a shiver run down her spine. Glancing around her living room, she didn't see anything out of the ordinary.

You're jumping at shadows, she told herself. She forced herself to remember her last conversation with Dr. Moria from their session the night before. Getting the wetted envelope had stirred something up again in Juliette and she'd voiced her concern to the therapist.

"Makes sense," Dr. Moria told her. "You found a sense of closure with this trial and then to have these notes show up and to see your picture on that woman's wall? You aren't getting a chance to recover."

"I don't know what to do to get closure. Whoever sent these notes is referencing the Triads. Will I ever be finished with them?"

"I have a suggestion that may help. What would you think about going to court to watch the verdict when it's announced?"

"It's not always clear when the verdict will happen."

"True. But with the amount of news coverage, there may be prep time."

Juliette had thought it over. "I suppose so. I've seen that with other big cases. But why go in person? Wouldn't watching it on TV be the same?"

Dr. Moria had crossed her legs and leaned forward. "Juliette, you were kidnapped from your own home, had to kill to escape your captors, then got shot. Twice. You suffered permanent damage because of the loss of your ear and you almost bled to death. I think you deserve to see this whole ordeal end. Watching from a distance will keep you detached. But really seeing it, up close, will prove that it's over, once and for all."

"But what about the notes? How can it end if other Triads are after me?"

"Think about this. Do you really believe they are from some new Triad and not just a stalker? If these other Triads really do exist, why would they risk exposure again by sending you notes?"

Juliette kept these words with her all last night and into work today. They made sense. And then, when she'd found the words carved into the wall of Bruno's brother's basement, she knew that Jasmine was merely crazy, not a Triad member. A team of elite women killers wouldn't make a shrine or carve words into walls. But copycats, stalkers, and broken people would.

Still, sitting on her couch, she felt a bit on edge. Triad or not, Jasmine had proved she was dangerous, as shown by her attack on Charlotte. Juliette grabbed her phone again and looked up her contact list, choosing a name at the top of the M's.

"Mags?" she said when someone picked up.

"Hey, girl! What's up?"

"Have you talked to Trann yet?"

"No. Should I. . . hold on, yeah, he's calling me right now."

"Call me again after you talk to him."

Juliette waited several minutes, scratching absent-mindedly at her fake ear. It still felt strange, almost as though she could feel it and not feel it at the same time. Finally, her phone rang.

"Hey Mags," she said into it.

Mags' words carried an edge of incredulity. "Sean just told me about Jasmine and what happened to Charlotte. In-sane."

"Yeah. I'm sure they'll get her. In the meantime, you wanna meet up for dinner or something? I don't think you should be on your own." *Or me either, for that matter.*

"Sounds like a good idea," she said. "I'm actually still at work—had some things to catch up on from my time off traveling."

"Okay, I'll pick you up. Don't take the bus or anything."

"You can't pick me up. I borrowed my sister's car. I'm moving some stuff to her place tonight. I'm going to stay with her over the weekend while Scott gets all his things."

Juliette could hear the catch in Mags' voice. "I'm sorry, luv. You'll get through this."

"I know. It's just. . .sorry, I gotta run. Millan wants to talk to me. I'll call you when I get to the car."

"Why don't I pick a place to eat and I'll message you?

You can just head over there right from work."

"That sounds great. See you soon."

"And Mags? Have someone walk you to the car. Just in case."

"I will."

Juliette hung up. She sat for a few moments, trying to think of where they could go to eat and if she should change, when a loud *bang* sounded behind her.

Juliette jumped up and whirled towards her attacker. Her breath heaved in her chest and her adrenaline shot through the roof.

"Don't move!" she called out.

To a chair.

Her kitchen chair had fallen over.

She'd forgotten she'd leaned it against the table that morning so she could clean under the fridge. She'd moved the appliance after she'd dropped a carton of milk and some of it splashed underneath. The chair never got returned to its normal position and gravity must have finally tipped it over.

With a shaky laugh, Juliette willed herself to calm down, but she still felt twitchy. The number of her clumsy accidents in the household had gone up significantly since the beginning of the trial proceedings. Juliette couldn't seem to keep her focus. Waiting around and hoping someone caught a crazy stalker didn't help either. She decided what she wore would be just fine. Getting out of the house felt more important than changing into a different outfit.

As she left, she headed down the hall, towards the front door. A reminder went off in her brain—she'd told a fellow officer she'd bring in some extra clothes for a clothing drive donation. Juliette had a feeling that if she didn't grab the bags now and put them in her trunk, she'd forget in the morning.

Turning, she changed direction and made her way to the side door, which led to the garage. Once inside, she pulled out her phone and turned on its small flashlight button. A ray of white streaked out across the area, highlighting boxes, random items, and furniture she kept stored here. Packed pretty tightly, she wondered if she'd ever actually use the space for her car. She scowled, the same way she always did when she worked her way through the garage, as she pushed herself around two mountain bikes.

"I have to clean this bloody place up," she said. With a serpentine movement, she wiggled her way through the odds and ends and found the bags at the edge of the space. Slapping a button on the wall, she heaved a bag in each hand and waited as the garage door slowly lifted from the ground up.

Once it reached eye-level, Juliette let out a gasp. A hooded figure wearing a mask rushed her, knocking her backwards into a stack of crates. Something wet splashed against her back and her feet slipped on a piece of cardboard.

Juliette's training kicked in and she defended herself, dropping the bags and driving an elbow into her assailant's body. The attacker, grunted. The noise sounded feminine.

"Jasmine?" Juliette cried out. *She found me!*

Before she could do anything more, someone else came through the door, a mask over their face as well, a syringe in their hand. Flashbacks of being kidnapped six months ago flooded Juliette's mind and she screamed. The sound was muffled by the hand of the first assailant covering her mouth. Juliette kicked out, coming in contact with a shin, and heard another grunt. Juliette's feet slid again and she lost her balance, clinging to the first assailant for support. The second attacker charged, pricking Juliette's neck. Within moments, Juliette became dizzy.

The first attacker retreated, disengaging Juliette's hand, and while rubbing her leg said, "She called me Jasmine."

The other simply said "Hmm. . ."

"We need to go. We don't have much time."

Juliette's eyesight faded, matching the growing darkness as the garage door closed behind the assailants.

41

October 10th
5:45 p.m.

Mags hung up the phone and rubbed her eyes. She couldn't seem to get enough sleep lately. Between catching up on work, long late-night talks with Scott, and being worried about someone who had her picture on their wall, even when she did sleep, she never felt rested.

"Mags?"

Mags glanced up at the voice. "Oh, hey Millan. I'm finally taking off for the day."

"Sean filled me in on what happened with Doctor Salla and this 'Jasmine' woman. You okay?" He coughed a bit and cleared his throat. "Do you need a police escort to your apartment?"

"No. I'm meeting up with Juliette for dinner. Just waiting for her to message me the place."

"All right. But I'd like to set up a patrol car to monitor outside your place tonight."

Mags felt her shoulders relax. "That would be great." She stood up and began collecting her things from the desk. "I'll call the station when I'm heading home."

"Sounds good." He put a hand on her shoulder. "We really missed you around here."

She patted his hand. "I missed being here, too."

"All this will be over soon, I promise."

"Thanks Millan." She swung her bag over her shoulder. "Oh yeah. Juliette asked if someone could walk me to my car."

"Sure thing, I'll just—"

"I'll do it!" Payne chimed in from across the room. He sprinted over. "I'll do it," he said again, his face a bit flushed.

"All right. Have a good night, Mags. We'll see you in the morning. Don't forget to call the station when you're on your way home."

"I won't. Night, Millan." She glanced over at Payne. "Well, let's go I guess."

The two of them headed outside and down the block to where Mags had parked. Since she didn't usually have a car, she hadn't been given a spot in the lot and had to park on the street.

Dusk had just hit the horizon and a slice of cold wind pierced the air. Mags pulled her coat tighter around herself.

"I had a nice time at lunch the other day," Payne said out

of the blue.

"Oh, yeah. Me too." She thought for a moment about this new addition to their staff. At first, she couldn't figure him out. Everyone complained about him. His brashness, his rudeness, his inappropriateness. But Mags hadn't seen anything like that. In fact, she sort of thought he was cute. He always seemed a bit nervous around her. It was refreshing. Scott was just as big and bulky, but he had a tendency to dominate the relationship. It was one reason why the breakup wasn't just about the time apart while she'd been on her trip with Charlotte.

Others had noticed a change in Payne, too. Juliette said he assisted her with one of her cases. Wilt said Payne offered to help him finish up his paperwork. And Sean mentioned Payne had brought him coffee the other morning. Apparently, these were previously unheard-of behaviors from him. Maybe he'd acted tough at first because he was new to the precinct? Or maybe being around these amazing people helped him act a little better? Mags wasn't sure, but she did feel intrigued by this Texan.

Payne cleared his throat while they walked, his boots clicking on the sidewalk. His words came quickly, the tails of them whispering bits of vapor into the cold air.

"I was wondering, if you wanted to, maybe, grab a coffee sometime? Outside of work, I mean."

Mags laughed. She hadn't meant to, but the sound emerged without her consent.

His face fell.

"Oh no," she said through giggles. "I promise I'm not

laughing at your suggestion. Truth is, I think I *would* want to get coffee with you. It's just the timing is so terrible, with Scott and everything."

"Who's Scott?"

"My fiancé. Well, ex-fiancé I suppose."

"Oh." She could see his face redden even in the darkening sky. "I asked Trann about you, I mean, just to see if you were available. He said you were unattached, but I didn't know you'd recently broken up with someone, especially an engagement. Sorry."

She smiled. One of the first genuine smiles she'd felt on her face in days. "You don't have to be sorry. Scott and I. . . we've had problems for a while. Everything that happened with the Spider case just cemented our issues."

"I was really impressed with what you did," he said. "I mean, I read the report when I first transferred here, about how you handled yourself when you and Tay were kidnapped. Tough stuff. I sort of liked you before I even met you."

"Well, thanks, I guess?" She let out a soft laugh. "Didn't think a traumatic experience would be attractive to members of the opposite sex."

"I didn't mean to bring it up."

"No, it's okay. In fact, it's sort of nice. Again, one of the problems with Scott. He just kept telling me I was fine and everything was over and to stop dwelling on it."

"He's a damn fool."

"Yeah." She paused. "I can't believe I just told you all that. I don't think I've talked that much to anyone about it, except Juliette."

He grinned, his teeth shiny underneath the streetlamp. "Then I'm glad I volunteered to walk you to your car."

"Speaking of, it's the white one, right there."

They stopped. "If you'd be obliged, maybe in a few weeks, we can talk again over coffee? No rush."

She pulled her keys from her purse and jingled them in her hand. "I think I'd like that." She paused, her grin widening. "See you at work tomorrow."

"Night, Mags."

Mags jogged around her sister's car and moved to the driver's door. She placed the key in the lock and turned it. Before she could open it, she heard a yell.

"Mags!"

She looked up at Payne's scream, terror in his voice.

Suddenly, someone knocked into her from behind. Pain surged in her wrist as it buckled against the car door.

"Duck!" she heard Payne yell.

Without thinking, she moved her head lower, and heard the shattering of glass. A dark, long bar had smashed through the driver's window right next to her face.

"You are nothing!" a voice rasped in her ear. "The Triads are *forever!*"

Mags heard the crunching of glass. She could see her assailant pulling out a crowbar from the busted window.

"No!" Mags said, struggling. Instinct took over. She grabbed the end of the crowbar and pulled it, breaking more glass. Jagged pieces sliced against her arm. The assailant lunged forward, pressing Mags further against the vehicle. She couldn't keep her balance. Her feet slid out from under her on the pavement, kicking wildly. Her foot connected with someone's shin before she hit her nose on the edge of the open window sill and lost her bearings, her face plastered against the car door.

The assailant released her and Mags could see out of the corner of her eye that she'd removed the crowbar. She watched it rise up. Mags held up her hands and covered her head, knowing the gesture would be futile, but survival kicked in and told her to do anything to protect herself.

She heard a grunt and then a thud.

Lowering her hands, she peeked out. Payne lay on the ground, face down. The crowbar lay next to him. The assailant was nowhere to be seen.

"Oh God," Mags said. She scrambled over to Payne's body, her eyes searching the street.

There. She spotted a woman running down the block, her long braided hair flopping against her back. A slight limp traced the edges of every few of her steps.

Mags looked back down towards Payne. Blood seeped from his head onto the street. He must have taken the blow meant for her.

"Oh God, no." The adrenaline in her body rushed out of her and she began to shake.

"Help!" she called out. Several passersby rushed over. "The police station," she said, pointing back the way she'd come. "Tell Sergeant Millan to meet us here." With a shaky hand she reached for her purse to get her phone. "911," she mumbled. She couldn't find her purse. She peered towards the car—it had fallen to the ground in the scuffle.

"I'll call," a voice said. A young woman stooped down and rubbed Mags' shoulder. "I'll call for an ambulance. You need to take care of him. And yourself."

Mags peered up into the woman's face. "Th-thank you," she said, her teeth chattering. She could taste the blood that dripped from her bashed nose. Her arm stung from the glass cuts.

The woman smiled, her dark hair framing her beautiful face. "Of course." She straightened up and made the call.

Mags tended to Payne, but wasn't quite sure what to do. She flipped him over gently and let out a sigh of relief at the rise and fall of his chest. She took off her scarf, folded it, and placed it under his head. He looked pale and ashen, but he still breathed.

"Hang in there, Payne," she whispered to him, swiping at the blood on her own face. "You have to hang in there. I can't have coffee with you if you don't hang in there."

42

October 10th
6 p.m.

Dr. Carla Moria hung up her phone. "Don't worry," she said to Mags. "An ambulance is on its way." A genuine look of concern crossed her face. She hated seeing innocents get hurt. Ironic, considering her past.

"Thanks," Mags said, peering up at her from the street. She returned to tending to the police officer on the ground.

Carla stepped away, melted into the crowd, then left the area. With quick steps, she headed towards her car, her eyes darting in the direction she'd seen the attacker flee.

Likely to run or hide? she thought. *I bet she'll hide, wait until she feels it's safe. She appeared injured. She'll need cover...* Carla noted an alleyway up a couple blocks. *There.*

She pulled out her phone, and made another call.

"Yes?" a voice said on the other end.

"You were right," Carla said. "Joslyn went after the receptionist. I didn't get here in time."

"Is she all right?"

"Yes, but an officer took the blow."

"Dead?'

"Unknown. An ambulance is on its way." Carla unlocked her car and got inside.

"You're sure Joslyn isn't Jasmine?"

"Not at the moment."

"Can you follow her for removal?"

Carla started up her car and peered down the street where the attacker had fled. "I'm on my way now."

"Good. Call me when clean-up has occurred."

Carla hung up the phone and cranked up the heat before driving off onto the street. She could tell it would be a very cold night.

43

October 10th
6:15 p.m.

Joslyn squatted behind a dumpster in an alley, rubbing her ankle where the receptionist had kicked her. Puffed-up skin greeted her wandering fingers, indicating that swelling had already begun.

Those fake Triad women, she thought, gritting her teeth. *I'll get them all. I got one in the courthouse parking garage. If that stupid cop hadn't stepped in the way, I'd have had two right now.* She picked at the side of the dumpster, peeling away a piece of rust. Several of her dark braids fell over her shoulder and she whipped them away. *That's okay, I'll get to her again.*

Pain snaked its way into her skull. She hated these headaches. They always came with periods of grogginess and blackouts. Sometimes she'd wake up in a strange place, unsure of how she'd gotten there. And then she'd remember. . .

Four years ago, a woman had approached her on the street.

"Are you Jasmine Stower?"

"Yes," she'd answered.

"I have a proposition for you. A job proposition."

Jasmine had stood there for a few moments, eyeing this woman. She appeared normal, even pretty, with pale skin, a gray business suit, a swirled blonde updo, light makeup, and sensible heels. But what place would ever want to hire her? Jasmine had had trouble with jobs her whole life. At 22 years old, she'd already been fired three times, suspended four, and arrested twice.

It was her stupid temper. She couldn't keep it in check. It always got her into trouble. Ever since she'd been little. Whether her bad mood crept in and made her feel envious of a coworker or jealous of a boss, frustrated at being told she'd done something wrong, or irate at inflexible rules, at some point or another, she would snap. Usually the emotional break ended with violence.

She had wished she could give up work altogether, but her mom's concentration had begun to waver and they needed a full-time nurse to take care of her. Her deadbeat father had died three years earlier from a drug overdose and her brother had moved away, ignoring their family as much as possible with his perfect wife and two perfect kids.

So, Jasmine kept trying for jobs. Anything that would last a couple months would work. Because of her track record, no one in their right mind, especially not this woman who seemed to work in a position *way* above Jasmine's paygrade, would seek her out. This woman must have made a mistake.

"You don't want me,'" Jasmine had said, turning away.

"On the contrary. I believe you are perfect for the job we have in mind."

Jasmine noted an uptilt in the woman's words which reminded her of what her mom would call "California Valley Girls." Why would someone like her be here in Boston, asking Jasmine to work for her? Unlikely as it may seem, she couldn't help but be intrigued. "Who's *we?*" she asked.

"A group of women who want to make a difference in the world. Make a difference with people. We think you could help make that difference."

"I don't care about other people or helping them. People suck. They're screwing up the world and don't even give a shit. Why should I help them? Or you?"

The woman held out a business card. "Because we agree with you. Come to this address tomorrow at one-o-clock, if you're interested in changing things." The woman gave a small smile, her teeth straight and white. One thing Jasmine had always liked about herself was her unmarred appearance, but she'd constantly been self-conscious about her poor dental care. She unconsciously ran her tongue over her crooked teeth as the woman continued.

"This is an opportunity to help your family, yourself, and

the world. I hope you'll consider it."

Jasmine hesitated before taking the card and putting it in her pocket, convinced she'd never even look at it again.

The next day, at 1 p.m., Jasmine found herself at the address listed. She wasn't sure why she'd gone. The rest of her life stunk so much she figured it couldn't hurt to check things out. Besides, with decent pay, she could handle any job for a couple months.

The building appeared ordinary—white brick, cement stairs, black shutters. Like any normal business building. For some reason, she expected a lavish hotel or grand mansion, based on the idea of some grandiose job. Jasmine scolded herself for getting her hopes up.

It's probably some "let's save the children" thing or something. I bet I'll have a phone glued to my ear for eight hours a day.

She made her way to the fourth floor, suite 422, which simply said Global Dynamic Change Corporation. Jasmine entered, not having any idea about how much her *life* would change.

After she met with the woman, who spoke about a Book and a way to help the world, Jasmine had a million questions. The woman answered all of them, dutifully, and didn't react when Jasmine sneered or brushed her notions aside.

"It just sounds crazy," Jasmine said for the third time.

"I understand. But it is a valid position. There will be training and perks and work hours, in a sense, just like a regular job. Except you only have to work once a month.

"This is a completely unique situation," the woman had continued. "We often don't let women stay in touch with their families. Your code name will be Joslyn. That's who you are now. When you awake, you will have to pretend to be Jasmine. She must still exist to the outside world, with that same name, but she will be a different persona. We will tailor her to function better in society, to stay under the radar, to keep her emotions in check. We will create her to preserve your secret. Do you understand?"

"I think so, yes." Jasmine, now called Joslyn, hesitated before her next question. "It'll really be like falling asleep and waking up once a month to work, while Jasmine uses up the rest of the time?"

"Yes. This is a way to give your life meaning while helping rid the world of those that keep hurting it."

"What if I change my mind?"

"You're welcome to change your mind at any time."

Joslyn had gone home, shaking. She wanted to talk to someone, tell someone about this woman's insane ideas, but she had no one to talk to. And that was sort of the point. She had no real life. Nothing to feel proud of. This work would give her that. She would live her life without any of her anger. She would be able to hold a job, provide for her mother, and keep herself out of jail.

The second reason she decided to take the position was because she felt like she would matter. Her whole life she'd believed herself to be a waste of space, sometimes thinking it would be better to fall asleep and never wake up. This way, she could be productive, make a difference in the world, and her life would *mean* something.

Joslyn had decided to try it out, go through the "training" process, which took three months, and see how she felt by the end.

After the training, she felt powerful, in control. She had a secret life, secret skills that no one else could know about. No one would expect *her* to be special, to be the kind of woman she was about to be.

She laid down to go to sleep in her own bed. . .and awoke in the guest bed at her mother's house.

Her phone lay ringing beside her, a strange song with an awkward repetitive beat. She answered it.

"Good morning, Joslyn," the woman said on the other line, her words lilting up at the end.

"Good morning." Joslyn checked her phone and gawked at the date. "Wow! It really happened! It's been a month. I can't believe it."

"Joslyn, this is important. You will have one day to complete your assignment. You will not remember anything that's happened during the last month. You'll have to check Jasmine's calendar and get as up to speed as you can. It is imperative you don't tip anyone in your life off about the changes."

"Got it." The deliciousness of the secret, held under the noses of the very people who considered themselves close to her, pleased her.

Her first assignment had been none other than a previous

boss. A boss who'd hit on her, then fired her when she'd turned him down. She'd made a fuss with corporate, which was quickly overlooked since she was considered a "troublemaker" anyway, and she'd ended up punching her boss in the face. That had been the first time she'd been arrested.

Joslyn felt completely nervous. The woman had provided exact instructions on what should happen, timing everything down to the minute.

"You can do this," she'd told Joslyn. "There's a reason he treated you the way he did. He's defective. He doesn't deserve to live and subject other women to the same thing."

And there he was. Getting out of his car, just like the woman told her.

The kill itself had been easier than she'd thought it would be. In fact, something inside Joslyn almost purred when she saw the look of surprise, then anger, then pain on his face when she'd slid the knife into his gut. It was almost as if all the rage she'd had for so many years now had an outlet, a purpose.

The next month, when she awoke to her ringing phone, she'd felt a sense of anticipation she'd never experienced before. Almost like a dog salivating at the sound of a dinner bell.

The "alternate persona" of Jasmine meant nothing to her. She was merely a placeholder, living a "good" life with those around her. Joslyn discovered her mother liked the new version of Jasmine better, that Jasmine had mended the rift with her brother, and had dated then eventually married someone.

It wasn't until six months ago that Joslyn knew something had gone wrong. She'd woken up the next day, not the next month. She hadn't returned into her Jasmine persona.

Joslyn didn't know what to do. She went to the address from the business card, but the sign had been removed from room 422, a *Vacant* sign attached to the window of the office.

What had happened? she thought. Finally, she overhead the news. One of the Triads had gotten caught.

Joslyn ate up any news report she could find. She devoured hours of television and hundreds of online videos. She needed some way to contact her own Triad group, or *any* Triad group, and let them know about her situation.

But nothing happened. Day after day came and went. She found herself in an odd situation—married to a man she didn't know, working a job she despised at a library, and having boring weekly talks with her brother about his wife and kids.

After about a month, something odd happened. She woke up sitting in the bathroom at the library with no recollection of how she'd gotten there. Used to waking up in strange places, she'd assumed a month would have passed, but only four hours had gone by.

The blackouts came more frequently. It was then she realized she was slipping back and forth between herself and Jasmine, except without anyone monitoring her, the changes were random and sporadic.

Terrified, her fear turned to paranoia and despair. How could the Triads have forgotten about her? Why would they have left her unattended for so long?

Joslyn needed a target to focus her anger. She fixated on the three women who had interfered in the first place: Dr. Charlotte Salla, Detective Juliette Tay, and Mags Stinton. These three women had come in and ruined everything, ruined Joslyn's perfect life!

Joslyn pulled herself from her memories, running her tongue over her aligned and perfect teeth. The smells of garbage from the dumpster and oil stains in the alley reminded herself to focus on her current situation. No one would make her lose all that she'd finally gained in her life. She'd showed those three women. The coroner had already been taken out. She'd try again soon for the receptionist. And the cop? Joslyn had already set something up at her house for a few "fireworks" to go off the next time she opened her door.

Joslyn tested her ankle. A bit of pain lingered, but she knew she could walk on it, run if need be. About to push herself up from her crouch, she paused. She heard the clicking of heels on the concrete. Someone had turned down the alley.

She held her breath, reaching in her pocket, and pulling out the switchblade she always carried on her person.

The steps came closer. They stood mere feet from the other side of the dumpster.

"Joslyn?" a woman's voice asked, low and soft.

Joslyn tensed. Who knew her code name? Unless. . .

Joslyn still felt anxiety itching across her skin, but she stood slowly. A beautiful Latina woman stood before her, wearing a flowy red skirt and a black sweater.

"Are you a Triad member?" Joslyn whispered, hoping

against hope.

"I am."

Joslyn nearly collapsed with relief. "Have you come to put me under? I want to go back to my regular life."

A sadness stole across the woman's brown eyes. "Unfortunately, no."

"No?"

"Joslyn, you made a bit of a mess. You've been exposed."

"What? No! How?"

"The basement," she said, "of your house. You left the pictures up. You carved words into the wall."

Joslyn remembered. The whole thing had felt like an odd dream. Putting up the pictures had given her focus. She'd kept slipping in and out of her states in a haze.

"I'll take them down," she said.

"It's too late. The police have discovered them."

Silence blanketed the narrow alley.

"What does this mean?" Joslyn asked. Fear slinked its way through her stomach, creating a knot, but hope still glowed warmly in her chest. She'd been found. Somehow, everything would be okay now. They'd put her back under and she'd wake up with a new target.

The woman's words cut, chilling any warmth she had left.

"You're broken," the woman said, twisting a wedding ring on her finger. "You should never have been created the way you were. It was only a matter of time. And where there's a mess, we clean it up."

"We?"

Joslyn had barely gotten the word out when something sharp pricked her leg. She glanced down to see a small dart sticking out of her thigh. It shined silver in the last remnants of failing sunlight.

"It'll be easy," the woman said. "A drug simulating an overdose. You'll just go to sleep."

Joslyn nodded. Her legs didn't seem to work anymore. She sat down. She knew it should have hurt, her rear end against the cold, hard ground, but it didn't. She felt peaceful. Peaceful as herself.

"I want to go to sleep again," she said.

"I know," the woman said, her tone sympathetic. "Goodbye Joslyn. Sleep well." She pulled out the dart and left.

Joslyn's last moments were of watching the beautiful woman walk away, of feeling content, and of hoping her mother would be okay.

44

October 10th
6:30 p.m.

Sean had just pulled up to Jasmine's mother's house when his phone rang.

"Yeah?" he said, answering the call.

"Trann? It's Millan. Where are you?"

"At the suspect's mother's house. The one who attacked Charlotte."

"You go there alone?"

"No. I called in for two officers to meet me here. They are sitting in a squad car, waiting for my instructions. Why? What's going on?"

"Mags was attacked at her car. Just up the block from the

precinct."

"What?!" Sean bolted upright in his seat. "Is she okay?"

"Yes, but Payne is in the ICU."

"Wait, *Payne*?"

"He'd been walking her to her car and apparently he dove between Mags and her attacker and got hit in the head with a crowbar. Most likely saved Mags' life, but we don't know how bad the damage is yet. He hasn't woken up."

"Do we know who attacked them?"

"Mags described a woman fleeing the scene. A woman with dark skin and long braids."

"Jasmine. Holy fuck, it was Jasmine." Sean rubbed his face. "Okay. I'm going to check in with the mother again and leave an unmarked car out here to see if Jasmine returns. We should put one at Bruno's house as well. We need someone at the hospital, too."

"I'll get someone over there ASAP."

"Where's Mags right now?"

"Waiting at the hospital. She's all right, a little beat up, but we made sure she got checked out."

"Jesus. First Charlotte, then Mags. This woman definitely has an agenda." He paused. "Millan, where's Tay?"

"That's the other problem. Tay isn't answering her phone and I sent someone to her house and there's no answer. Wilt said he'd just pulled up outside the house when it happened."

"What happened?"

Millan's words came out curt and carrying more anger than Sean had ever heard from the man. "An explosion. Apparently rigged at the front door when the officers forced their entry."

All the feeling left Sean's body as his blood ran cold. "Anyone dead? Tay?" he whispered.

"Two officers dead. There's a lot of rubble. Once Wilt arrived, he and two other officers wanted to search the place, but they decided to wait for the Bomb Squad in case there's another explosive. They haven't found Tay yet."

"Holy shit." Sean took a deep breath. "Okay. We need to do this one step at a time. Check in with me when you find out *anything.* I'm still going to follow up with the mother."

"Let me know what the mother says. She may be covering for her daughter."

"All right."

Millan paused. "That's my other line. We'll talk soon."

Sean hung up the phone, his head spinning.

Ten minutes later, Sean left Jasmine's mother's house, frustration coursing through him. The mother seemed thoroughly confused, although Jasmine had told them previously that she'd recently suffered a stroke and was having difficulty remembering things. Still, Sean couldn't rule out that she was hiding her daughter, so he had the officers remain to watch the house until the unmarked police car arrived.

Sean called Millan and let him know the update.

"Any news on Tay?" Sean asked.

"Yeah." A pause. "We found her."

45

October 10th
6:30 p.m.

Something rumbled the boxes behind Juliette, shaking her awake.

Her eyes didn't want to open. They begged at her to remain closed, to stay in the safe darkness of drug-induced sleep, but Juliette's brain kept trying to tell them she needed to be awake. It was important.

Juliette finally pulled herself from the darkness and looked around. She sat, alone, on her garage floor. Something cold and damp had sunk into her pants and her mouth tasted like salty cotton. The edge of the garage door appeared bent inward, shining a bit of light into the blackness. She'd been propped up against a stack of boxes and was sitting quite comfortably, considering her attack. Next to her lay her purse. She pulled at it with sleepy fingers and rummaged through her things. Everything looked in order: keys, wallet, phone.

Phone.

With a few weak shakes she forced her hands to work. They did so, grudgingly. After a few taps, she managed to call the station. The evening receptionist answered.

"This is Detective Tay," Juliette said, her voice thick and syrupy. "I need someone to come get me. I'm in the garage at my house. I may need an ambulance."

"Someone is already there, Detective. Hang on and I'll send your message through dispatch."

Two minutes later the heavy door screeched open. Wilt, with two other officers helping to lift the door, stood silhouetted in the darkening sky.

"Tay!" he called out. He rushed over to her. "I found her!" he yelled over his shoulder. "Are you hurt?" he asked, checking her face and shoulders with his hands.

"I don't think so," she said. "Drugged."

"We should get you to the hospital. You may have injuries you don't feel. I'll drive you there."

"How did you get here so fast?"

"We were already here. We thought the explosion got you, but maybe you just hit your head and fell?"

Juliette's head swam. "Explosion?"

"Your front door was rigged to explode. Two officers got the main blast. They. . .didn't make it. We were waiting for the Bomb Squad to arrive, but before they did, I heard you called the station." He paused. "Why are you in here?"

"Clothing bags for donation," she said, nodding towards the spilled contents on the ground. A flash raced through her mind. "Two women!" she yelled out, grabbing his arm as he attempted to help her to her feet. Her legs felt wobbly and she wasn't sure how, but they managed to keep her up. "They attacked me, injected me with something."

Wilt nodded. "It was Jasmine. She went after Mags as well."

Terror gripped Juliette's heart. "Is she. . .?"

"She's okay, but Payne took a hit to the head."

"Payne. . .?"

"It's a long story. I'll tell you on the way to the hospital."

As they moved down her driveway, Juliette kept talking. "You said Jasmine did this?"

"Yeah."

She shook her head, regretting the motion as the world swayed. "I thought it was Jasmine at first, but then a second figure came in. They said something about Jasmine. Like they were surprised I thought one of them was her."

Wilt helped her down off the curb. "Two women? Are you sure?"

Juliette gave him a look which made him laugh.

"Sorry, sorry. I know you hate when I make you repeat yourself. All right. Sean's at Jasmine's mother's house now. We have someone going to Bruno's to stake out the place. If she returns to either of those places, we'll get her."

The more she walked, the better she felt. "That's just it," she said. "I don't know if either of those women were Jasmine."

Wilt paused, helping her into the front seat of his car. "You mean you think two *other* women attacked you? Was it random, like a robbery or something?"

"I don't think so. They didn't take anything that I could tell."

Wilt shut the door, ran around to the other side of the car, and hopped in. He radioed dispatch and filled them in on the situation. Then he shifted to Juliette. "Then what did they want with you?"

She laid her head against the headrest, staring at the wreckage of her blown apart front door. Tears stung her eyes. Why attack her and then rig a bomb to explode?

"I have no bloody idea," she answered, letting the tears streak down her face as Wilt pulled away from the curb.

46

October 10th
6:35 p.m

Dr. Carla Moria answered her phone about half a block from the alley near her parked car. The setting sun shone into her eyes, making her cast her gaze downward towards the sidewalk. "Yes?"

"Is it done? With Joslyn?"

She swallowed against the lump in her throat. "It's done."

"Great. Things with Detective Tay have been taken care of as well."

"That's wonderful."

The woman on the other line must have heard the sadness in Carla's voice. "Carla?" she asked.

Carla remembered the look on Joslyn's face. "I just prefer it when we can adjust their memories or remove their trigger."

"I know. But her Jasmine persona was compromised. She would have been sent to jail, unaware of what she'd done. We don't—"

"—punish the innocent," Carla finished for her. "I know."

"It's why if there is no alternative, when we determine their trigger, we always use it, so they are the person who committed the crimes."

"I know," she repeated, twirling her wedding ring on her finger. "Is everything set then? For Violet?" Carla had reached her car, got in, pulled down the visor, and took off down the street.

"Yes. She was clever, returning to the Veronica persona, believing she could escape from her crimes. But everything is set. She'll be returned to Violet. Then, after her sentencing, whether she ends up at the medical facility or prison, she'll be taken care of. It's all been arranged."

Carla pulled up to her apartment. The moving truck sat outside, full of her things. "Is there anything else before we're done here?"

The woman replied, "Just the last loose end, but I'll deal with it."

"Wonderful. I'll talk to you in a week unless anything changes." Carla hung up the phone.

47

October 11ᵗʰ
1:45 p.m.

Sean paced in front of his desk. Charlotte, Payne, and Tay had all been admitted to Mass Gen hospital the previous night, plus an officer who'd gotten injured in the explosion at Tay's house. Four people injured, two dead. All because of one woman.

Jasmine.

Who they then found in an alley near where she'd clubbed Payne with a crowbar, dead from a drug overdose.

Sean couldn't believe it. It was over. The woman was dead. At first, he'd been surprised to find she'd OD'd, but from the description of Charlotte and Mags and the obsessive nature of the photos in the basement, the woman seemed un-hinged, so drugs made sense.

Still, he felt on edge. Something didn't quite feel right. If Jasmine had been responsible for all the attacks, who was the second woman with her who'd attacked Tay? And how could the timing have worked out? The assault against Tay happened close to the same time as the incident with Mags and Payne. Maybe if Jasmine had driven, but she'd run and hid, as if she hadn't brought a car. She couldn't have made it all the way from Tay's house in time. So, if Jasmine hadn't been there, who were the two other women who'd attacked Tay? And why had they done nothing except sedate her, only to set an explosive at her front door?

Too many questions still remained unanswered. But Sean didn't care about that very much at the moment. He had two other things on his mind. The first, that Charlotte would be released soon and he was going to pick her up from the hospital and take her home and the second, the verdict from the case against Violet was going to be announced later that day.

Sean wasn't sure what he wanted the verdict to be. Either way, the woman would be locked up for a long time, whether in prison or an insane asylum, and that had to be a good thing.

The clock on the station wall clicked over to 2 p.m. and Sean grabbed his jacket from the back of his chair. He headed into Millan's office.

"I'm heading over to the hospital to pick up Charlotte," he told the sergeant. "I'll see if there's been any change with Payne and let you know."

"Sounds good." Millan paused. Sean noted the leanness

of his cheeks, the sunken nature of his eyes. "I saw on the news about the verdict coming today. What are you hoping for?"

"I just want that woman locked up. I don't care how or where. I just want it to be done."

Millan grunted.

Sean's forehead wrinkled. "You don't feel the same way?"

Millan rubbed against his shirt pocket, the one with the cigarette pack in it. His words came slowly, almost as if he were not fully aware that he spoke. "After I heard the news about my daughter's death, I hated the world. I mean, *really* hated it. A man had decided to get drunk and drive his car. And my daughter is dead."

He raised his gaze to Sean, his dark eyes hollow, yet piercing. "The woman on trial, Violet, decided to kill. Even if some Triad created a whole other person inside her, her core is a killer. She doesn't deserve to live. If my daughter can be dead, Violet doesn't deserve to live." Millan's head drooped, then he slowly pulled the pack of cigarettes from his pocket, stared at them with a blank look on his face, and chucked them into the trash can next to his desk. "I'm tired of them winning," he muttered. "Those women made me kill some-one. That's not all right."

Sean stood there, unsure of what to say. He hadn't really talked much with Millan these past few weeks. He'd been too busy and Millan hadn't really been a part of the investigation anymore. He'd forgotten that Millan had been responsible for the death of someone based on Violet's in-depth mode of murder six months ago. The victim would have probably died anyway, but Millan had gone into the house before the victim was fully dead and a contraption Violet built had pulled the man apart, literally quartering him, removing any chance of survival. There had been no way Millan could have known, but apparently it had eaten away at him more than he'd let on.

Add to that the death of his newly-found daughter and Sean couldn't imagine the pain Millan must be feeling.

Sean remained there for several moments, wishing he had some words to placate the older man, but nothing came. He felt useless. "Well, uh, I gotta go. I'll see you tomorrow," Sean said, inching towards the door.

"Tell Doctor Salla I hope she's okay," Millan said as he'd already resumed his paperwork.

"I will. Thanks."

Sean left the precinct and headed towards his car. As he got in and started it up, a feeling of emptiness stole over him. His job sucked. There were always so many losses, not just someone's life, but emotional and mental losses and bruises and blows they had to take as cops. Every day they saw the worst of the worst in people. They had to always be on edge, never knowing if someone they were arresting would randomly strike them or flee, never knowing if helping would end up hurting.

Sean knew the police authority system was far from perfect. He'd met cops who went too far in investigations, who profiled for no apparent reason, who had little respect for most of the criminals they arrested, even if their crime was as minimal as graffiti. He'd always despised those officers. But Sean could also understand them. And that scared him. He always believed he'd be fair, do his job to help people, and keep things positive. The idea that he could understand the desire to just stop giving people second chances, stop believing that they would come quietly, stop thinking he could *ever* really make a difference terrified him.

After all he'd been through the past six months, what would keep him from becoming one of those kinds of cops? What would keep *any* of them from wanting to take matters into their own hands?

To counter that dark path, Sean focused on the positives he still had left. No one he cared about had died. Everyone would be all right. The criminals hadn't won. He had to put that in the plus column, no matter how much shorter that column looked in comparison to the negatives.

A half hour later, Sean helped Charlotte into the front seat of his car. They'd just left the hospital after Sean quickly popped his head in on Payne, whose condition remained the same.

"I can manage," she said, clutching the door for support.

"I know you can," he said with a grin, "but maybe I just want the excuse to touch you."

He saw the edges of her mouth move upwards.

"We had your car towed to your apartment," he told her while getting into the driver's seat, "so there's no need to take you to the parking garage."

"I appreciate it," she said. "Returning there is not something on my to-do list anytime soon." She shifted in her seat and winced.

"Back still hurting?" he asked as he pulled away from the hospital.

"It is not as terrible as I thought it would be. The pain-killers are wearing off, though. I am only supposed to take ibuprofen from now on. I will take some when I arrive home."

"Do you need me to help you with anything? Is it hard to reach for stuff?"

"No. My arm is fully functional. The stiches pull a little bit when I reach too far forward, but I can manage. But thank you."

Sean rubbed his chin. "Did you hear that the verdict is coming back soon? They are going to air it in a few hours." He turned onto a side street.

"I did. I watched the news in my bed this morning."

Silence descended as Sean thought for a few minutes about his conversation with Millan. He wondered how Charlotte felt about the situation. "Do you care what the verdict is?"

She didn't answer until they pulled up to her apartment. "I am unsure. I do not know what to believe anymore."

Sean could hear her breathing quicken as she reached for the door handle.

"Are you okay?" he asked.

"I just. . .need. . ." She finally got the door open and spilled out onto the sidewalk, gasping for air.

Sean bolted from his side and ran around the car. "Charlotte what's wrong?" he asked, moving to help her stand up straight.

She waved him away, but stayed hunched over. He stood

there, a couple feet from her, shifting from one foot to the other until she rose.

"Sorry," she muttered.

"Are you all right?"

She ran her fingers through her hair. Sean could see them shaking.

"Yes," she said. "And no. I have been experiencing panic attacks since the day before I returned from my trip with Mags."

Sean stood there. "Uh. . ." he uttered. He didn't know what to say. She'd said it so matter-of-factly, like she'd had ringing in her ears or throbbing in her foot. But what do you say to someone having panic attacks? "That sucks," he finally said.

She smiled. "Indeed." She began to walk towards the building.

Sean caught up with her. "Have you ever had them before?"

"No."

"Oh."

She sighed. "They are. . .embarrassing."

"We don't have to talk about them."

She stopped just short of the outside door, keys in her hand. "I am a grown woman. I am a doctor. I have dealt with cadavers and seen repulsive and horrific things. I have never *once* had a panic attack. Logically, I know they are created by my own mind and therefore, I should be able to stop them. But I cannot!" The last word came in a huff. Charlotte shoved the key into the door lock and twisted it.

Sean just stood there, silent. He felt like this might be one of those times that anything he might say would only make things worse.

Charlotte's shoulders dropped as she let out a breath. She winced again. "Apparently what I think about panic attacks does not matter. They happen anyway. It is time to stop pretending I can make them go away on my own. Sean?"

"Yeah?"

"Are you free tonight? I would like to propose that I stop here to shower and change, but perhaps return to your apartment for dinner? I would not mind talking through some of the things I experienced on my trip. Maybe it would help with these attacks."

Sean lit up. "Yeah? That would be great." He nodded at her shoulder. "If you think you're up for it?"

"I do. I am." She opened the door. "I will come by in about an hour."

"You got it," he said, a big grin splitting his face. He returned to his car and made a call to fill in Millan on Payne's condition at the hospital.

"It's the same," Sean said, once he'd connected to Millan. "Still unconscious. The doctor said it doesn't look like brain damage, but until he wakes up, they can't be sure. Mags was sitting with him when I left. Her nose looked puffy and her forearm was bandaged, but she said she was all right."

"I guess there's nothing to do but wait." Millan hacked a cough before continuing. "I just saw they are announcing the verdict in a couple hours. Tay and Wilt already went down to be in the courtroom when it happens."

"I'm not surprised Wilt wants to be there. This was his first major case and what a *huge* mess it's been."

Millan let out a scoff. "Yeah. I don't envy him." He paused. "Listen, we'll have to talk on Monday if Payne is still out of commission. I'm hoping for the best, but we need to figure something out if he isn't going to be your partner for a while."

Sean nodded, then remembered he was on the phone. "I get it."

"Great. Well, enjoy your night. You deserve a break. As for me, I'll be glued to my TV."

"It'll be great for all of us for the trial to be over, one way or another."

48

October 11th
4:00 p.m.

Sean heard the buzz of his apartment's intercom and clicked a button to open the connection.

"Hello?'

"It is Char—"

Sean sighed at the still broken line and hit the key to unlock the entrance on her end. He cracked his door, took one last look over the place, which he'd hastily cleaned up, then pulled the door fully open to welcome her.

She entered, her hair tousled and still looking a bit damp. The scent of fresh soap and something that smelled a bit like honey hit Sean as she moved past him. She smelled incredible.

"Have a seat," he said, gesturing to his sofa. He'd already turned on the TV to the news station, but had it muted since a break in the trial story hadn't occurred yet.

"Thank you," she said. She laid her coat along the back of the couch and slid onto one of the cushions.

"I thought we could order a pizza?"

"Sounds wonderful."

He grabbed his landline. "What do you want on it?"

"I am flexible."

Sean swallowed hard. The statement seemed benign, but the idea of Charlotte's flexibility unwillingly drifted through his mind. "How about sausage, onion, and mushroom?"

"Perfect."

Sean made the call. The pizza would be there in about 45 minutes. Plenty of time for them to talk and the food would probably arrive before the verdict was announced.

Sean hovered for a bit, unsure how close to sit to her. He wanted her to feel comfortable talking about whatever had been on her mind lately. He remembered all too well when he'd passed out six months ago because of an anxiety attack. Nothing like that had ever happened to him before, or since, but he could relate to the uncomfortable feeling it gave him. Not to mention the embarrassment. He felt bad she'd had to experience anything like that.

"You want something to drink?" he asked.

"Just water. The painkillers are out of my system, but I would prefer not to risk drinking alcohol yet."

Sean had already forgotten that she'd just been released from the hospital. The way she looked right now, he would never have guessed she'd been stabbed in the back yesterday.

"How's the shoulder feeling?" he called over from his kitchen while filling up a glass from the sink.

"Stiff, and a bit achy, but not as bad as I thought it would be. Apparently, the blade slid in at an odd angle, so the cut was long, but shallower than it could have been."

He found himself curious to see what the wound looked like, but then thought it would be weird to ask to see her bare back.

"I'm just glad you're okay." Emotion welled up inside him unexpectedly. She could have been hurt much worse, or killed. In six months, she'd been attacked twice. She was a lot stronger than he thought anyone really knew. "I'm *really* glad," he added.

"As am I." She nodded at the TV. "Anything new?"

"Not yet. They seem to think the verdict will come in pretty quickly, so everyone is on standby. Wilt and Tay went. Maybe we'll get to see them if they pan over the spectators."

"Thank you for letting me come over to watch the end of this trial."

"You know, you could come by even if we *aren't* going to watch the end of a trial."

Charlotte smiled. "Good to know." She settled back into the corner of the couch. "This whole situation. . .it has affected me in ways I was unprepared for."

"Like what?"

"I thought I would find other Triads during my travels. I failed."

Sean squirmed a bit. He'd never been the best at saying

the right thing with women, but he really wanted to get things right with her. He let out a mental sigh. The only way to know was to try.

"I thought you'd find other Triads, too." Charlotte frowned, so Sean quickly continued. "But when you didn't, I didn't think it meant you failed. I thought it meant that maybe they didn't exist after all."

"But Truth told me—"

"Truth told you a lot of things. She'd also been living underground in a bunker for three years believing that she should murder people for stupid reasons like a heart condition. Just because she said things, doesn't make them real."

"I have thought about that. I really believed. . ." Charlotte paused and tucked her hair behind her ears. "Truth told me I would save them. She called me their Messiah."

"I remember you mentioning that before you left."

"I. . .I believed it. I thought that because I did not die when Violet threw a knife into my chest that somehow it made me. . ."

"Special?" he finished for her.

She nodded. "I love my job and I love my life. But having someone tell you you are destined for a greater purpose. . .? For someone like me, someone who strives for perfection, it felt. . .flattering." She shook her head. "I hated myself for thinking that. For using that horrible situation as a way to feel superior. I do *not* want to feel that way.

"Then," she continued, "when no other Triads were found, I felt. . .betrayed. Let down. Small and insignificant. I started jumping at shadows and seeing things that were not there. My irrational mind kept trying to find proof that all of it was real." She took a sip of water.

"And now?" Sean asked.

"It appears everything was orchestrated by Truth, Violet, and Anya. Three delusional women who believed in something larger that did not exist, convinced by women before them, also clearly delusional. I have even figured out the others in the bunker, the scientists. Clearly they must have met or seen other Triad members, since they had been brought in to decipher the Book before Truth took over. But there is no proof they ever met anyone else, or even saw the Book prior to Truth's involvement. They say they were involved earlier, but cannot produce any other woman they previously worked with.

"When the notes began to arrive," she went on, "I thought it was another Triad and once again, I would have proof. But it ended up being a drug-filled ill woman with delusions of her own." She gestured towards the television. "And now, when the trial ends, it will be over. All of this will have meant nothing and simply have been a waste of everyone's time and energy. And I will return to my normal, un-special life."

Sean was struggling to make sense of what Charlotte meant. "Did you want to *be* their Messiah?"

"That is the odd part. No, I did not. I wanted it to all go away and wanted my life back. But it felt like being told Santa was fake. Something I believed in was ripped away and the reality was that there was nothing fantastical, just someone telling me a lie."

She sat up on the couch, her cheeks flushed. "Why did I care what Truth told me? Why did I believe her in the first place with such ease? I do not consider myself a gullible woman, so why was this so important to me?"

"I don't know," Sean said. "I don't know you well enough to answer those questions." He moved closer to her on the couch. "But I'd like to *get* to know you better to help you answer them." He took her hand. "Charlotte, you're one of the most fascinating people I've ever met. You're passionate about your work, you make me look at things from different angles, and surprisingly enough, you're easy to talk to. Do you know how rare that is? You don't have to be some 'messiah' for a bunch of crazy killers to be special and have a purpose. Besides, perfection is overrated. I like your flaws."

Charlotte cocked her head. "No one likes someone's flaws. That makes no sense."

Sean laughed. "Well I do! I like that you're stubborn, because it makes me really think about my side of a discussion. I like that it bothers you when you fail, because I know that means you give your best with everything. And I like that you're sometimes stand-offish because it means that when I do get through, it's real. You might want to be perfect, but then you wouldn't be all these other things, either."

Charlotte stayed quiet and Sean wondered if he'd said too much. He couldn't take any of it back and he didn't really want to. He enjoyed her company and as the seconds ticked by, he realized he wanted to be closer to her, to see what else she had to offer.

The intercom buzzed, making them both jump.

"Pizza," Sean said, remembering. He pulled his wallet out of his pocket. "I'll be back in a minute." He told the delivery person he'd be right down, jogged down the stairs, got the food, and returned. When he reentered his apartment, Charlotte had unmuted the TV.

Sean had a sudden flashback to when his ex, Angellica, had been sitting on the same couch six months ago. He'd thought about how beautiful she'd been, just sitting there.

He'd been so wrong about what beautiful was.

Sean cleared his throat to announce his presence and put the pizza onto the coffee table, a new addition he'd gotten over the summer from someone at work who'd been trying to get rid of it. Having a place to put his snacks and beverages, other than tucking them into the couch next to him and hoping they wouldn't fall, made a huge difference in the cleanliness of his apartment.

"Hungry?" he asked.

"Famished."

Something flashed in Charlotte's eyes as Sean took a seat on the couch. A note of invitation in her eyes at the word "famished."

Sean swallowed, hard. The speed in which she could entice him—just a word or simple-seeming motion—amazed him. He grabbed a slice and motioned to the TV with his piece of pizza. "Anything new?"

"They keep saying the verdict will arrive any minute now. Until then, they are simply showing previously taped video from the trial."

Sean saw her frown slightly and muted the TV. "Let's just

eat until something new pops up."

They dug in. Sean hadn't realized how hungry he was. He'd barely touched the sub sandwich he'd gotten for lunch at the station as he'd been too distracted by picking up Charlotte from the hospital. Melted cheese and spicy sausage hit his tongue, striking his taste buds with delight. He sighed and sank into the cushions.

"I enjoy your flaws as well, you know," Charlotte said.

Sean halted, mid-bite. Every part of his skin tightened at her words. He glanced over at her. "You do?"

She nodded.

"That's impossible."

Her forehead wrinkled. "So, you can like my flaws but I am not allowed to like yours?"

"Of course not. It's impossible because I don't have any flaws." He held the joke as long as he could.

They both burst out laughing. Her laugh rung in his ears. He loved it. He loved *her.* The notion didn't scare him as much as he thought it might. Not that he planned to tell her that right now, but maybe someday he could. Still, he liked the idea that in this moment, not in some huge romantic gesture or because she said or did the "right thing," but just sitting here, laughing with her, was the moment he realized how he really felt.

Charlotte finished her slice and put her plate on the table. "I really mean it, though. I value your flaws. You make me think outside the box and do silly things that may seem ridiculous, but are just fun. I have not always done that in my life—had fun for the sake of fun. I appreciate that." She looked at him again and this time Sean could almost *feel* the heat coming from her gaze.

Don't screw this up. It may not mean anything. Don't make a move. Don't screw this up! This was always the hardest part. Women were tough to read. Some liked it when men made the first move. Others liked to be part of the decision. Sometimes a woman would just fling herself at a guy. So what type of woman was Charlotte?

Sean thought about her. She was direct, upfront, and honest.

"I'd like to kiss you," he said. "You and all your flaws." The words sounded a bit cheesy, but he didn't care.

"I was thinking the same thing," she said, a smile spreading across her face that seemed to light up the whole room.

He hardly remembered moving closer. But he wanted to remember. He wanted to savor every second of this. She wasn't someone he wanted to just be with for the pleasure and the fun. He wanted to experience her. Her mouth. Her skin. Her hair. Her scent.

So, he slowed himself down.

He gathered her face in his hands and brought her towards him. That same explosive shuddering feeling shot through him when their lips met. He pushed his hands into her hair, the still slightly damp locks clinging to his fingers. Pressure mounted on his biceps as she returned the pull. His fingers traveled to her shoulders, drawing her closer, then slid down her back.

Charlotte let out a hiss of breath and pulled away.

"Oh, God, I'm sorry!" he said, realizing he'd just felt her bandage. "I forgot about your cut!"

She shook her head. "It is all right," she reassured him. "You merely grazed the area."

He paused, feeling bad he'd hurt her.

With a slow but deliberate motion, she took his hand and placed it around her waist. "Just keep your hands lower and it will be fine." She smiled again, that joyful smile, and he immediately slipped once again into the moment.

They began to kiss again, his body itching to do more. He trailed away from her mouth, his lips kissing the edges of her jaw, sucking for a moment on her earlobe, then traveling down her neck. She ran her own fingers through his hair and dug her fingertips into his scalp.

"More," she whispered in his ear. That one word sent a shiver through his entire body.

He started to lean her against the sofa, but remembered her injury. She must have sensed his hesitancy because she gently pushed him backwards instead. With his hands still on her hips, she gave him a teasing grin, and he helped lift her up to straddle him.

Their kissing intensified. He couldn't get enough of the taste of her—salty and tangy at the same time. He kept up the kisses, spreading them to her neck, her collarbone.

Suddenly, she rocked her hips against him.

His body responded faster than he thought possible.

She grinned again and nibbled on his lower lip. He tucked a strand of hair around her ear and stared into her eyes.

"Do you want to move off the couch?" he asked.

She nodded.

She stood up, he took her hand, and they headed towards the bed. She took a seat and began to unbutton her blouse, waiting for him as he headed to the bedside table. His body ached.

Don't go too fast, he thought, but he didn't know if his body would listen.

While she carefully undressed so as to not disturb her stiches, Sean rummaged around in his bedside table drawer. He then pulled his shirt over his head, removed the rest of his clothes, and made sure safety precautions were in place.

Naked and stunning, she patted the bed next to her.

He sat down, scooted against the headboard, and allowed her to straddle him once more. This time though, he slid inside her.

The pleasure was almost instantly unbearable. How could this one motion feel so unbelievably good?

The two of them rocked together, their hands wandering, their mouths connected. All he could hear were the sounds of them breathing, of them moaning every once in a while. Sweat dripped down her chest, beaded on her forehead.

The pace quickened. Sean didn't think he could hang in much longer.

Charlotte let out a gasp. Her whole body trembled, twitching and shaking.

"Oh," Sean said, realizing what was happening. He increased his pace once more, excited that she'd finished so quickly, but also that it meant he didn't have to hold on much longer.

"I did not realize," she said, out of breath.

"It's okay. It's *great*," he said with a grin.

His own moment was mounting and with one last strange twisting rock of her body, he climaxed. His eyes rolled up and everything rushed forward towards his groin. Except instead of the normal explosion of pleasure, the moments ticked by, and a sense of shuddering overtook him, holding him in the explosion longer than he ever thought possible. Finally, it ended and he gasped for air, unaware that he'd stopped breathing.

"Holy. . ." he said, the adrenaline draining away.

Charlotte laid down next to him, being careful of her shoulder, and he let out shaky breaths. She was so beautiful, so gorgeous with her glistening hair and heaving chest.

Suddenly, he stirred again.

What? he thought. His body responded fitfully, wanting more from her. This had *never* happened before, not this fast.

He quickly reached again into his nightstand, applied a new safety measure, and turned towards her.

"Already?" she asked, her eyes wide.

He grinned. "You said you were famished. I want to leave you more than satisfied."

An hour and a half later, Sean's leg cramped. He'd been dozing off and the muscle spasm woke him. The second time around between the two of them had been even better, although he wouldn't have thought it possible. They both took their time, the minutes sliding by, building each other up, then pulling back, until they finished at the same time. It had been the most incredible sex of his life.

He reached down and rubbed his cramping leg, jostling her. She opened her eyes.

"Didn't mean to wake you," he said, pulling her closer.

"I fell asleep?" She sounded surprised. "I must have been comfortable. And completely sated."

"Sated is a good word," he said, kissing her softly.

The corners of her mouth rose. She blinked a few times and then a worry line creased her brow. "What time is it?"

Sean rolled over and checked his clock. "Just before 8 p.m."

"That is later than I thought."

A small tug pulled at his belly. "You aren't leaving, are you?"

She ran her fingertips down his temple and across his cheek. "Not because I want to. I was not prepared for this, or for spending the night. I will have to go home."

"Why?" He pulled her closer.

"Things I need to do before I go to bed, including taking another antibiotic for my wound."

Once again, he'd forgotten that just yesterday she'd been stabbed. Everything rushed over him, all they'd been through. It had been so wonderful to exist outside of the world for a while.

"I get it," he said, releasing her.

She drew him back in and kissed him deeply. "But I would like to return, maybe tomorrow night?"

Sean smiled. "I would *really* like that."

He watched her get up and get dressed, admiring her curves and smooth skin. "I'll call you," he said.

Once she finished, she kissed her fingertips and brought them to his lips. "Sounds wonderful. I will see you tomorrow, Sean."

"I'll hold you to that."

"You better." She paused at the door, a Cheshire grin spreading across her face. "I have a feeling my appetite will return."

49

October 11th
6:15 p.m.

District Attorney Jordan Parker sat quietly at the table in the courtroom, her attention wandering. The rest of the room murmured and whispered, having waited several hours for the conclusion to this prominent trial. It didn't really matter to her one way or another what the verdict ended up being against the defendant. Besides, she had a feeling the result would be "not guilty by reason of insanity." There had simply been too much evidence presented that shed reasonable doubt on a guilty plea.

If it mattered to her, she might think about the grander scheme of things court-related, that this would be a precedent for cases in the future. The idea of "brainwashing" had never been believable in the courts. It felt too farfetched to some, too science fiction.

But Jordan knew the truth. Influencing others, hypnosis, and brainwashing were all powerful tools. She'd seen it firsthand. Been a part of it firsthand.

Jordan still remembered the day she'd been recruited to her unique position by Dr. Carla Moria. Having spent her youth in beauty pageants, Jordan wanted to do something else with her life, so she'd gone to law school. When Carla came into the picture, Jordan had already established herself as a DA in the south, with quite a decent win record.

Even with her newfound career, Jordan had never felt fully appeased in her job. She'd witnessed too many odd cases that didn't add up and no one seemed to care. It was more than having to be okay with the fact that sometimes criminals went free. Some of the cases were just. . .weird.

Jordan started digging around and asking questions. She began to see a strange pattern—a pattern that would have been difficult to notice if she hadn't been looking for one.

Cases against women. All over the country. Women claiming blackouts. Women claiming amnesia. Women claiming temporary insanity. All related to murders.

Even stranger, of the women who'd been convicted and went to prison, none were still alive. Different reasons, nothing out of the ordinary—a shanking from a cellmate, a flu that took a bad turn, an infection from a cut. Things of that nature. But no matter the reason, they were all dead.

Two of the convicted women, however, had escaped

death. Except they weren't in prison—they were in mental institutions.

With curiosity brimming to its edge, Jordan went to visit them. She found what appeared to be completely sane women who simply didn't remember committing the murders they'd been accused of.

"I feel like I'm in a bad dream," one woman said. "Like I keep waiting to wake up and my life will be normal again. But every time I wake up, I'm always here."

On her return home from one of these trips, Jordan found an envelope in her mailbox. It spoke of an agency that wanted to make a difference in the world. And it looked for recruits who wanted to do the same. Based on Jordan's work record, would she be interested in an interview? If so, she needed to call the number listed and ask for Carla.

That had been the beginning of everything. Jordan was introduced to a world she couldn't have imagined in her wildest dreams. She met Carla, who explained that they monitored women who fit the pattern Jordan had discovered. When the group recognized that Jordan had visited both women in each mental institution of her own accord, they knew they had to bring her in.

"Is there more than one of you?" Jordan had asked.

"Currently, it's just me and one other woman," Carla replied. "We just started working together. For what we have planned, though, the smaller the group, the better. Except we are always willing to expand for the right recruit."

Carla then proceeded to explain what she did and why.

It seemed ridiculous. Crazy even.

"You hunt down these. . .'Triad' women all over the world? Women who murder others because they've been brainwashed and programmed to do so?"

"You misunderstand. The women choose to kill. They are reprogrammed as innocent women and hide behind these personas. We. . .adjust this."

"You expect me to believe what you're sayin'?" Jordan had asked, incredulity in her voice.

"I can prove it."

Jordan couldn't help herself. She didn't know why, but she needed to see if this absurd notion could be proven. She drove separately, following Carla to the mental institution of the last woman she'd visited. The whole time, Jordan kept trying to convince herself to turn around and go home, that she was following a woman who must be crazy as well, but a sense of curiosity pulled her forward. She'd recognized the odd pattern in these crimes herself. If this woman could offer a real solution, implausible as it may seem, she needed to see it through.

They arrived at the facility, signed in, and entered.

"Well hello again," the amnestic woman had said to Jordan. "Did you have more questions for me?"

"Hello Patrice," Carla said.

The woman frowned slightly. "I'm sorry. Do we know each other?"

"I know who you are."

"Forgive me. Maybe we met at the trial? I don't really remember much of my life."

"No. I know you from a file I recovered. It told me what

your trigger was." Carla held up a small digital device.

"Trigger?" Patrice asked.

"It'll wake you up." Carla clicked on the device.

Jordan listened to a quiet song she'd never heard, with a funky, rapidly tapping beat.

Carla leaned over to Jordan. "Watch her eyes," she whispered.

Jordan focused on Patrice's eyes.

They blinked. Then again. Then a few times rapidly. Her pupils dilated and constricted in an instant. She then blinked again a few times.

"Pamela?" Carla asked, clicking off the device.

The woman in front of them seemed to. . .change. Jordan couldn't think of a better word for it. Her mouth tipped downwards into a frown. She slouched down in the chair, her lids half-closed.

"Yeah?" Patrice asked. Suddenly Patrice looked around. "Aw fuck, where am I?"

"In a mental hospital, Pamela," Carla said.

Jordan wondered why she kept calling Patrice a different name.

Patrice bit her bottom lip. "I got caught?"

"Yes."

Her eyes twitched back and forth inside their sockets as she took in her surroundings. The movement reminded Jordan of a trapped animal.

"You here to take me back?" Patrice asked.

"No, Pamela. What you did was not okay. You chose to kill and you have to stay here, now, and serve the remainder of your time. Because you're ill."

Patrice scowled. "Whatever. They can't hold me here."

Jordan couldn't believe it. This Patrice woman, something about her had definitely shifted. Demeanor, facial expressions, even her word choice.

Carla sighed. "I thought you'd see it that way," she said to Patrice. She paused. "Very well. Good luck to you," she said, then reached out her hand and Patrice took it.

Patrice had time for a crease in her forehead to show before she snatched her hand away. "Ow! What the hell?" She sat there, rubbing her palm.

"Goodbye Pamela." Carla stood. "Let's go, Jordan."

"Tell them I want to come back!" Patrice called out as Jordan and Carla walked away. "Tell them I'm ready! I just messed up the once. They have to fucking know that!"

The two of them left and Jordan stopped in the middle of the parking lot. Her knees shook and her mind swirled with thoughts. "That really happened. Just like you said it would. She really was someone else? This. . .Pamela woman?"

Carla's eyes softened. "Basically, yes. Her rewritten persona had no knowledge of what she'd done. But, like I mentioned before, unlike normal brainwashing, these weren't decent women tricked into becoming killers. They were women who *were* killers or wanted to kill and decided to hide behind the personalities of innocent women. They are guilty from the beginning, forcing someone else to take the blame for their crimes."

They arrived at their separate cars. "I have another appointment somewhere else," Carla said. "But if you think you're ready to learn more, call me tomorrow at that same number. I will answer any questions you have—who these women are, why they kill, and why we want to find them. If you don't call, then after tomorrow the number won't work and you'll never be bothered again. And you must understand, you cannot tell anyone else. Ever." Carla placed her hand gently on Jordan's arm. "I hope you'll help us."

Jordan had tossed and turned the whole night, her head a whirlwind of confusing thoughts. The next day, she returned to work as usual, but things felt different. Her coworkers were oblivious to what she'd witnessed. And who could she tell? Who would believe her?

Jordan wanted to do more. She'd always felt that way, her entire life. And this could be a way to do just that.

On her lunch hour, she called Carla. They met that evening and Jordan learned about the Book, the Triads and their purpose, and about how they'd lost their way. About how the women involved were unstable from the beginning. About how they were abusing their power. And file after file of evidence showing her the involvement of these women in multiple murders.

The police couldn't stop them. They had tried. The only people who could end this were the same women who knew about it, who'd been a part of it, and who wanted to make a difference.

"But I've never been a part of it," Jordan said. "So why ask me to join?"

"Because of your connections with the law. Because of

your desire to create change. And because we believe you are willing to do what is necessary to stop women from killing and getting away with it. We employ several tactics to nullify the danger from these women, but the end result must be the same: to stop them from hurting others and to extinguish exposure."

"And that woman in the mental institution, Pamela? She can expose the Triads now. She can escape. She can kill again."

"She's unable to do any of those things." Carla rubbed her palm.

Jordan remembered how Pamela had pulled away in pain when she'd shook Carla's hand.

"You did somethin' to her."

"Yes. I gave her the chance to live out her sentence. She made it clear she would escape. She wanted to kill again."

Realization hit Jordan. "You killed her? You didn't have to do that!"

"What was the alternative? Leave an innocent woman in a mental facility? What a horrible life. Besides, Pamela had already been tried by the law for her crimes. If we explained the situation to the authorities, the Triads would have been exposed, and they do what they have to in order to cover their tracks. Our goal is to exterminate knowledge of the Triads and remove the threats. The less people involved, including the law, the better."

Fear crept into Jordan's chest. "What about me? I know about the Triads now. What if I don't join?"

"As long as you don't reveal any of this, you will be left alone, to continue your life. But you'll always wonder, in the back of your mind, about cases you encounter if a Triad is behind them. If an accident really isn't an accident. If these women are being allowed to roam free to kill."

Jordan had wrestled with the decision for a week. She did her best to poke holes in their practice, but she couldn't see a way around it, especially because she knew the law. She hardly believed when seven days later she called Carla and said, "I want to help." She then began her journey into her current position—part of a team that "cleaned up" anything related to the Triads—and had been doing so for two years.

Today, Jordan sat in a courtroom, awaiting the verdict against Violet, who was currently in the persona of Veronica. Jordan had been taught how to recognize the different traits of these characters. The clean-up team never terminated someone when they were in their innocent personality. Until they determined someone's trigger, they merely kept tabs on the woman, making sure she stayed in her innocent state. As for Violet, they'd found her trigger. Veronica would not have to suffer for Violet's crimes.

The door to the jury room opened and the twelve jurors resumed their positions in the jury box. The judge asked the defendant to rise.

Jordan picked up her cell and messaged two words to a long-distance number.

-It's time-

"Ladies and gentlemen of the jury," the judge said. "Have you reached a verdict?"

"We have, Your Honor."

"What say you?"

"We find the defendant 'not guilty by reason of insanity.'"

The courtroom burst into a commotion. The judge banged her gavel. The racket started to die down just a bit. Veronica sobbed into the defense attorney's shoulder. The defense attorney held her up.

Jordan just sat there, waiting.

The judge continued. "The defendant will be held at Bridgewater State Hospital for rehabilitation. Case closed." The judge banged her gavel again and everyone stood and filed towards the exit.

Jordan stood, nodded at the defense attorney, and peered to the rear of the courtroom.

There she stood, just like Carla had said she would.

Detective Juliette Tay.

Jordan picked up her phone again, entered a set of numbers into it, and hit *Send.*

A song began to play from the back of the room. A strange song no one would recognize, with a frenetic background beat to it that made you feel a little on edge.

50

October 11th
6:20 p.m.

Juliette sat squished on a bench between Wilt and some older man with a thick white mustache and a completely bald head. They'd been able to get seats in the courtroom, but at this point, the place was filled to capacity. Body odor and the combined breath of all the spectators hung like a humid cloud within the room. Sweat pooled beneath her arms underneath a red sweater and she'd watched Wilt remove his outer jacket and then his blazer.

Juliette didn't really care. Dr. Moria had been right. She wanted, no *needed*, to see the verdict. To be here for when this nightmare ended.

"My first big case, almost done," Wilt whispered next to her, a toothpick wedged in his mouth. She could hear the excitement in his voice. "I'm not going to lie—this has been hell."

"You're telling me," she whispered in response.

"That woman is as nutty as a fruitcake," he went on, adjusting a bit against the wooden bench.

"Agreed. She deserves to be locked up in a tiny cell for the rest of her life," Juliette said. *Just like they locked me up in their compound.*

"Well, I'm not sure that'll happen, but at least she'll be off the streets and drugged up in Crazy-Town."

Juliette scowled. "You don't think she'll go to prison?"

"I'm not sure. There is a lot of evidence that points to her being psycho. They may just send her to the looney bin."

Juliette honestly didn't think that would happen. Violet had killed a cop and attempted to kill two others. She'd kidnaped people and tried to kill Dr. Salla. There were just too many things to dismiss.

Right?

Suddenly Juliette's stomach turned. She knew a mental facility wouldn't be freedom, but she didn't like the idea of that woman being treated like a victim. Of not being punished for her crimes.

The door to the jury room opened and her body seized up for a moment. Either way, it would all be over soon.

Juliette grabbed Wilt's arm and he nodded at her. The tension in the courtroom spiked. Everyone seemed to be holding their breath while the foreperson read out the verdict.

". . .not guilty by reason of insanity."

The courtroom exploded with a mixture of angry shouts and sobs, applause and sounds of disbelief. The judge announced the sentence and decreed the case closed.

People stood, shuffling around each other, and filed towards the door. The room would be cleared first, then Violet would be taken out of the courthouse and brought to Bridgewater State Hospital.

Juliette just sat there. She couldn't believe it. After everything she'd gone through, that woman wasn't going to jail.

"Jewels, come on, get up," Wilt said, helping her to her feet.

Juliette let him help her, still in shock.

Then, a small buzzing noise sounded from her left. She turned towards the noise, but it continued to move with her.

"What the. . ." she mumbled.

All of a sudden, a song blasted out, as if someone was holding a radio up to the side of her face. She cowered and covered her ears, the prosthetic one unable to feel any pressure. The music continued, a frantic beat which pulsed through her. She turned her head, trying to find the source of the noise, but everyone else was staring at her.

The sound came from *her*.

My ear, she thought.

She reached up, unsnapped her prosthetic ear, and removed it from the side of her head. It was the source of the music.

"What's going on?" Wilt asked, pointing to her ear.

"I don't know. But I better get outside." Juliette pushed her way through the crowd and had just burst through the courtroom doors when the song silenced itself.

Juliette held the ear in her hand, now aware of the deep quiet around her. She slid into the crowd, past the media, down the steps, and out the doors. She didn't know what had just happened, but she didn't want to stay in the middle of all those people if it happened again.

She waited for Wilt to finally catch up with her.

"What the hell was that?" Wilt asked, pointing once again at her fake ear.

Anger burbled up inside her. "I have no clue. But I'm going to bloody well find out."

51

October 11th
6:25 p.m.

Violet's head felt heavy. She recognized the sensation. It had happened almost once a month for the last three years or so. But she hadn't expected to ever feel this way again.

She was coming out of her other persona, Veronica.

Her eyes cleared, though tears filled them. Veronica had been crying. She found herself being supported by a woman. People milled around her. Smells of wood and soft perfume filled her nose.

Violet pulled away from the woman and got her bearings. She'd practiced in the past on how to not reveal that she was changing personalities. She'd woken up in strange situations before. She'd perfected the art of pretending.

Violet could hear the remnants of her trigger song floating through the courtroom and then ending abruptly as the sound moved away.

Fury flared up inside her. Who had done it? Who could have possibly brought her back? This isn't what she'd planned. She'd decided to go to sleep, let Veronica serve out the punishment. So who had triggered her once again into herself?

Violet stared at the defense attorney. No, her puppet hadn't gone rogue. No acknowledgement or searching to see who Violet really was penetrated those dark eyes. She then searched around the room. She didn't have much time. Two officers stood on either side of her, pulling her arms behind her, about to escort her from the courtroom. But to where? Prison or a hospital?

Her eyes frantically examined the room, needing to find who had triggered her. Stares from dozens of strangers fell on her. They all judged her as to whether worthy or unworthy of her sentence, but she didn't care. She didn't want to see judgement. She wanted to see. . .

There.

Recognition.

The district attorney.

Violet averted her gaze, but she could tell she'd been identified. The question was, for what reason?

"What happens now?" Violet asked the defense attorney.

"They'll escort you to Bridgewater State Hospital. Don't worry. I'll meet you there later to make sure everything is in order."

So. Insanity. Violet quickly adapted to the new situation. At least the security would be minimal. She would be able to break out in a couple weeks at most, maybe even sooner.

One of the officers took her by the arm and moved her forward, past the now empty benches.

Violet took one last look over at the district attorney and memorized her face. She'd be on guard if she ever saw that woman again. Until she found out if that woman was friend or foe.

52

October 11th
6:30 p.m.

Millan muted his television with a grunt. "Better sentence than she deserves," he muttered. He stretched, his 58-year-old joints protesting. He felt old lately, older than he should for his age. It was more than just an achy back or stiff legs. More than the persistent cough and trouble sleeping. This type of "oldness" sunk into his very core, pulling him down, making him feel weak and tired through every fiber of his being.

"I'm getting too old for this shit," he joked to himself, quoting one of his favorite movies. Yet the sentiment rang true. He didn't think he'd ever want to leave the force until he'd gotten to the required retirement age, but these past several months had worn him down like never before.

Millan pushed himself up off his couch with another grunt and made his way to the kitchen. He opened the fridge and stood staring at its sad contents for several minutes, not really knowing what or *if* he wanted anything inside. Finally, he settled on another beer and returned to the couch, hoping to find an old Red Sox game on a sports channel.

"Triads," he said to the empty room. "Bad enough we got rapists and child molesters and people who kill for money or love or revenge. But killing people cuz they look different?" He shook his head. Yet the suffering of people throughout the centuries from this same motive didn't really surprise him. He rubbed his own dark arms, marveling anew at the fact that something literally skin deep could be motive enough to kill.

His phone beeped at him. He still had voice messages from work he needed to listen to. After Trann left to pick up Dr. Salla from the hospital earlier that afternoon, Millan had decided that he, too, wanted to leave work early, so he'd sent his work calls to his cell and gone home.

Except home didn't make him feel any better.

Everyone at the station had been through so much these past six months, himself included, but they all had each other to talk to. Though Millan prided himself on his team, he kept most of his personal life private, making sure there was a little distance between himself and the officers. But one detail had come out: when he'd learned about the daughter he never knew existed. He'd been so excited, he'd told everyone.

And then she'd died. Just like that. Some drunk driver

and a missed stop sign.

After he told his staff about the accident, Millan kept quiet once more. What he *hadn't* told the rest of his group was that he'd been reprimanded at work for late reports and that his wife moved out a month ago. She currently lived with her sister, telling Millan that she couldn't help him if he wouldn't help himself. That he needed to deal with his loss.

Millan let out a sigh. He probably should have seen the precinct's counselor, Dr. Moria. From what he'd heard, she seemed decent.

Maybe I'll give her a call on Monday, he thought.

Until then, he might as well continue going through the motions. With another sigh, he checked his voicemails. The first two were basic and he made a note to send follow-up emails to them after the weekend, but the third caught his attention.

Sergeant Millan. This is Brett Chules, returning your call. We went ahead and traced the cell number you gave us in regards to the messages that were being sent to Detective Trann's phone. The towers pinged concentrated the call to come from someone named. . .uh. . .Marina Beguilous. Her address is. . ."

Millan scribbled down the address and apartment number. He paused, staring at the name. Why did it sound so familiar? He glanced once again at the TV, which still showed recaps from the trial.

The pen fell from his fingers.

There.

The defense attorney.

Violet's attorney's name was Marina Beguilous.

Millan rubbed a dry hand over his grown out salt-and-pepper stubble. *She* had sent those cryptic messages to Sean? Why?

Thunder rumbled in the far distance. Millan stared at the paper on his coffee table. An inkling of motivation trickled through him.

Only one way to find out.

53

October 11th
7 p.m.

A half hour after she'd returned to her own persona in the courtroom, Violet was roughly pulled from a police van.

"This is too good for you, you fucking cop-killer." The officer, an older man with graying temples and weather-worn skin yanked her by the arm then spit in her face. He turned her back around to face the front of their destination. Bridgewater State Hospital loomed before her. The brick building looked like an oddly-shaped, overly long high school with razor-wired fence surrounding it.

Violet had decided on a new plan while they traveled. She wouldn't last long inside. She'd somehow end up "sick" or an "accident" would happen. No one liked cop-killers.

After a few steps, Violet faked a stumble, leaning forwards. The officer grabbed her and pulled her backwards, into his own chest.

"Walk straight, you whore!" he snarled at her.

Violet easily pulled the tie pin from his tie, her fingers grasping at it on his chest, and then let her knees buckle.

"I can't!" she gasped. "My ankle!"

She took those few moments on the ground to shove the pin into her handcuffs, rolling it around in the lock, and felt satisfying relief when the cuffs clicked open.

"Get up!" the officer screamed. He grabbed her by the arm, so tightly she knew she'd bruise later, and wrenched her to her feet. She pretended to hobble, favoring her left ankle.

The other officer, younger with olive-toned skin and a square jaw, came over. "Man, chill!" He held onto her other arm so she could steady herself.

Violet flashed him a look of thanks. She would honestly regret this part.

In a quick motion she freed her arm, arced it around, and shoved the tie pin into the younger officer's eye and kneed him in the groin. The older officer barely had time to register what had happened before she whipped her other hand around and shoved the end of the open cuff into his throat, ripping across it, and gashing his neck.

The younger officer screamed, holding his eye. The older officer gurgled and fell over, clutching his throat.

Violet quickly assessed the situation. Staff from the hospital, who waited on the other side of the fence, began to notice a problem. They yelled out, some running towards the fence, others running away to the safety of the building.

Violet took the guns from each officer. She fired two shots towards the oncoming staff members, who ducked and covered. She left the officers on the ground. One she could tell wouldn't live and the other. . .well better to have lost an eye than be dead. She didn't want to waste the bullets.

She raced towards the van. The driver, however, already had a radio in his hand. She quickly fired two bullets: one that broke the window and the other that burrowed into the driver's forehead.

Unlocking the door through the broken window, she jerked the body out of the front seat, and hopped in. She pulled off, tires squealing.

She needed to think, lose this soon-to-be targeted vehicle, and find a different car. A deep fire burned in her belly while she drove, searching for someone whose car she could steal. She knew she needed to get out of town, and fast. The district attorney had somehow triggered her into being Violet again. But why?

"This wasn't supposed to be this way," she said out loud over the roaring engine. "I was supposed to go to sleep and not wake up. Why the hell did you bring me back!" Violet pounded on the dashboard, spittle flying from her mouth.

"It was all perfect," she continued, turning onto a side road. She spotted a white sedan driving in front of her. "I had everything planned. Until that fucking detective and that stupid coroner ruined everything." Violet swerved, cutting off the sedan, forcing it off the road. She jumped out, leaving the engine running. The women who drove the car also got out, cursing and waving her hands.

Violet promptly put a bullet through her skull.

She got in, turned on the car, and peeled away. She still needed one more car switch, but it could wait a bit. She'd take a few out-of-the-way roads and find someone who wouldn't be reported for a while.

Violet knew she should head towards the state border. She'd be free and clear in a matter of hours. No one was *quite* looking for her yet. This was her moment of escape.

But escape to what? Violet had arranged everything. She'd have been on top, leading a Triad, deciding people's fate. The detective and coroner had taken that away from her. And while she could've hidden as Veronica, she now existed again as Violet.

With a sharp yank on the wheel, she turned the car and headed north, into the city. She couldn't leave things this way. She needed to know why she was Violet again.

White spots popped across her knuckles from her grip on the steering wheel.

But before talking to the district attorney, she wanted payback from those who'd ruined her plans. And to get rid of any loose ends.

54

October 11th
7:15 p.m.

Jordan yawned. It had been an exceedingly long day. She'd done her part—turned Veronica into Violet—so she would get to relax for a while.

Except something tugged at her thoughts. Violet had definitely realized Jordan had been staring at her. The moment had been fleeting and most anyone else would have missed it, but Jordan had spent the better part of the year working on face cues and their meanings. It helped her with her job, to identify which persona a Triad member existed in.

The clean-up process, though, as they called it, was so slow. Currently, they didn't have the technological skills needed to keep up with all the Triads. They needed more help. And she had an idea who might be able to help them.

Jordan remembered her meetings with all four of the main witnesses: Detective Trann, Dr. Salla, Detective Tay, and Mags Stinson. They'd all been fairly straightforward when she'd asked them the questions designed by her Triad. Her group wanted to make sure none of the four planned on pursuing the other Triads after Violet's trial ended. Everyone needed to believe the Triads were a one-shot deal—that Truth, Violet, and Angellica were on their own. Otherwise police and others would continue to meddle and eventually get themselves killed.

Carla had become their therapist for this very reason. She'd tested the officers emotionally, guiding them ever so slightly, making sure none of them really *believed* other Triads existed. And if they meandered onto that route, Carla would steer them once again onto the correct road.

This had been the first instance where all three women from the clean-up group had worked in the same city at the same time. But then again, no other Triad had been exposed the way Truth's had.

Jordan's job had been to test Sean, Charlotte, Juliette, and Mags logically. Often responses to tough questions revealed more about a person than in a therapeutic setting. Less time to lie, to craft an answer, to analyze their responses.

Their reactions to her line of questioning, under the guise of cross-examination preparation of course, had revolved around anger and of wanting justice. Each of them also seemed tired of this case and wanted it to be over. Very normal responses and nothing to indicate they would pursue other Triads after the case finished.

But something in her last interview made her think. Something about Mags.

There'd been an. . .energy about her. Something on the cusp of exhaustion mixed with sadness.

Intrigued, Jordan had done some research on her own. She discovered that Mags and her fiancé had separated due to this case and that lately she spent most of her free time in the hospital with Detective Payne, who still hadn't recovered from his head injury.

That woman has a lot of pain, Jordan thought. And pain could be a motivating factor.

She decided to call Carla.

"Jordan?" Carla said, answering with a breathy voice.

"Yes. I have a proposition."

"I'm so glad you called!"

Jordan frowned at the abnormal breathing sounds. "Carla? What's wrong?"

"*Ay Dios.* Haven't you heard?"

"Heard what?"

"Turn on the news!"

Jordan grabbed the TV remote and flicked on the screen. A news bulletin flashed across the top reading:

BREAKING NEWS: SPIDER KILLER HAS ESCAPED HER WEB OF CUSTODY

"What the hell?" Jordan said, turning up the volume.

We have breaking news that a half hour ago, Veronica Chasis, also known as Violet, escaped custody right outside Bridgewater State Hospital. She killed two officers, including the driver of the police van, and blinded a third officer in one eye. She stole the van and took off. The vehicle was found about five miles east, abandoned on the side of the road. A woman was found dead along the side of the road next to the van, a gunshot to the head. We learned she'd been driving a white sedan. A general alert has been issued regarding the car. If seen, please call the hotline.

A phone number flashed across the screen, with photos of Violet from the trial and her mug shot beneath it, plus the car's license plate info.

If you see this woman, call the police immediately. Do not approach her for any reason. She is considered armed and extremely dangerous.

"This can't be happenin'," Jordan said into the phone.

"I know. But it happened."

"What are we goin' to do about it?"

"The same thing we would normally do. Track her. If she jumps states, we'll find her."

"But you're not sure she'll leave?"

The other line went quiet for a moment. "I wouldn't."

Jordan knew Carla didn't like to reference her time in her old Triad. "Where do you think she'll go?" Jordan paused. "Where would *you* go?"

"I'd do one of two things: go after the people that interfered—"

"—meanin' Detective Trann or Doctor Salla—"

"—or after the person who brought me back into my persona."

It took a moment for Jordan to realize what Carla meant. "Me."

"Are you safe?"

"I'm at my apartment." Jordan whipped her head around, checking all the possible entrances to her place. "It seems secure."

"Stay there. I'll come to you."

"What about the detective and the coroner? Who will protect them?"

"That's why there are three of us."

Jordan let out a breath of forced air. "Okay, head over. I'll call her and fill her in. And when you get here, remind me to tell you about my proposition."

"Will do. Stay safe."

Jordan hung up and made one more phone call.

"It's me," Jordan said into the phone.

"I just saw the news," the woman on the other end answered.

"Carla's on her way here."

"All right. I'm already heading towards the detective's apartment anyway."

"I figured you'd be at the coroner's. Weren't you goin' to approach her when she got out of the hospital?"

"He checked her out and she wasn't home. Neither was

her car. I'm guessing she went to his place."

"Okay. Be careful. Call me if there's an update."

"Same."

Jordan hung up, double checked the deadbolt, and waited for Carla to arrive.

55

October 11th
7:45 p.m.

Millan pulled up to an apartment building on Malden Street and parked his car. He plugged the meter, hoping this wouldn't take too long, and headed towards the front door. He knew he should wait. He should have called for an officer to join him. But technically the defense attorney hadn't done anything wrong. She'd merely sent strange messages to Trann.

Still, he felt a little uneasy.

However, he needn't have worried about being alone. When he rounded the corner, two police cars sat in the street outside the entrance.

Millan flashed his badge. "What's going on?" he asked the

lead officer.

"Homicide." He pointed at the body being wheeled out inside a body bag on a stretcher.

Millan's joints stiffened. "Name?" The word came out in a rasp.

"Uh. . ." the officer said, flipping open his notes. "Marina Beguilous."

A woozy feeling came over Millan and he gritted his teeth to steel himself. "What happened?"

"It looks like she opened her door and was shot point blank in the head." The officer nodded over his shoulder when someone called his name. "I gotta go. If you need more info, you can call our precinct in the morning." The officer jogged off.

Millan turned and trudged back to his car. He'd been too late. If only he'd listened to that message earlier, he could have saved that woman.

Marina. Her name was Marina.

Another death.

The first time because he'd been too impatient, now because of his apathy.

Millan climbed into his car and headed home.

"I'm too old for this shit," he mumbled. The phrase that usually made him crack a smile this time rang sickeningly true.

He had a lot to think about.

56

October 11th
8 p.m.

Violet crept forward through the alley. She'd already abandoned the white sedan and had made the remainder of the drive into Boston in a black SUV, the owner of which lay dead somewhere in a ditch without a shirt and pants. The new car currently sat on the street at the other end of the alley, parked next to a giant dumpster.

Violet had just returned from taking care of a "loose end"—Marina Beguilous. When she'd arrived at Marina's apartment and buzzed her intercom, the defense attorney immediately let her in. Violet knew this would happen, all based on the hypnosis she'd done to the defense attorney during their visits at the prison.

Though not as skilled as Truth, Violet had learned the basics of hypnosis and one key factor had been trust. In an unknowing participant, this trust is even more important, as they will often be receiving suggestions unwillingly. Violet programmed this concept into the sessions with Marina, along with the rhythmic repetitious beats, and after a couple of their meetings, she began to notice Marina's compliance.

The plan had been so simple: use Marina as an outside puppet to set things up for after the verdict. That way, whatever happened, Marina would have helped Violet plan an escape route from the courthouse.

But then Violet realized Marina wasn't as submerged under the hypnosis as she should have been. She'd caught her sending messages to Detective Trann, trying to warn him about what Violet's intentions were. Violet had realized at that point that her skills weren't enough to keep the defense attorney on a leash. Changing tactics, Violet realized there was no way out, so she opted for the next best thing: retreat into Veronica's personality and let *her* serve out the punishment.

Except the district attorney had triggered Violet.

Unsure if Marina had anything to do with it—perhaps she had remembered the hypnotic experience and somehow told the DA or the cops—Violet needed to make sure Marina was silenced once and for all.

So when she'd arrived at the apartment, Violet needed to test Marina. Buzzing the intercom, she announced her name and trigger word to invoke trust and Marina let her in. Once outside her apartment door, as soon as it opened, Violet shot her in the head.

Moving quickly, Violet fled the building, shifting her attention to the next task. Between the detective and the coroner, she chose to visit the detective first. He'd merely been a thorn in her side. She wanted his death to be quick. Not like the medical examiner's. The so-called "Messiah" of the Triads. She wanted to kill that woman slowly, make her realize that nothing would keep her alive because she was nothing herself.

Violet currently hovered near the end of an alley, two blocks from Trann's apartment, casually leaning against the edge of a brick building next to her. She looked like she could have been waiting for a ride or to meet a friend. No one would notice her or care. She was excellent at blending in while still being visible.

The low rumble of thunder, fairly close, sounded in her ears. A storm was on its way and would be here soon. Even better. Rain would make it more difficult for anyone to see her.

With a deep breath, Violet left the edge of the alley and headed towards the detective's apartment. She already knew exactly where he lived. She knew pretty much everything about him. She'd researched him thoroughly when he'd thwarted her clues the previous year.

This time, the only death he'd have to deal with was his own.

Before she stepped off the sidewalk and onto the street, she saw the most enticing thing she'd ever seen in her life.

The coroner. Walking to her car.

Violet grinned.

Change of plans. Time to play.

57

October 11th
8:10 p.m.

Charlotte left Sean's apartment, her body still tingling. Never in her whole life had she had an intimate encounter like that. Not that sex defined a relationship, but she did know things would never be the same between the two of them from this point forward. The idea made her smile.

She definitely had *not* expected anything physical to happen. That had been the most surprising part—how much she'd felt drawn to him, and so quickly. Logic and reason dictated so much of her life, but in this case, her emotions had driven her. And yet, she'd still felt in control. It wasn't as though she'd gotten drunk or threw caution to the wind.

Opening up to him, both emotionally and physically, felt safe. More than that, it felt right.

A streak of lightning lit the sky, followed by a low roll of thunder. She wasn't worried about the rain—her car sat parked only two blocks away. A few other people hustled by, getting off the street, their gazes flickering up to the darkening sky. Several popped open umbrellas, but the sidewalks quickly emptied for a Friday evening. Perhaps they knew the rain would be stronger than a brief shower. Charlotte wasn't sure—she hadn't paid attention to the weather. She'd been otherwise. . .occupied.

The first drops of rain hit the pavement, heavy and plump. Charlotte picked up her pace. She could see her car just ahead. A wet drop plunked onto her cheek, like a random tear from the heavens. Keys jingling in her hand, she wiped the drip from her face, then unlocked her car and opened the door. Just in time as buckets of rain suddenly dropped from the sky, soaking her in moments.

Before she could get in, a force behind her slammed her forward. Her forehead smashed into the rim of the car's door. Pain seared through her eyebrow and temple from the contact. Dazed, she felt herself being whirled around. Inches from her face hovered the eyes of her nightmares: Violet.

Charlotte barely had time to wonder how Violet could be here.

"You ruined *everything!*" Violet hissed, shoving her again. Charlotte's legs buckled and she fell back into her car through the open door, her calves hitting the seat. She shook her head, clearing it, and scrambled backwards. Something warm trickled down her face, mingling with the rain.

"Oh no you don't," Violet said, yanking Charlotte out by her ankle.

"Leave me alone!" Charlotte yelled, kicking out with her unhampered leg. She connected with Violet's shoulder and her attacker stumbled a little, loosening her grip.

"I would've had it *all* if it weren't for you!" Violet's eyes widened and almost seemed to pop out of her head.

"Help!" Charlotte screamed. Her cry was covered by another boom of thunder, this one louder. Her gaze desperately searched the area for someone to aid her, but she couldn't see anyone. The clouds had rolled in, black and heavy, and had blotted out the remaining sun. Rain poured down in sheets, obscuring much of her view down the street.

Violet regained her grip and pulled again. Charlotte shrieked, sliding out of the car and onto the wet pavement. Water pounded her face and she blinked fiercely, trying to clear her eyes. Another substance, most likely blood, had trickled into her right eye, causing it to burn. She could barely see.

"I'll kill you, you *bitch*! I'll make you pay!" Violet yanked again and Charlotte's body skidded across the road, her shirt shimmying up to her chest, her skin scratching against the rough surface. Charlotte's head hit the ground and the rain-streaked world swam. She could feel her stiches stretch on her shoulder and pain flared throughout her back.

She was going to die, right here, a couple blocks from Sean's.

A little voice screamed inside Charlotte's mind: *Don't be scared! Get mad. Fight back!*

Charlotte let out a grunt and swung her free leg again,

this time connecting with Violet's face. Violet let go and shook her head, her nose bleeding freely, then spat a gob of blood in Charlotte's direction. Rain soaked her hair and body, making her appear like a wet, rabid animal.

"I'll make sure you stay dead this time, *Messiah*," she said, the word snapping at Charlotte like a viper.

Lightning streaked the sky again, this time catching the glint of a gun in Violet's hand.

I'm dead. The thought popped into Charlotte's head against her will. The image of Sean's face danced in her mind for an instant. She opened her mouth to scream.

Violet's eyes widened and she grunted. Her body jolted. She fell forward onto Charlotte.

The scream emerged from Charlotte's mouth, but once again thunder covered it. Charlotte's breath caught in her throat as she waited for Violet to turn towards her, put the gun to her temple, and pull the trigger.

Nothing happened. Violet simply lay on top of her, not moving.

"Oh God," Charlotte said, struggling. Her right eye remained closed, still fighting the sting of blood. Rain still battered her face. Pain throbbed in her head. She could barely think. She pushed Violet off of her, scuttling backwards on her hands and feet. Once far enough away, pressed against her open car door, she forced herself to focus and saw blood pooling around Violet's head.

Charlotte's breath came in ragged gulps. She still could barely see. She wiped her face and it came away smeared with red. It must have been a bad cut to bleed so freely amidst all this rain.

A figure appeared next to her. "Come with me," a voice said. Someone helped her up and the two of them began to move.

"No," Charlotte mumbled, her steps wobbly. She wanted to return to Sean's. Or climb into her car. Anything to get off the street. Violet's body lay on the ground, growing distant.

"It's all right," the voice said, sounding slightly familiar, leading her down the street, supporting Charlotte as they walked. "You're safe now."

They went in through a door. "Stay here. I will be right back," the person said, releasing her hold.

Her savior let go and left. Charlotte stumbled forward, finding a bare table to catch her balance, and squeezed her own head, willing the world to stop spinning. *Concussion?* she wondered. She worried about how much rattling one brain could take. The dizziness slowly receded and she got her bearings. She stood inside some sort of warehouse—abandoned by the looks of it. A streetlight from outside shone through the window of the dark room.

Moments later, before she could contemplate a plan of action, the door reopened and whoever had helped her stepped through.

"Are you okay?" the voice asked.

Charlotte lifted her head to face whoever had just saved her life.

58

October 11th
8:30 p.m.

Charlotte stared at the woman. "You!" she cried out.

The figure stepped further into the light, her short, dark hair dripping from the rain outside. Though on most it would be an unflattering look, on this woman, it seemed more like a sexy shampoo commercial. Large, dark eyes, liquid and full of hope stared at Charlotte. Her full lips curved into a tentative smile.

"Yes, Charlotte, it's me."

Charlotte couldn't believe it. Isabella. The grad student who had lunch with Sean, who'd shadowed her at her office.

"How? Why?" Charlotte sputtered.

Isabella said nothing at first, merely slipping a backpack from her shoulders and placing it on the table. She unzipped it and tipped the open end towards Charlotte. Curiosity took over and Charlotte took a step forward, peeking into the bag.

In it sat the Book, wrapped in plastic, and next to it what appeared to be a manila file folder.

"You are one of them," Charlotte said, pulling away from the bag, her hands balling into fists.

"I am, yes and no."

"Explain."

"I don't have much time." She glanced backwards at the door. "I placed Violet's body in a nearby dumpster, closed your car up, and called the police to report the body. They will be here soon and I can't be here when they arrive."

"I do not *care* about you and your time."

Isabella held up her hands in submission. "I will tell you what I can, but I'm afraid it won't be enough. You will have more questions and I will gladly answer them for you another time. Until then, here are the basics." She lowered her hands slowly. "First, other Triads *do* exist. I'm sorry you've had to suffer, believing them not to be real."

Charlotte's chest constricted. No. She'd just let go of the Triads. She didn't want to hear this.

"Second," Isabella continued, "there has been dissension among our Triad sects for several years now. Lack of communication and autonomy kept us separated and unaware of the others. With the invention of the Internet, things changed. We could safely connect with other groups, but we found. . .problems. Many problems. A major one for most was the realization we weren't making a difference."

"Murdering tens of thousands of people does not make any difference?" Charlotte snorted a laugh. "You are an egotistical fool."

"On the contrary," Isabella said, moving forward hesitantly, then re-zipping the bag. "The Book speaks of women helping to maintain a balance. We bring life and therefore have the right to remove it. The translations are meticulous and cannot be argued. Every new set of linguists brought in every ten years reconfirms what the Book says: target those who should not reproduce or exist, lest their imperfections create havoc among other humans.

"But after access to the Internet," she continued, "and when we could monitor the world on a larger scale, the interpretation of 'imperfections' changed. The Triads had always assumed they were physical. But why?"

Thunder sounded so loudly that Charlotte jumped. The storm raged around them, wind rattling the windows and whistling outside the door.

"So, what was the alternate interpretation?" Charlotte asked.

"Mental imperfections."

Charlotte stood there, stunned. "I do not understand. Truth told me that those in the sects were recruited because of their sociopathic and psychopathic tendencies. They *wanted* to kill and so would be perfect choices to perform those deeds."

"Exactly!" Isabella said, running a hand through her hair. "And look what happened. Violet."

Charlotte's mind raced. "You believe Violet's coup was because of her mental instability?"

Isabella nodded. "It's not the first time something like this has happened, but a Triad was never exposed like this until now. Violet crossed too many lines. Her ego became involved. Her pride. She played with civilians and exposed our very existence. She was careless and ruthless. But it's because she didn't have any conscience telling her to stop."

"Why are you telling me this?" Charlotte asked. A shiver ran through her as the coldness around her set in, chilling her wet skin. A tiredness sunk into her bones. She wanted to curl up and sleep for a week, wake up and know this was all a dream.

Isabella's eyes flicked again towards the door for a moment, then to the watch on her wrist. "When the split between the sects happened, the factions still remained autonomous. They did what they saw fit. There was no one to monitor them or keep up with their progress. It's why Violet happened at all—no one was notified of any problems with Truth's group. But Truth's announcement that she'd found the Messiah caught everyone's attention. There'd been claims throughout the decades, of course, all over the world, but we always research each claim. You fit. Everything. Every item on the list the Book claimed about the Messiah was true in you. Except, of course, not being able to be killed."

Charlotte's heart actually skipped a beat. "Except. . ." she mumbled.

"Except Violet tried to kill you and you didn't die," Isabella finished.

Charlotte's hand instinctively went to her chest, right where the scar remained from the knife that had been thrown into her from Violet's own hand. She should have died. The doctors told her she should have died. But she hadn't.

"I am not the Messiah," she whispered.

Isabella shrugged. "The question is not 'are you the Messiah?' You are the Messiah no matter what you think. Whether you believe in it or not does not make it any less true. The question is 'if you had the power to save others, would you let it go to waste?'

"Just imagine," she continued, "the idea of women who choose to kill, not because they like killing, but because they see the purpose to it. They won't ever be tempted to kill for any other reason."

"Psychological studies show that once you have killed, it is easier to do so in the future."

"True. But when you feel like you aren't being manipulated, when you're killing for a reason instead of just to kill, it's different. Soldiers kill in wars, but they don't start shooting people left and right when they return home."

Charlotte's heart pounded in her chest. It didn't matter what this woman told her, killing was wrong. *Then why are you so happy right now, knowing Violet is dead?* The thought stabbed at her, breaking open her sense of right and wrong.

With a gentle push, Isabella nudged the bag towards Charlotte. "This was stolen from the police while on its way to the courthouse. It's from the trial, although not needed anymore as evidence since Violet is dead. It's now yours, to do with as you see fit."

Charlotte stared at the bag in horror, as if it were Pandora's Box.

"I'm giving you the chance, Charlotte. These women around the world will keep killing. The police can't stop them. They tried. You can't stop them on your own. You can't even find them. You tried. You traveled around the world and found *nothing*. But you *can* stop them with our help."

Isabella retreated a few steps. "Think about it. The damage being done to our world is *not* from physical imperfections, but from mental ones. The very women we originally found to weed out those bodily imperfections are the exact women who must be stopped. Our justice system here couldn't even handle Violet's case correctly. What chance does the rest of the world have?"

"So this whole split persona thing was just a hoax?"

"Oh no. You would have sent an innocent woman to a mental institution if we hadn't stepped in and made Violet her true self again. We are different than the Triads. We don't murder innocents. We stop the women who are killers."

"But—"

Isabella held up a hand. "You have questions. I know. But I'm out of time. You'll have to make a choice. I promise I will answer everything—who we truly are, what truths and falsehoods did Truth actually tell you, and what is really going on in the world with the Triads."

She swung the door open, the streetlights barely visible in the downpour. A streak of lightning lit up the sky behind her, outlining her body. "You can have the control, Charlotte. You can help lead us. I'll be in touch soon to find out your decision. If you choose not to help us, so be it. We will continue to right the wrongs of the Triads, with or without you. If you tell anyone about our meeting, we will do what we need to in order to keep the Triads a secret. That's our job. To clean up after the Triads, no matter the cost."

She paused at the door. "Besides the Book, there is a file in that bag. A file about your brother. About his death."

Charlotte's knees shook. "What. . .?"

"You have the power to save others," Isabella said, pointing to the bag, the rain falling in sheets behind her silhouette. "Are you going to let it go to waste?"

Isabella closed the door behind her, leaving Charlotte alone in darkness with nothing but the sound of the rain pounding on the roof and the sound of her thoughts pounding inside her head.

59

October 11th
9:30 p.m.

Thunder shook Sean awake.

"What the. . .?" he said, trailing off. He hopped off his bed, rubbed his aching arm, which reacted to the weather, and opened his shades. Rain poured down his windowpane like a curtain of water. It must have been storming for some time.

He glanced at the clock. A half hour had passed since Charlotte left. A smile touched his mouth at the thought of her. Another boom sounded, rattling his windows.

Well, he thought, *I'm not going back to sleep now.* Sean threw on a pair of boxers and made his way to his couch. The leftover pizza called to him. He shoveled a piece into his mouth and peered over at the TV, which still remained on.

"Oh yeah," he murmured. The case. They hadn't even watched the verdict. They'd been a little. . .busy.

Sean unmuted the screen and turned up the volume to compensate for the random bursts of thunder above. He dropped the pizza at the breaking news.

It's been confirmed. The body of escaped mental patient, Veronica Chasis, also known as Violet, also known as the Spider killer, has been found in an alley dumpster off Hancock Street. A stolen black SUV was parked nearby. The call reporting the body came in anonymously. There are currently no witnesses to the crime.

Police so far have said it appears to be a mugging gone wrong. Veronica was hit in the head and killed, then the body left in a nearby dumpster. Police are unsure if the killer even knew who she was at the time of the attack. An investigation will be pursued.

There has been no speculation yet as to why Veronica returned to the city after escaping custody earlier this evening from Bridgewater State Hospital, but it seems that she met an untimely death.

This reporter will have more as the investigation reveals itself.

Sean muted the television. Violet had escaped. And died a couple blocks from his apartment.

She'd been coming to kill him. He knew it in his gut.

But someone had killed her first.

She'd been so close to him. To his apartment. To. . .

"Charlotte!"

Sean's stomach twisted. He raced over to his landline and dialed Charlotte's number.

Ring.

"Come on."

Ring.

"Come on!"

60

October 11ᵗʰ
9:45 p.m.

The past couple of hours felt like a blur. After Isabella left, Charlotte just stood in the warehouse, shivering from both the cold and loss of adrenaline. She felt frozen, not from the chill, but from moving forward. Too many thoughts battled each other in her mind, racing and jumping out of control. She couldn't decide what to do. The bag with the Book and the file sat on the table in front of her, like a nightmare and treasure all wrapped in one.

Eventually, Charlotte heard sirens.

The police.

Isabella had said she'd called them, to lead them to

Violet's body.

Charlotte had taken a step towards the door, ready to go to them, to find solace in an officer and tell someone everything.

But she'd stopped. What would she tell them? Isabella had made it clear that no one could know about the Triads and if they did, they'd be a target.

I need some time to think, she thought. *And I cannot do that here.* With another swipe at her bloody forehead, which had pretty much slowed to a stop, she once again headed towards the door, intent on going home.

But again, she'd stopped. As if the movements weren't hers, she twisted around and stared at the bag which contained the Book. She knew if she touched it, even for a moment, she'd take it with her.

You do not want that, her mind told her.

But it's the only proof.

Is it? Proof of what? There won't be fingerprints, you know that. There won't be any indication that another Triad member gave this to you. What will be the point of giving it to anyone? What will it accomplish?

What about the file?

Her mind had no logical response to that one.

Charlotte walked slowly towards it, her mind screaming at her the whole time not to do it, to run before the police found her, to forget everything and return to her life.

Instead, she picked up the Book.

Now, she sat on the bed in her apartment, having cleaned her superficial wounds, hair wet, feet up on her toes.

Her phone rang.

Mechanically, she answered it. "Hello?"

"Charlotte? It's Sean. Are you all right? Are you home?"

"Yes, I am sitting on the bed in my apartment."

She heard him let out a sigh. "I just saw the news, about Violet's escape, and how they found her near my place. I was worried..."

"No need to worry. I arrived home safe and sound." The words came, but she couldn't feel any emotion behind them. The whole thing felt like a bad dream and if she could convince him she was all right, perhaps she would wake up.

But she wouldn't wake up. Because it wasn't a dream. It was real. All real.

A pause. "You sure you're all right?" Sean asked again.

Charlotte placed her hand on the plastic-wrapped Book on the bed next to her, her gaze resting on the opened file beside it.

"I'm fine," she lied. "Perfectly fine."

ABOUT THE AUTHOR

Christa Yelich-Koth is an award-winning author (2016 Novel of Excellence for Science Fiction for ILLUSION from Author's Circle Awards) of the Amazon Bestselling novels, ILLUSION and IDENTITY. Her third book in the *Eomix Galaxy Novel* collection is COILED VENGEANCE.

Christa has also moved into the world of detective fiction with her international bestselling novel, SPIDER'S TRUTH, the first in the *Detective Trann series*.

Looking for something Young Adult? Try the YA fantasy *Land of Iyah* trilogy, starting with book 1: THE JADE CASTLE.

Aside from her novels, Christa has also authored a graphic novel, HOLLOW, and 6-issue follow-up comic book series HOLLOW'S PRISM from Green-Eyed Unicorn Comics. (with illustrator Conrad Teves.)

Originally from Milwaukee, WI, Christa was exposed to many different things through her education, including an elementary Spanish immersion program, a vocal/opera program in high school, and her eventual B.S. in Biology. Her love of entomology and marine biology helped while writing her science fiction/ fantasy aliens/creatures.

As for why she writes, Christa had this to say: "I write because I have a story that needs to come out. I write because I can't NOT write. I write because I love creating something that pulls me out of my own world and lets me for a little while get lost inside someone or someplace else. And I write because I HAVE to know how the story ends."

You can find more about Christa and her other books at:
www.ChristaYelichKoth.com

www.ingramcontent.com/pod-product-compliance
Lightning Source LLC
Chambersburg PA
CBHW020917110726
47900CB00001B/188